I0730535

NO *perfect* SECRET

IMPERFECTION SERIES BOOK 4

Award-winning Author
DD LORENZO

return to your favorite ebook retailer and purchase your own copy.
Thank you for respecting the hard work of this author.

The Karas family and all who are fortunate enough to be loved by them.

Note from Author

This story is written to honor all the women and the
inter strength that they possess, but in particular one
who I will never meet but have long admired.

Gracie Allen ~
Your love story with George Burns continues to inspire
me. Paige's tale was birthed from my desire to see you
wear a strapless dress.

Prologue

Paige

The heat is visible as it rises from the Vegas strip. It wiggles like a black-tar genie from a lamp. I stand in one of my favorite spots—the overpass between the New York-New York and the MGM Grand hotels. It embraces me where I am, nestling me in its warmth like a long, lost lover. Each time I come to Vegas I find myself in the same place. It's become as much a habit as breathing. Here is where I decompress. Like most people, my life is filled with stress from work and home. Good stress, but stress nonetheless. The hot embrace of the city caresses my skin and strokes me day by day until my body responds and the tension releases. Most people think it's hot here; I prefer to believe the energy makes me glow as the pulsing beat deepens our affair.

To most people, it seems I have it all together. I'm financially independent and have all the material things everyone hopes for. The truth is, it's all an illusion. I've always fancied myself a mistress of deception, and Vegas and I are the same in that, we are imposters. Each presents an alluring outer shell while disguising our true intent—we both want to sell you something.

I look out at hotels—concrete behemoths. They surround me with their architectural magnificence. The distinction of the respective properties pours itself into my senses until I'm esthetically drunk. With their open arms they break my resistance, and I'm no longer alone.

Each building is unique, and their careful alignment makes them stand as sentries in the world in which I languish. I've been coming here for so long I've witnessed many of their births. Masculine steel mates with feminine glass, and, together, they deliver the most sensuous bodies of architecture. This is a city dedicated to self-indulgence and it invites me to be one of its disappearing souls. Vegas and I are kindred spirits, sharing a cliché, appearances can be deceiving.

Anything can happen in Las Vegas, and I embrace its unpredictability. This place is my mecca; my holy ground. I left the church of due diligence behind to find peaceful obscurity in the land of smoke and mirrors. Vegas is the temptress that floods my soul, and I am happy to be in her arms again. Somewhere between the east coast and the dessert, at thirty-five thousand feet in the air, I left behind my constant introspection and relentless self-examination and traded it for sinful anonymity. With each complimentary and carefully measured airline cocktail, I left behind the woman inside of me who guards and approves everything I do. On any normal day I check myself from appetite to asshole, but not here in Sin City. As my desires remain incognito amongst hundreds of tourists, Vegas and I share another trait, we were both opportunists.

I take in a deep breath, inhaling toxic fumes of car exhaust mixed with particles of dust carried on the hot dessert breeze. This trip is both business and pleasure. If I focus on the business, the pleasure will be a sweet indulgence. A balance of the two. That's my purpose.

Chapter 1

Paige

The Realtors Conference and Expo were being held in Vegas, and I had to dedicate a portion of my time toward business in order to write off the trip. Necessary but boring. Most times the networking required was tolerable, but lately I'd been working my ass off and I needed the break. That's where my friend Elizabeth came in.

Elizabeth Santiago was my second best friend. The number one spot belonged to my lifelong friend, Aria Sinclair. By choice, I didn't have many. I'm private. Most people read me as shy. Though I was an introvert by nature, in my professional life I was a masterful extrovert. I could sell you anything. I kept company with a small circle of people, but, because of the social aspect of my business, there were some who believed themselves to be my friends, but, in reality, I was still deciding if they'd make the cut. Aria and Elizabeth were the two people who'd proven their friendship and loyalty to me. I trusted them with anything.

I'd known Aria since childhood. We'd met at the beach during our families' respective vacations. Elizabeth was a more recent friend. We'd met several years ago. She was much more an extrovert than me. A gorgeous Latina who I would've described as a serious party person. She's seen me at my worst! But, then, Vegas was known for bringing that trait out in people.

It was during a night of partying, while I was puking my guts out in a nightclub bathroom, that Elizabeth handed me cool, wet paper towels under the stall door. Though I didn't know her, it was a true bonding moment. She stayed with me in the bathroom, talking to me while I emptied the contents of my stomach. She resided in Vegas and had nowhere special to be that night. She took care of me, nursed me with a big glass of ginger ale and Angostura, insisting the concoction would settle my stomach. As she walked me back to my hotel room, she handed me her business card, all the while making me swear to call her the next day. The next morning I was terribly hung-over but I respected her request and called her. She insisted we meet for lunch, and somewhere between our iced teas and salads, my gut told me her sincerity was genuine. We've been friends ever since.

Today I was late. I hurried down the Strip to the Hard Rock Hotel to meet Liz for lunch in a quirky little restaurant there called the Pink Taco. As I approached the hostess I gave her a quick description of Elizabeth. After telling me she hadn't yet arrived she led me to a table. I wasted no time getting into my Sin City frame of mind. The waitress came over to my table a moment later.

"Mojito." I paused, then smiled at her. "Actually, make that two."

"Sure thing."

As she went to get my drinks, I positioned myself so I could see Liz when she came through the door. Of course, while I waited I couldn't help but eavesdrop. It was a talent of mine that had proven to be most beneficial. I'd honed the skill over time. Bits and pieces of conversations wafted through the air and traveled to my ears. I dissected information as I enjoyed my drink. I'd learned much about people over the years by breaking down tone and verbiage, and had learned most people had an agenda, and most were opportunists—just like me. This ability drove my success while showing homes to prospective buyers. I'd peel away their kind words to reveal what they really loved or hated about a property. But, now, I needed a vacation.

My head was filled with many loads of bullshit, and I needed a place to dump the old information so my mind would be fresh when I returned. The best cure for what ailed me was alcohol. I rarely indulged at home because I was always working but had more than my fill while on vacation. I was just about ready to order my third drink when Liz came rushing toward our table.

"Where have you been?" I held up my empty glass. "I'm two ahead of you!"

"Sorry, chica! The traffic was terrible!" She seemed a bit frazzled but wasted no time launching herself at me to give me a big hug. "I missed you, Paige!"

"Yeah, yeah." My tone was very blasé. "I haven't been here *too* long," I said, rolling my eyes at her.

Our waitress returned to the table. "Whatever she's having? I'll have the same." Elizabeth pointed to my empty glass, a smartass smirk on her lips. "And she'll have another."

"You're going to get me drunk, Liz. I haven't eaten yet."

"So, we'll fix that! As soon as she comes back with the drinks, we'll order food." Her bossy but animated expression matched the excitement in her voice. Elizabeth had a way of infecting people with delight. I liked her carefree personality more than I cared to admit.

"I am happy to see you!" I said, placing my elbows on the table and leaning in so she could hear me above the chatter. "What've you been up to?"

"You're very chipper!" She grinned, avoiding my question, and circled her finger over the top of my two empty glasses. "My guess is this is why you're in such a good mood." Sarcasm dripped off the words as she playfully winked at me.

"I needed something to take the edge off." I shrugged and straightened my spine. "All I've been doing is working." I inhaled dramatically and then let out a sigh. "You know all that shit in the paper about Marisol and her husband?" Liz nodded in reply, and I continued.

"Well, all of her real estate transactions were done through me and my company. It was a real mess. We bought properties for her company—which I didn't know was her company—and then as soon as her husband came into the picture he wanted them all sold, immediately. Those two are evil. Pure evil."

A twinge of anger sparkled in her eyes. "When I saw that on the news I just knew it had something to do with your company!" She leaned in and lowered her voice. "Was this connected with Marisol's attack on Aria? When Marisol's sister was killed?"

"Yes." Though I spoke in a low tone there was a hard edge in my voice. "It's all connected."

"That's what I thought! The paper didn't give all the details, but I remembered you saying that's how you wound up in the hospital. I still can't believe you look as good as you do! Shit! You went through a glass window! It's a wonder you didn't need some plastic work." Her eyes widened, and her head bobbed up and down, as she looked me over.

I laughed at her. "Now, how do you know I didn't have work done?"

"Did you?"

I laughed at her question, holding my glass high to toast that statement. "I'll never tell."

She grew more serious. "How is Aria? You said she was coming along really well."

Her concern touched me, considerably lightening my mood. "She's great. Wonderful as a matter of fact. She and Declan are expecting a baby. I'm going to be an aunt!"

"No! Really?" She squealed. Her excitement nearly matched my own.

"Really. She also asked me to be godmother." I recalled the day Aria asked me to stand for her daughter. "She's been my best friend forever—more like a sister really."

"You two have known each other a long time, haven't you?" Her eyes softened, as did my heart.

"Yes. Since we were kids. Aria's family and mine vacationed in Ocean City every summer for two weeks. Her family owned two apartments, the Skipjack and the Rosemont. We always stayed in the same building—her family in the upper apartment and ours in the lower one. I was shy, but Aria was very outgoing. I guess we were so opposite we attracted." I took a sip of my drink. "Looking back, I'm sure Aria's parents worried about her. We'd be playing on the beach while our parents caught up. She'd walk up and talk to anyone and everyone. She offered hugs to complete strangers without reservation. Scary." I shook my head. "There's no way she'll let her child do that. It's too crazy these days." I paused for a moment. "I think that if it weren't for Aria I might not have had any friends growing up." I reached over, patting Liz's hand. "Now, I'm lucky enough to have two of them."

The melancholy moment passed quickly. I didn't want to dwell on the past, for the past is where my demons lived.

Chapter 2

Falcon

I was sitting at the blackjack table when I saw a woman who looked familiar walking through the lobby. I would have called out to get her attention, but a winning hand diverted my attention.

"Blackjack."

With a smile on my face, the dealer pushed a tall, colorful stack of chips in front of me. I cupped my hand over the stack, swallowing it into my palm. Rising from the chair I tossed a shiny, purple one to the dealer.

"Buy yourself a good meal. I'd recommend Gallagher's, but I'm sure you already know that."

The man lifted his chin and nodded appreciatively.

After a quick glance around the room I found her again. *So, it was Paige!* I watched her for a moment, my eyes softening as I enjoyed the sight of her walking from the front desk to the elevator. The effect she had on me hadn't diminished in the last few months. I put the remainder of the chips in my pocket and discreetly adjusted myself. *Yeah, I remember her.* She was as beautiful as I recalled, although the last time I'd seen her she was bundled in layers of sweaters. This time, the cute, yellow dress she wore fell over her curves and swished back and forth as she walked. She provided an entertaining view with that sway, one that distracted me from my chase a little longer than I'd planned. The elevator doors opened, and I tried to dodge through the crowd to get her attention but just before I arrived they began to close. When I got there I saw her through the tiny sliver that remained open, but she didn't look up to see me, robbing me of the opportunity to make eye contact.

Damn it!

Frustrated, I twisted away and headed for the front desk. If I hadn't been so focused on watching her I would have reached her before she went to her room. I closed my eyes for a minute then headed toward the front desk. The fact that I could get information on just about anyone was going to come in handy right about now, and that knowledge made me smile. Being a security expert had its perks. I was well aware that hotel policy was to keep guest information confidential, but my credentials were impressive, giving me a certain amount of clout. Though I rarely exploited my authority to gain leverage, I only had to flash my badge, and the hotel would be more than accommodating.

Fortunately, the short walk to the desk was enough time for common sense to kick in. I wouldn't gain any points with her if I invaded her privacy. It would be a sensitive point for anyone, and I didn't want to give her a reason to be defensive with me, especially since I hadn't seen her in a while. *Shit!*

She looked as good as I remembered. Hot, stacked, and blessed with curves I'd like to ride. We hadn't seen each other since the past Christmas holiday at our mutual friends' cabin up on Deep Creek Lake.

Paige had been easy to talk to. We'd hit it off right away, and by the end of the weekend I'd definitely been interested. I'd meant to call her but never got around to it because I'd been swamped with my new business. MarSin Falcon, Inc. is a security firm I'd started with Carter Sinclair and another friend, Marcus Bainbridge.

Since then, my life had been crazy and time consuming. I seldom had downtime, but when I did, Paige had a way of creeping into my thoughts. It had been less than a year since the party but seeing her now brought all the pleasant memories back.

CARTER AND HIS GIRLFRIEND, *Aimee, had planned something special during the holidays for their friends and family. The two of them had gone through a rough year, and Carter thought a party would lift Aimee's spirits. Of course, he'd enlisted the help of both his partners, namely Marcus and me, and because we'd been such good friends we'd been invited to the party as well. It wasn't just because we were friends, though. We'd known each other a long time.*

We'd met at a local bar when I got out of the Army. I'd just wanted to have a few beers and a place to decompress, and that bar was the first place I'd walked into.

Most of the patrons were law enforcement or military. I ran into an old friend while I was there, Marcus. We were just shootin' the shit and catching up. Carter had come there with Marc before I'd arrived, and he called winners on the game. Before the night was through, we'd bonded over pool sticks and Budweiser. Our friendship grew more solid through the years. When Carter's wife had died, Marc and I stood by him. On the flip side, when Aimee had come into town, we ragged on him about the new girl.

Aimee was the best thing that had happened in a long time to all three of us. She was a pretty, little thing and loved getting her hands dirty renovating busted furniture. Once we figured out she was the same model we'd seen in the magazines, we nearly shit ourselves! Who would have guessed grouchy ass Carter Sinclair could land someone as beautiful and sweet as she was? But, then, stranger things have happened. I couldn't blame Carter one bit for falling for that girl. Hell, I would've tried to hit on her myself if Carter hadn't threatened to rip my head off! By the time Marcus and I put all the pieces of the story together, Carter and Aimee had a solid thing going. She became his sole focus after she nearly died.

Like most people living in unfamiliar territory, when Aimee first moved to Deep Creek she didn't know her way around. The story goes that she and Carter had a fight and she stormed out. She tried to take a trail through the woods to her house but was viciously attacked. Carter found her and carried her all the way through the thick forest back to his house. He felt responsible for their fight and moved Aimee into his house while she recovered.

The way Carter handled the whole incident gave me a new respect for the man. Aimee's wellbeing became Carter's duty. When he couldn't be with her he enlisted us to stand guard over her. Marc and I looked *after her like she was our little sister. I have no idea what possessed the two of them to have a Christmas party, but I'm glad they did; that's where I first saw Paige.*

All the out-of-town guests had been invited to spend the weekend. Marcus and I were going to our own houses since we lived nearby. By the time we'd arrived on the first night of the festivities, the party was in full swing. Carter put a beer in my hand while Aimee made introductions. It was just the normal routine, shaking hands and returning hugs. There was a shift in the energy in the room when I laid eyes on Paige.

From the moment I first saw her, I knew she was different. Normally I'd have checked out her tits and ass first, but when Aimee introduced us, the first thing I noticed was her smile. She had killer dimples, and I could've fallen head first into them.

Always on guard and overly cocky, I shocked myself when I tripped over my own name.

Paige's eyes were brown and gorgeous. Little gold flecks around the rim of warm color reminded me of the sparks in a fire. Her hair was pulled to the side in a ponytail. Long waves hung over one shoulder and nestled inside a fold of her sweater. She was reserved and even seemed a little shy, but the fire in her eyes told me she was confident as hell. She played coy, tucking her head down, but when she looked up and rested her gaze on me, I could tell the shyness was all an act. There was an instant attraction. I'd never met anyone who I'd sized up so quickly. She was a fucking lethal weapon—sweet and sassy—and I knew I was in trouble.

Most of the crowd was in from Ocean City, Maryland and all of them were friends. Marcus and I were the only outsiders but, by the time two in the morning rolled around, we felt like we were old friends. But it was late, and Carter was shutting the night down. Aimee was worn out and it showed. One by one, everyone excused themselves and the huggy bunch started with the affectionate goodnights and went off to the bedrooms. All except Paige. She came over to me.

Something inside of me stirred, something I couldn't identify. Her coy act made no fucking sense to me, but some things can't be explained. As she approached, she tucked her chin down and peeked up at me through dark, thick lashes.

"Are you coming back tomorrow?"

"I'm planning on it."

"That's a good thing. I'd like to get to know you better, Mr. Falcon Grey."

The way she'd addressed me was respectful, but her tone was playful. If she was trying to get my attention, it worked. I watched her backside swing all the way up the stairs.

The next day Marc and I arrived in time for break-

fast, and the first thing I saw was that killer smile. I'd lain awake the night before strategizing how I'd get her number before the weekend was over. That was before I met Blake Matthews.

When Blake had arrived he'd acted like Paige was a claim he'd staked. I hadn't wanted to back off, but I was unsure if I was treading on some other guy's territory. I sure as hell didn't want to be messing with some other guy's girlfriend. When I'd asked Carter about it, he'd said that, as far as he knew, Paige and Blake were just friends. Blake, however, seemed to have a different opinion.

The knowledge that Blake was a friend of Carter's brother was the only thing that had kept me from decking the son of a bitch. He'd acted like a dick the entire weekend, and his attitude put a damper on some of the livelier conversations. But it was Carter's house, and he seemed to have everything under control, so I'd restrained myself. Of course, that hadn't stopped me from keeping an eye on the guy. I watched everything he did for the remainder of the weekend, especially when it had involved interactions with Paige.

Paige said she wanted to get some fresh air, and I took my chance. I joined her as she explored the grounds. Once I had the opportunity to be alone with her during our walk, we exchanged numbers and said *we'd keep in touch. A week passed, and we rang in the new year.*

I fully intended to contact her, but then business had exploded.

MarSin Falcon's good reputation was spreading and we had more work than we had hours. I fell into bed exhausted most nights, but the business card I'd been holding onto reminded me every evening she was someone I wanted to know better. But time kept getting in my way. As the days passed my promised phone call to Paige became one more thing on my never-ending to-do list, because every day, one more thing always came up.

Until today.

When I was young, my mom used to talk about "signs." If *this* happened, it was a sign; if *that* happened it was a sign. According to my mother, a sign usually preceded anything that was supposed to happen. Maybe today I got a sign myself.

Back in my room, as I pulled my clothes from the closet, Paige's card fell out of my pocket. It flipped and hit the floor. I bent over to pick it up and when I stood it slipped between my fingers, falling to the floor a second time. Grabbing it again, I cupped it in the palm of my hand. I dropped the clothes on the bed and, once again, the business card landed on the floor, face up, Paige's name and phone number staring me in the face.

Maybe this was the kind of shit my mom was talking about. Like, really? What are the chances of me and Paige being in Vegas, in the same hotel, at the same time?

Signs.

Memories of my mom and her superstitions made me chuckle to myself. *What the hell?* Fate was a fickle bitch, but she might just be intervening to tell me to get off my ass and go get the girl. And I had just the way to do it. After all, what good is information unless you force somebody to share it?

Chapter 3

Paige

Spending time with Liz was always fun, but my feet were killing me from the high heels I was wearing, and I couldn't wait to stand under a hot shower. Although I was still relaxed as I strolled through the lobby of my hotel I wasn't sure if the buzz in my head was from the noise of the machines or the residual effect of the Mojitos.

Unlike the quiet of home, the Vegas environment was nothing but hyperactive. Bells rang, machines chirped and whooped, and music played everywhere. It was exactly what I needed; a welcome change from my overextended existence. I loved my work, but some-times it could really be a pain in the ass. The pressure mounted when twenty-some contracts were going on at the same time. To say it could be chaotic would be a gross understatement, and the stress it created was not my friend.

The headaches I got as a result of the chaos always felt as if a vise was gripping my head—and when I did too much and didn't get enough sleep it became overwhelming. *And then I self-destruct.*

I tried to toss the dark thought away before an old, internal pattern had a chance to emerge, but it came back like a boomerang. I reminded myself I had the ability to think and act and told myself they were merely thoughts, before a caustic pattern emerges. One where my focus turned inward, and I began to mentally check off boxes of self-incrimination. It, by no means, was a healthy habit, mentally or physically. The topics ranged from perfectionism with my work to beratement of my personal life. For the most part I was far more lenient with the professional part of my life than I was with the personal one. What began as innocently as making sure my outfit was well put together, usually ended with me belittling myself for every tiny flaw I believed I had. I walked an uncharitable tightrope during those episodes as I tried to find a balance between being fussy and self-abusive. I tiptoed on a fragile, threadbare line. Over the years I'd come to recognize when that rope was about to snap and drop me into a black pit. It was at that pivotal point I had a choice. I could internalize the darkness or take them to a place where the lights shone brightly twenty-four hours a day, seven days a week—Las Vegas, which would save my sanity and distract me from my murky thoughts.

I could lose myself in the activity of that city. The vibe took me to a place where the mundane falls away to let the magnificent shine. The crazy thing was that when I was in Sin City the words of an old hymn came to mind, it is well with my soul.

It was my mother's favorite hymn. I had sweet memories of her singing that song when she was besieged by things beyond her control. While my mother's faith was admirable, mine was nowhere as steadfast. Instead of going to a religious service, I turned to things I could see and feel, and I boldly approached the altar of the almighty dollar. In Las Vegas I purged my muddled thoughts by confessing my sins in the tabernacles of Prada, the mosques of Tiffany, and the cathedrals of Dior. I paid my penance not with prayers but with currency. I hated the sins I'd committed against myself and I'd thought I was done with inflicting punishment on myself, but a demon made them rise from the dead. An unclean spirit, who I'm convinced came from the bowels of hell—Marisol Franzi.

I hated that it was my encounter with Marisol that

unearthed my long dormant disorder. Marisol and I were nothing alike. Whereas I made my money behind the scene of real estate transactions, she plied her wares before the public.

As an international model known for her flawless physical form, Marisol could be seen on every television and in every magazine. But she was living proof that beauty really *is* only skin deep. Her soul was a black pit where happiness went to die. Though I'd never met anyone like her before, I've learned much about evil from her. Marisol's kind of nasty crept out through the pores of her beautiful skin. She was a woman possessed by psychotic manipulations that, unfortunately, had threatened the lives of my friends. Marisol's madness created an illusion of aesthetic normalcy while it disguised a web of deception. She sucked the lifeblood of any poor soul who showed vulnerability. I knew firsthand, because I was one of them.

Never again.

I closed my eyes and erased the mental pictures. I had to stop marinating in what was behind me and look forward to the future. I needed to purge the negativity, and the only one who could do that was me. If I wanted to enjoy this mini vacation I had to delight in what was right in front of me and leave the stressful things behind. At that moment, all I could think about was getting a hot shower and a good night's sleep. Exhaustion was not my friend. The shadows of my self-critical nature tended to take control when I wasn't well rested, and travel days were the worst. Fortunately, that was an easy fix, because the bed in room 1022 was calling my name.

ONCE INSIDE I closed the door behind me. I leaned against the backside of it and took a deep breath. I hadn't been able to enjoy much solitude before meeting Liz for drinks and I couldn't wait to get settled in. My bags had been brought to the room upon my arrival. The valet had smiled at me as he brought my luggage in, but I'd seen strain in his face as he lifted the largest suitcase. The problem? Shoes and accessories— but mainly . . . shoes.

I had to stifle a laugh at the recent memory. He'd been so polite when I'd tipped him, but I'd known he'd suspected what was in there. I hadn't tried to explain because I didn't have to. Men could never understand how or why women were obsessed with footwear, but, to the female of the species, the beauty of shoes was an unspoken language—not to mention that when we wore them they made our legs look fabulous!

Opening the suitcase, I laid my clothes out on the

bed to arrange my outfits. I thanked my mother for my love of clothes and accessories. My mom was, and always has been, beautiful and stylish. I'd inherited her fair skin and deep brown eyes. Growing up in an upper, middle class family, my parents had lived on a budget. My mom had been resourceful and dressed us so well people thought we had more money than we did, even after my accident. That was when her true talent came into play. She'd been creative when it came to hair and make-up, so much so that it should have been her profession. When I'd become a teenager, my mom had taught her skills to me.

The memories associated with my childhood accident were jumbled. I was such a little girl when is occurred. For years I'd heard the details. I had knowledge of the actual event but what I most remembered was that there had been pain. Lots of pain.

I winced at the memory of the agony. Blistering hot oil on tender skin. How it had made me scream.

As I'd recovered, my mom had diverted my attention from IV drips, bandages, and medication by turning the pages of hairstyle and fashion magazines. Though I'd been barely beyond being a toddler, I'd loved looking at pictures of the pretty ladies, and the constant, comforting attention of my mother. My mom would flit through the pages as she sat with me in bed, often until I fell asleep from the painkillers. It had been just a diversion; something to pass the time. I'd never dreamed that the distraction of pretty things would be a lifeline for me.

As I looked at my wardrobe I said a silent prayer for my mother and how she'd weathered that time in our lives. Like most children, I'd been resilient. I'd healed physically, but the scarred skin had continued to hurt and itch. My mom would apply cream several times a day and would gently massage the soreness away. During a recent conversation she'd disclosed that every day I'd spent in the hospital, she'd been secretly planning how special my first shopping trip would be. I honestly don't know how she did it. I mean, how do you console your child when you are agonizing for them? When I'd been well enough, her way to help me heal had been to spend some girl time with me. Just Mom, pretty clothes, and me. She'd thought a big-girl lunch would right my world to its former, happy axis. I guess it sounded silly, but unless you've been in that situation you couldn't possibly know what you would have done. What I did know was that my mom was the best friend I could ever have hoped to have, even above my girlfriends. She'd tried to prepare me for everything that was to come so I'd know how to fight it.

. . .

"Sweetie, one day, people may not be nice to you. You mustn't pay attention to them." My momma's expression was tender. I carefully put my little cup of hot chocolate on the saucer. My nose wrinkled up, my forehead furrowed in confusion.

"Why would they be mean to me, momma? You always say I'm nice with my friends." She reached across the table and held my little fingers in her palm.

"Baby, they might not see you the same way that Daddy, Ricky, and I do. We know you're a brave girl, and we think you're beautiful, but some people . . . they only look at the outside. They shouldn't, but they do."

I touched the edges of my bandages, my little fingernails sparkling from the polish my momma had applied.

"Momma? If you kiss the boo-boos, will they go away?" My mom seemed to swallow a lump in her throat, surely wishing she had that power. She moved a tendril of my silky hair, pushing it behind my shoulder.

"Baby, if I thought that would work I'd give you a million kisses—no, a billion kisses. Dr. Dylan said it would take time. Then we'll see how you heal."

I reached up and placed my hand on her cheek. "I want to be pretty like you, Momma. Daddy says you're boo-ti-ful."

I noticed tears against my mother's lashes and wanted to console her. Laying my head against my *mother's chest, I coiled my little legs around her waist and hugged her.*

"I love you, Momma," I whispered.

THAT WAS one of my first memories from my time in the hospital. It was one I'd revisited many times, but I wished it hadn't surfaced just then. I was tired. Bad things happened when I was tired.

Though I tried to keep the sweet recollection from becoming a nightmare, remembrances of helplessness, both mine and my mom's, wielded the power to put me in a funk. It was imperative to my peace of mind to keep the bad thoughts at bay.

I exhaled the unconscious breath I'd been holding and placed the last outfit in the closet. My shoes were snug from wearing them all day, and I sat down on the bed to pry them from my swollen feet. It didn't matter how high they were or how uncomfortable I felt after wearing them for ten hours, the Vince Camuto's were one of my favorite pairs. Surely, some psychologist could have analyzed how accessories camouflaged my insecurities, but I didn't care. For years the pretty things I'd bought and wore were my magic. When I was little, their power canceled out hospital smells, painful bandage changes, and pitiful stares. I thought I'd placed the pain of those thoughts in the dark recesses of my mind, but, unlike the scars on my body, they'd resurface at the most inopportune times.

Like that moment.

Images I couldn't erase clouded my thoughts. I still heard the name-calling, the taunts, and saw the ugly expressions. They'd made me feel like I didn't measure up and never would. Although my mother was my angel, she learned the hard way she couldn't protect her little girl from a broken heart. The worst offenders had been children. Though they'd had cherubic faces, they became devils when they weren't monitored. Mean girls.

I stretched, flexed, and pointed my toes to distract myself while I tried to put the sad thoughts back in the dark where they belonged. I had many such boxes inside my mind. All were childhood memories, some pleasant, some not, but neatly catalogued nonetheless. As I'd grown up, part of my healing had been through counseling. They'd taught me to concentrate on the present to avoid the pain of the past, but I hadn't always been successful. It was a work in progress, and I was still working on it.

My thoughts were beginning to get muddled, and I felt scuzzy from the recirculated air on the plane. Shower. Sleep. Now. It was an easy formula, all I had to do was follow it.

As I closed the closet door and placed my clothes

on a hook I caught a glimpse of my reflection. Just like Narcissus, I was drawn to it, but there was one big difference between us; I wasn't in love with myself. Not at all. Quite the opposite in fact.

As I looked in the mirror *she* stood before me. The one I despised. The girl that never measured up. The one everyone hated. The one who lived inside of me, birthed into being by ugly comments. The hidden insecure girl whom *they* brought to life because they hated *her* imperfection. In my sleep-deprived, maudlin state, my mind weakened. I couldn't see the successful woman I'd created. The feminine, smart, and well-dressed phoenix that rose from the ashes of physical pain and tortured confidence. No. I wasn't on top of my game today where I could fight back the arrows of incrimination. Tiredness weighed down my limbs. Weariness and alcohol muddled my thoughts. I was weak and in a stressed state I looked at myself—her—through their eyes. All I could see in my own reflection was the victim, not the victor. A wave of disgust rolled through me, twisting my stomach.

I pushed the dress off my shoulders and tried to look away, but I couldn't. It was her who looked back at me. *Her* eyes watched it flutter to the floor, but it puddled at *my* feet. The girl in the mirror was the object of their cruelty. She fixated on the lacy bra and panties I wore beneath my dress. I loved them. That part of me that had healed. That part of me who was rational. But she—the girl that they'd said was a freak—was disgusted by something so pretty against a body so foul.

I should have recognized that I was double-minded from exhaustion. I should have shifted away from the mirror, or at least warned her, the child inside of me, to look away. We didn't coexist peacefully. I chastised myself because all I'd needed to do was to take off my underwear and step into the shower. Instead, the little girl inside of me was hooked through my peripheral vision like an unsuspecting fish. She knew I was weak when I was tired, and she took advantage of it and gained the upper hand. I wanted to turn away—but I couldn't. Like a shark she fixated on the massacred flesh. The waters of exhaustion were the perfect opportunity for her to wade through my wounded mind. She swam in the waters of my anxiety, compulsion, and ritualism, while I stood helpless on the shore. As a child, they'd ripped her spirit apart with their blood-thirsty appetite for cruelty, and, in my exhaustion, she surfaced through the dark seas of my mind. The voice in my head screamed for her to fight, to turn away from the perilous waters, but, instead, she swam in a sadistic ocean. No matter how hard I tried, I knew I didn't have the ability to pull the broken girl from the riptide. Not when sleep deprivation drowned me.

Lost in past sadness, I watched a tear warm her skin as I reached behind my back to undo the clasp of my bra. I wished I could turn away, but I was hypnotized by the girl in the mirror. The breath I was holding burned my lungs as it begged to escape. She watched the garment loosen on my breasts. It slowly danced down her curves, hitting the floor at my feet as I surrendered to the strength of painful memories. My perfectly manicured fingers caught the edges of lavender panties as she watched with sick fascination. For one brief moment we were connected by our love of the color purple and we shared a smile in the mirror, but it wasn't strong enough to hold us together as we danced a macabre striptease. I pulled them down over her hips, and they added to the pile of clothing on the floor. The logical side of my present life was sacrificed to the unlovely girl of my past. I was beaten by a whip made of memories, both of us victims of an event that should have never taken place.

I stood while she watched with sick fascination. Memories emerged with crystal clear accuracy as if leather braided strands were flaying my confidence until blood was drawn. I'd been witness to this scene many times before. No good ever came from it. Years of both of us staring at the scars only exacerbated the self-judgment. Her gaze traveled up, connecting with mine, and I felt her. Every cell carried pain as it misfired deep in the dark synapses of our mind. Overtiredness had claimed me, and I numbly watched as she examined her skin. A fleshy star was mapped as identical fingertips traced pinkish-white flesh. In the mirror, she cupped my breasts. Implants corrected their inconsistencies and won an aesthetic victory by improving their shape and size, and had minimized the appearance of the scarring. Normally I noted these as achievements, but I was too tired to fight this insecure beast who only saw inferiority.

A scarred trail traveled over the shoulder of the body we shared. It snaked down the collarbone in multiple shades of red and pink until it reached the nipple. We fixated on the imperfect skin, patches of mismatched widths, lengths, and ragged edges. The front and back of her body looked like a devil's mark. It mimicked the shape of claw marks, its appearance condemning us both to a purgatory where strapless dresses and bathing suits are nonexistent. I breathed through the emotional pain, running my fingers through my hair. Big mistake.

The sore spot on the backside of my head gave her a new path to roam. I looked up, and she looked back at me. We glided eager fingers through the chestnut strands. There, in a carefully disguised hiding place, was a hairpiece attached to my scalp with skin-safe glue. It was slightly larger than a silver dollar, as was the bald spot it covered. *She* griped and pulled as I winced. With a nearly silent popping sound, the suction released it from my skin.

Defiance rose within me in. This was my life. My pain. Mine! I owned my appearance. The girl whose thoughts took over my reflection was my enemy. My anger toward her was nowhere near abated. Hatred diluted my blood. My carefully guarded serenity was crushed, and rage took its place. Though I hated the children who'd created the fractured girl, I hated her even more for unraveling my self-assurance. As I ran my fingers through my hair for comfort, all I felt was the residual pain from their revulsion. It buzzed painfully down the thread-like strands, through the follicles, each hair shouting in my head a recalled taunt. I wasn't thinking rationally and I knew it was a lifetime ago, but I still held a great deal of hatred for what they'd done.

I.

HATED.

THEM.

I LOST track of time as I humiliated the insecure girl. With each hair I ripped, I regained more and more control. With each strand I felt a little less pain and a little number. I looked down at the small pile of hair lying on the floor. It was over.

For now.

Chapter 4

Falcon

I struck the most intimidating pose I could muster in the hotel security office that morning. I stood tall at six foot four inches, with shoulders wide and thick from my high school football playing days. I'd worked out in the hotel gym just an hour before, so my biceps strained a nice bulge against my clothes. By anyone's standards, I didn't look like a guy you wanted to mess with. I steeled my eyes with an intense glare so there was no mistaking the level of my determination to get what I wanted. And I always got what I wanted.

As a Navy SEAL I was a home grown, loyal to the bone, American made fighting machine. I had served several tours of duty and during my last one I'd been sidelined by an injury. I never saw another tour but chose to improve my physical strength and educate myself in cybersecurity. The knowledge I'd garnered while in the employ of Uncle Sam, combined with my efforts, had birthed some ideas for what I could do when I was discharged.

I served out my commitment and decided not to push my luck re-enlisting. Because of my stature, my skills were rarely tested. On those occasions when they were, I loved a good fight. But today I'd play the professional card instead of the pushy one.

The man in front of me was very chatty—and was testing my patience. He was much smaller than me, which made me wonder how he'd become the head of hotel security. I mean, he didn't have an ounce of muscle on him. I smirked when he introduced himself and I hoped I'd wiped it off my face before he had a chance to see it. Maybe his daddy got him the job.

"Sir, it isn't the habit of this hotel to surrender information on a guest."

I anticipated resistance, so I reached into my pocket for another form of identification. I snapped open the leather displaying my government issue.

"So, will this do it for you?" I gave him a lopsided grin. "You know, as one professional to another?" He looked at the ID and then back at me. He smiled.

"Of course, sir," he nodded. "Anything for Homeland Security."

As the man went to the computer to get Paige's information for me, the office assistant approached. Her look was shameless. Like a cougar eyeing up her prey, she stalked toward me. As she looked me over from head to toe, I catalogued her reactions. I was blessed with an eidetic memory. Reactions such as hers were filed in a mental file cabinet for a time when they could prove useful.

I returned my attention to the man whom I'd already formed a poor opinion of. Even if his actions suited my purpose, what he was doing for me was wrong. In my world, security was a necessity, not a luxury. Though I appreciated his initial reluctance, he'd given in to me too easily. Opportunist that I am, I categorized all the things this man was doing wrong for a time when I approached the owners of this hotel/casino. With a guy like this in the department, they needed to beef up or be vulnerable.

Currently, cyber security was an area of great concern for major corporations as well as small businesses. Hackers grew savvier each day. They exposed the economic structure to frequent attacks within a wireless world. Everyone was at risk, and, because of that, Marcus and I had initiated a covert force under the MarSin Falcon umbrella. The corruption of international securities and investments could collapse governments. While Carter saw to the day to day operations of our business, the three of us founded an organization that would utilize the talents of everyday people. Though innocent enough to the eyes of the outside world, each person involved was a link in a chain. Their specific skillsets were unique, and each person on the secret team took an oath to deny any existence or connection to each other if questioned or incarcerated. Although we hoped that the services of this special team would rarely be required, we knew that unique circumstances required exceptional skills in order to protect the innocent. It was a service available for the direst situations. Luckily the need for that service was rare. For now we were content to run the storefront of MarSin Falcon and provide help to increase the safety of businesses large and small.

This was supposed to be a business trip, pure and simple. The Securities Trade Show. When I'd made my reservations the clerk also mentioned that a real estate convention was being held at the same time. Paige had mentioned she was a realtor. Though I didn't seriously consider that our paths would cross, I was pleasantly surprised that I'd spotted her. I blamed the sudden improvement in my mood on that little, yellow dress she was wearing. Much skimpier than the last time I saw her wrapped in layers against the mountain's winter cold. If this plan worked out, hopefully I'd get to see her.

"Here you go, sir." The security officer handed me a piece of paper with Paige's room number and telephone extension.

"Thanks, man. I appreciate it." I extended my hand for a shake and gave the guy my business card. "Give me a call if you guys need a consult. I'm sure you have the latest and greatest, but it never hurts to hear about what's available out there from an objective point of view." I tucked the paper into my inside jacket pocket. The blonde cleared her throat to get my attention. She'd waited long enough for her boss to disappear into his office. Rolling her chair from behind the desk so I'd have a better view of her, she crossed her long legs and bent over to give me a glimpse of what lay beneath her blouse. She ran her finger down her throat and gave me a hungry look.

"If you need anything while you're here, sir, please, give me a call."

She stood. The skirt she wore barely covered her ass. She sauntered toward me and took my hand, slipping a business card into my palm.

"My number's on the back, sir. Call me. I'll make sure you have a good time while you're in town."

I smiled back at her. "I'll keep that in mind."

I POSITIONED myself on the casino floor, right across from the elevators. If Paige left the hotel she'd have to pass me. I figured I'd pass the time by throwing a little money at the tables. Seeing Paige had been a lucky break. Maybe I'd have another.

I'd been playing for about an hour and a half and was about to play my last hand when I saw a dash of yellow. *Paige?* I swiveled in my chair, but my view was blocked by an approaching cocktail waitress.

"What can I get for you, sir?"

"I was just about to leave." My words were clipped and sharp. I looked around the waitress for a better view, but Paige was nowhere to be found. *Damn it!* I looked up at the woman. "Scotch. Rocks."

Though we'd only spent a few days in each other's company, seeing her revived the feelings I'd had when I'd first met her. Something about her was different. At first, I'd thought she was hot. She'd made my cock twitch. I would have tried to entice her for a one-night stand, but we'd had too many friends in common. If I'd acted on impulse, a scenario like that would have had the potential to bite me on the ass. When the weekend was over, I was glad I hadn't extended the invitation for a quick fuck because she had more depth than I was used to. I even liked her name—Paige. It was short and sweet and didn't at all sound like the names of the women I was used to, like Bambi or Trixie— the twins whose last name was Starr. I'd bet my last dollar Paige wasn't a wham, bam, thank you ma'am kind of girl. She had class. There was a different air about her.

I'd been a perfect gentleman around her, so she'd get the impression I was a nice guy. What she didn't know was that while she'd appreciated the winter scenes around the lake, I'd been inspecting how tightly her jeans hugged her ass. What I hadn't expected was the way she made me feel. Like a lovesick teenager, I noted all her details, how the sun filtered through the trees and caught the shine of her brown hair and how the braid in her hair hugged her neck. On someone else Paige's style that day might have looked juvenile, but on her it looked simplistic and sexy. She didn't need to use a bunch of makeup and low-cut clothes to make her beautiful. She already was.

"Your drink, sir." The waitress handed me a glass that was more ice than alcohol, but I didn't care. Thoughts of Paige had mellowed my mood and I slipped a hundred-dollar bill to her. Her face beamed when she noticed the denomination. "Thank you, sir. Can I get anything else for you?"

"No, darlin'." I drank the scotch down in one gulp, enjoying the burn and chill of the mix. "I'm calling it a day."

Chapter 5

Paige

Mental note: *Take a nap when you change time zones.*

IT WAS my first reflection of the day. What had happened last night was unacceptable, and I refused to let myself get so tired it would repeat. Whenever I was weary, dark thoughts ruled my judgment, they were triggered by exhaustion and stress, and that episode was the first I'd had in a very long time. Even though I'd slept well when it was over, this morning I felt somewhat defeated. No matter how many years passed, self-incrimination met my fatigue and divided me between insanity and lucidity. I became two people when I was drained—the little girl who felt responsible for her injuries, and the woman she grew up to be. In the middle of them both was a confused person who still felt the hurt of not fitting in. Although it was unlikely to hit me again, a dark shroud had already invaded my vacation. I wouldn't make the mistake of getting so exhausted again. I'd worked too long and hard to escape its grip and I refused to willingly give it a foothold.

Over the years I'd become somewhat of a health nut to fight back against any toxic shadows. . I'd put in the time and effort it took to live a lifestyle that promoted a fit body and mind. It worked well for me and helped cancel out negative thoughts. It also dove-tailed nicely with my orderly life. The only time I strayed from my routine was when I was on vacation. Alcohol, at least in the quantities I'd consumed yester-day, wasn't beneficial to a sensible mind. I should have restricted myself and stuck with one, maybe two, Mojitos. Unfortunately, I was suffering the brunt end of my enthusiasm overriding my common sense. It wasn't the first time I'd exercised bad judgment in Vegas, and it certainly wouldn't be the last. But today I had to be good. After last night's macabre scene, I needed a break.

I walked over to the window and pulled the curtains aside. It was a beautiful day. The mountain view from my room was spectacular. Sunshine skimmed the edges of the peaks making them look like inverted ice cream cones. Slowly, the Coney Island atmosphere of the hotel colored my opinion and my mood, and I relaxed into the cozy feel. I walked into the bathroom and grabbed a large towel for a makeshift yoga mat. I stretched out in a pose in the stream of light that enveloped me in its warmth. As I arched my back and bathed in the morning's color, I bore the stiffness that gripped me like a vise. The strained muscles relaxed with the familiar routine. It hurt good. The tightness in my scarred skin rebelled and then surrendered, and, when I was finished, I felt like a different person, longer, leaner, and lighter.

I promised myself that today would be a casual one. I decided on stylishly cuffed skinny jeans, a white, short sleeved, oxford shirt, and black pumps. I'd made plans with Liz and my clothes promised I'd be comfortable for them. Following my routine, applying my makeup was next, and I was relieved when I looked at my reflection. I felt whole; unlike last night there was no more disengagement, and I relaxed.

Dipping a brush into a creamy puddle of foundation, I was once again thankful that my face hadn't been scarred. Cosmetics could hide a multitude of sins and they were such a guilty pleasure. When I was little, my mom had a silly saying for when she opened her makeup bag, powder and paint makes you pretty when you ain't.

My mother had helped me create beauty from ashes, and I would be forever grateful. She'd let me experiment with makeup from the time I was young, and I'd benefitted greatly from her lessons. I was just a little thing when I would sit in the bathroom and watch her "put on her face." She used pencils, blush, and lipstick like an artist to create a glamorous illusion. Sometimes she'd lay out a magazine featuring an actress made up in a new trend. Mom had an eye for spotting something different, even if it was as subtle as a different arch in an eyebrow. A few brushstrokes here, a lip line there, and poof! Instant beauty!

With my makeup now complete, I prepared my hairpiece. I was still a little emotional about tearing it off the night before. Ripping my hair out, my own or my "falsie," wasn't something I was proud of. I didn't discuss it with anyone. Ever. The hairpiece was made to fit the bald spot left from the accident, and Aria was the one who'd designed it. She'd seen the spot when we were children, and when we grew up, she went into a career where she could help me. Formerly, before using her creative talents to flip houses, she was a hairstylist and specialized in the art of hair replacement. She'd helped hundreds of people before she'd switched careers. Many of them suffered from hair loss and she bore their pain like her own. I was her only remaining client.

I remembered back to when I was very self-conscious about wearing the piece, Aria and my mom had said something that helped me accept wearing one. Hair was an accessory.

It was that frame of mind that helped me to experiment today, and I teased the top of my hair for a little fullness. I dressed quickly so I wouldn't be late and smoothed my clothes in the mirror. A little perfume, a dab of gloss and the final touches were complete. The remnants of last night's mental storm faded from gray to white, and as I closed the door I reminded myself it was going to be a good day. Eat. Register. Shop. Everything on my list in its proper order.

I closed the door behind me and walked down the silent corridor. I was the only rider in the elevator, and the white noise hugged me within its silence. I made a mental checklist as I descended and everything I wanted to do was in order by the time the doors opened. Oblivious to the crowd around me, I made my way through the maze of people to get to the taxi station. The line was long and tangled, and I was forced to wait. I almost jumped out of my skin when a large hand reached around my shoulder.

"If I remember correctly, you like a little cream."

The sound of the familiar voice startled and

thrilled me at the same time. It was deep and rich and, just like the brew in his hand, it jolted me like a shot of caffeine. I spun around so quickly I was dizzy, and he quickly cuffed my arm to rescue me from falling.

"Falcon? What are you doing here?" My smile was genuine, and his eyes danced with my response. They crinkled at the corners when he was amused. Although my memory of that feature was rare, I loved it.

"I could ask you the same thing, sweetheart. I'm here for business, the Securities Convention. I heard there was a real estate convention in town and I wondered if you'd be here. Is that where you're off to?"

"I am. I never expected to run into you here, of all places." I stared into his handsome face. *Damn he was gorgeous.* "How are you?" *And why didn't you call me?* He shrugged casually.

"I've been good—and before you say anything, I'm sorry I haven't called. Business doubled after the first of the year. It's been busy—crazy busy—but it's all good. The three of us have been working our asses off. But I'm looking forward to some downtime." He tilted his head toward her. "What about you?"

His eyes never left me as he raised the cup to his lips. His hands were large, and nothing but the lid showed within his grasp. I remembered how small mine felt inside his as we'd walked through the woods. It had been electric then and it still was. I tried to act casual, but the connection I'd felt to him in the mountains was still there.

"I'm good. I've been really busy too, and I get what you mean about downtime. It's rare that I get any. I must come all the way across the country to get it. Anyway, I am here for business as well but I'm making time for pleasure. This is a working vacation for me." His eyes and smile widened, and, gauging from his reaction, it seemed he liked what he heard.

"Then maybe you'll have time for dinner with me." I felt a warm flush creep over my chest. Maybe some women wouldn't like how forward he was, but, despite my body's reaction, I appreciated he didn't play around and got right to the heart of the matter.

"I think that could be arranged."

"Good. What about tonight?" He wore a mischievous expression, and a laugh escaped me.

"You don't waste time, do you? I don't think I have plans but let me check with my friend. I usually spend most of my time here with her, but it shouldn't be a problem. I just want to make sure she didn't buy tickets for a show or something." I removed a business card from my purse. "Here." I placed the card in his palm, closing his fingers around it. "It's my cell." Oh, we had a connection all right, I could see it in his face. He narrowed his eyes and turned his head to give me a side-glance. It was a seductive look.

"Oh . . . I'll call." His voice lowered to a husky depth as he lightly took my hand. "When I do, I hope you can arrange it. I'd really like to see you." I tilted my chin to hide the flush that, once again, washed over me.

"I'll see what I can do."

He lifted my fingers to his lips and kissed them. "Don't forget."

Dayaum!

As he walked away I couldn't tear my eyes from him. Of course, neither could any other woman near me. I was usually so aloof around men but with him I didn't stand a chance. He'd been so polite that weekend in the mountains, I'd taken him for a quiet, soft-spoken man, but I'd been mistaken. He was raw sexuality. There was nothing passive in his demeanor today. I followed him with my eyes as he disappeared down the street.

I KNEW I was late when I approached the hostess and saw Liz out of the corner of my eye. She was sitting at a table, smiling as she sipped a tall glass of iced tea. The best I could do was to muster an apologetic look.

"Sorry."

"Honey bunches of oats, you don't have to apologize. I was enjoying the show."

She made me laugh with her terms of endearment. "The show?" A wicked smile appeared on her face.

"I was there, at your hotel. I was going to meet you, but then I saw that gorgeous man run after you, so I stood close enough to hear but far enough away to be inconspicuous. *Where* have you been keeping *him?*"

I blushed, saying nothing as the waitress approached and took our order. Once she left the table, Elizabeth stared me down. "So?"

I was nonchalant. "So, what?"

"Chica, don't play games with me," she teased. "Who is he, where'd you meet him, and is he single?"

Really? I rolled my eyes and let out a sigh. "His name is Falcon Grey."

"And?" She pried.

"And what?" Exasperated, I answered. "I met him at a Christmas party. The one at Carter and Aimee's." The look on her face told me she wanted more details.

"Dear God, woman!" she said in an exasperated tone. "It's like pulling teeth! And?"

I snapped my napkin in the air and laid it on my lap. I looked her straight in the eye. "And he's single. Satisfied?"

"Well, yes. Yes, I *am* satisfied." Her shoulders stiffened, and she gave me a smug look. I lifted the glass to my lips and hid a smile behind it.

"What? There's more isn't there." She obviously

wanted more because she didn't divert her intrusive gaze.

"He asked me to have dinner with him."

Elizabeth grinned. "And are you going to go?"

"I don't know. I told him I had to check with you. That we might have plans."

"Oh, no, you don't, girl! You're not using me as an excuse to escape the clutches of that gorgeous man. We do not have plans." She smirked at me, her lip curled with attitude.

"I didn't even tell you when he wanted to go!"

She shrugged her shoulders and gave me a matter of fact look. "It doesn't matter. Whatever time he wants to take you—we don't have any plans. How's that? You're off the hook." She winked at me.

Really? "Oh my God . . ." I sighed and sat back in my chair.

"What? I have a reputation to protect. If you like this guy, do you really want his first impression of me to be as your buttinsky friend? No. No. No. You go to dinner with him."

"He's just a friend." My irritation, although slight, fed Liz's humor. I could tell by the look on her face. She was acting like she hoped Falcon would become more than that, but she also knew me better than that. I liked him, but I never let a guy get too close. I liked men, and Falcon was certainly one I'd like to go out with. But more than friends? That would make me vulnerable. No. I wasn't that stupid. Too much chance of getting hurt.

Thankfully, for the remainder of our meal, we moved on to other topics, especially what we wanted to accomplish over the next few days. Interestingly, Liz didn't bring up the topic of Falcon again, but she didn't have to. I knew she hoped for more, but I knew my limits. I'd have to be careful. Dinner and drinks. Nothing too involved. We lived on opposite sides of the state, a six-hour drive away. There was no chance we'd run into each other, so a little fun was okay. Once we returned to the reality of our very busy jobs, the distance between us would suffice to keep us apart.

And for me, that was just fine.

Liz and I spent the remainder of the afternoon registering for the convention and shopping. Thankfully, we hadn't done so much damage to our wallets that carrying our shopping bags was a hindrance. As we walked back up the Strip from the stores, time passed by quickly. We were lost in conversation, and a block or two away from my hotel, when my cell went off. On the display was an unknown number. Liz grinned and raised an eyebrow, then walked a comfortable distance away.

"Hello?"

"Hey, beautiful."

A smile played at my lips. "You greet all the girls like that?"

"Nope. You're the first." He paused. "Are you free for dinner?"

Even though Liz was standing five feet away from me she was shaking her head up and down, encouraging me to accept. I tilted my chin and glared at her.

"I think so."

"Great. How about Gordon Ramsey at eight o'clock?"

Elizabeth had moved closer and she could hear the deep rumble of his voice. When she heard the name of the restaurant, her eyebrows raised, she formed an "O" with her mouth, and she nodded more vigorously.

"That sounds good," I answered, and tried to walk away from my friend. "I'll meet you there at eight."

"That won't be necessary," he objected. "I'll pick you up. We'll drive over together."

Elizabeth smiled from ear to ear.

"Well, okay. I'm in room 1022." Instantly, I regretted the anxious way I'd told him my room number and I tried to backtrack. "You know what? Why don't I meet you outside the lobby? Near the taxi stand. I'll be ready around seven-thirty." He didn't answer, and I thought he might have been offended by my dismissive tone. "Are you still there?"

"Yes, I'm here. I just left a meeting. Sorry, I was preoccupied for a minute."

The tone in his voice told me something was wrong, but I didn't know him well enough to press the issue. "I'll meet you in front of the hotel."

"That sounds good. I'll see you then."

His odd pause in our conversation disturbed me. Maybe I was overreacting. I gave Liz a puzzled look. "Is it me, or was that a little weird at the end?" She shrugged.

"Maybe he forgot something at his meeting. Anyway, you're going to Gordon Ramsey tonight! That place is great!" When she looked at my face she could tell by my expression I was reading too much into the hesitation in his voice.

"Paige . . ."

She read me very well. I overthought everything, but one thing I did well was read people. It was almost a survival technique. Growing up as a victim of bullying, I'd learned to pick up subtle things. She was probably right, so I played it off.

"I'm fine. I promise."

Like two eager puppies spotting a squirrel in the yard, our conversation changed quickly when we saw a woman wearing a fantastic pair of shoes. That, more pleasant, topic sparked a discussion that lasted all the way back to the hotel. I waited outside with her, so she could take a taxi home. As soon as one approached, she hugged me.

"You relax and have a good time tonight, okay?"

I nodded. "I will. I'll call you tomorrow.

"And be careful," she warned. "Even though I was teasing you about him, I don't know this guy. Call me if you need me. Crazy things happen in this town."

"Liz! He's in security, and he was in the military. He isn't going to let anything happen to me, and he's not going to try anything, okay?" I gave her a peck on the cheek. "Now, go home! I'll see you tomorrow."

Chapter 6

Falcon

I couldn't remember when I'd taken such pains to look good for a woman. Then again, I met most women in bars and had them in bed the same night. But this wasn't one of those bars, and Paige certainly wasn't one of those women. This entire situation was different; she was different, and I was too when I was with her. I checked my appearance in the mirror, black suit jacket, white shirt, open at the neck, and no tie. *Damn right, no tie!* Ties were for business. Tonight was about pleasure.

"Hello, sir."

Prompt as always, Jorge had the car right in front of The Aria hotel where I was staying. He opened the door, and I stepped in. He was my go-to person when I was in town. Another ordinary person who wasn't quite so ordinary. I'd met Jorge on a trip to Vegas several months ago. I'd needed a car and someone reliable to take me where I'd had to go. Jorge was always on time, friendly, and knew the best ways to get around Vegas in a hurry. I'd vetted him well. I didn't impress easily, but Jorge was more than a driver, he was a man of exceptional, hidden talents.

"Where are we headed tonight, sir?"

"New York-New York. We're picking up a friend of mine, then going to Gordon Ramsey for dinner."

Jorge looked at me in the rear view mirror. "Gordon Ramsey's, sir? Must be a special friend."

"She is."

The two hotels were Paige and I were staying were neighbors on the Strip, but Vegas traffic was heavy. It could take twenty minutes to get from one hotel to the other. That was okay. It gave me some time to strategize our evening plans.

I was pleased Paige had agreed to have dinner with me, but, reading people as well as I did, I sensed some hesitancy on her part. I had some as well because I'd seen Blake Matthews on the casino floor in my hotel. *Does she know he's here?* It seemed an odd coincidence to me. It was obvious from our last encounter he had a thing for Paige. The thing that seemed most odd was that he'd been with Manuel Vallega and his wife, Marisol.

I rolled my neck and cracked away the stiff tension. Blake Matthews had been nothing but a pain in the ass the entire weekend when we'd met. It had been the same weekend I'd met Paige. If I hadn't asked my friend Carter about her, I'd have thought Paige and Blake were an item. The entire weekend Blake's attitude darkened every time I engaged with Paige. The minute I'd start a conversation with her, Blake would be right in my face. Though I realized that Vegas is a place where the house played against you, I didn't like how the odds were stacked in this game. Though I'd bet bank Paige had no knowledge the three of them were here, I also knew there was a chance she did. It just didn't add up. Those three together. Blake gambling and having drinks with Manny and Marisol. I didn't like it. Especially where Manny was involved.

Manuel Vallega had a story of his own, and none of it was good. His name was linked to many illegal endeavors. Unfortunately, very little proof to convict him of anything concrete existed. Manny is very careful. The lack of evidence left in his wake had frustrated law enforcement for several years. It's rumored his fingers have dipped into everything. Drugs, guns, and human trafficking—all of it bore a smudge of his mark, but not enough to identify him and make anything stick. Every time the DEA, FBI, ATF, or Marshal's service think they have something on him, witnesses and evidence disappear.

Marisol isn't much better. She's become notorious in the tabloids. "Manny's Mannequin" they called her. She's Manny's trophy wife to the media, but close sources believe there's more. So much more that Manny is extraordinarily protective of her. She flew under my radar until she'd been locked-up for an attack on Carter's sister-in-law. Her release was secured by an unprecedented technicality. Now Marisol's name pops up on any intel regarding Manny. Earlier, while I was talking to Paige on the phone, the three of them walked together through the lobby of the hotel. Whether Paige was aware they were there or not, I didn't know. What I did know was the three of them made a nefarious cocktail.

Jorge made the turn under the New York-New York hotel portico. As he pulled the car up to the front, Paige breezed through the revolving door. *Damn!* As always, she exuded class and style. The black dress hugged her curves, and I appreciated that the length showed off her toned legs, but not too much. Most women in Vegas, either local or visiting, exposed as much skin as they could. Not Paige. That's what made her stand out.

Jorge came around the front of the car and opened the door. I stepped out.

"You look gorgeous." The compliment was rewarded with a pink flush on her cheeks.

"Thank you. You look very handsome yourself."

"No, sweetheart, thank you. I thought this would be a boring trip, but you're making it anything but."

She entered the back of the car and slid all the way to the other side of the seat. As she did, I took note of the back of her dress, sheer across the shoulders, with just a hint of sexy. I unbuttoned my jacket and got into the car on the opposite end of the seat. As I looked at her beautiful face, she smiled. Those dimples were killer. *That* was the kind of smile she'd given me in the mountains, and it slayed me. I hadn't realized how much I'd wanted to see her until that moment.

"Have you ever been to Gordon Ramsey?"

"No, but I mentioned it to my friend, and she said it was a nice place. I'm looking forward to going there."

"She's right. It is a nice place, but there are many nice restaurants in Vegas."

"I come here for business several times a year, but I can count on one hand the number of five-star restaurants I've been to. Usually I'm busy, and by the time I'm free to have a little fun, we go somewhere for a late dinner that has a club nearby."

"Then you should go more often. I'm not too much for the club scene but I enjoy a great meal." I added a suggestive tone to the conversation. "I could name a few for you, but then, I'd rather take you to them." She tried to hide it, but her eyes sparkled at the suggestion of future dates. "Is it the town that's making your eyes light up?"

"It's the lights. They get to me every time I come here. Reminds me of Christmas, only here you get to see it every night." Her expression softened. "Have you ever flown into Las Vegas at night?"

"If I have, I was probably sleeping."

She rolled her eyes, a smirk on her lips. "Then you really should make an effort to fly here at night, even if it's one time. Stay awake and look out the window as you're landing. The lights in the dessert look magical from above. With all the glitz and glamour that Vegas has to offer, I think it's really one of the most beautiful sights.

I felt the corners of my mouth rise in a smile, but my thoughts were focused on something other than brilliant bulbs and flashing neon. "I don't know about that. I think I'm looking at one of the most beautiful sights Vegas has to offer." Again, she blushed like a schoolgirl.

"I'm not going to be able to eat if you keep this up."

I frowned. "Why, because I think you're beautiful? I thought most women loved compliments."

"I'm not most women."

She shrugged, then regained her normal composure. That didn't prevent her from changing the subject back to me, and it didn't escape my notice

"So, how was your meeting?"

"The one today?" I was surprised she'd remembered. "It was good. Two new contracts."

"Isn't your company comprised of just you, Carter, and Marcus? I thought I remembered hearing that at the Christmas party. How do the three of you keep up with it?"

"We've just expanded," I explained. "As a matter of fact, we've hired seven people. Carter, Marc, and I had a come to Jesus moment after Aimee got hurt. He wanted some time for a personal life, and Marc and I wanted to grow the business. It was a no-brainer."

Her eyes widened. "Wow! I thought the business was relatively new. That's great!"

"We had planned for expansion six months ago. Initial interest told us that we had something to build on. None of us expected the response we've gotten, so we're pleasantly surprised."

Jorge slowed then stopped the car as we pulled up in front of Paris Las Vegas. I gave Paige a smile as I touched her hand. "We're here."

We waited for Jorge to open the door. When I got out I extended my hand to her, and she slipped hers into mine. A strange kind of possessiveness seared into me as her hand fit perfectly against my palm. I wasn't used to that kind of proprietary feeling, but I could get used to it.

"Thanks, Jorge. I'll call when we're finished."

"Have a good time, sir. I'll be ready when you need me."

Paige giggled.

"What's so funny?"

"You'll have to forgive me." Her voice was low, and the tone was sexy. "I don't think of you as a 'sir.'"

"No?" I looked down at her and placed my other hand at the small of her back. "I might be offended, but I'm happy to know that you think of me at all."

I led her through the lobby of Paris Las Vegas, and then to the restaurant area. The host took my name and then led us to a nice, private table. He then held out the chair for Paige while I seated myself.

The aromas mingled, creating a scent that caressed our senses. I noted the approving expression on Paige's face. Apparently, I'd made the right choice of restaurant. From the neon British flag on the ceiling to the rich, dark wood, the entire restaurant oozed indulgence. Once I ordered a cocktail for her and a beer for myself, I watched as she scanned the menu. She really was the most beautiful woman I'd ever met.

"Everything looks delicious." She peeked at me over the top of the menu.

"I would recommend the steak. It's excellent."

Our server approached. She took my advice, ordering the steak, but when she said she wanted it cooked "so well done it was charcoaled," it earned her a horrified look from both me and our waiter.

"Give us a minute." The waiter nodded, then disappeared. I could feel my forehead crease as I raised my eyebrows. "You're killin' the flavor like that, sweetheart. At least give the beef a break and order it medium or medium well."

She pursed her lips as she struggled to decide. When her mouth relaxed she gave me a cute little smirk.

"You win. I'll try . . . but if I don't like it—"

I didn't give her a chance to finish. "Then we'll send it back."

I relished the small victory. I stood when she rose from her seat. "Be right back," she said as she excused herself. Her soft smile was a clear indication she appreciated the gentlemanly behavior. My mother would be proud.

I watched as she walked away. When she'd taken only a few steps, she double-backed. When she reached the table, she looked down, and when she did, I saw a question in her eyes. I followed her gaze to a member of the wait staff folding the napkin she'd placed on the table just moments ago. Taking her hand, I gently pulled her down to whisper in her ear. "Every time you leave the table, they service your seat."

Her mouth formed a little "O" as she nodded. "Forgot this," she said as she picked up her clutch bag. I watched her walk toward the restrooms as the waiter refilled our water glasses.

"Beautiful lady."

"Yes, she is," I agreed.

When she returned a few minutes later, I leaned in, reached for her hand across the table and took it into mine. "I know a little about you from the last time we were together, but I want to know more."

She leaned into me, closing the distance between us. "There isn't much to tell, really. I'm still listing and selling properties. It keeps me busy since the shore area is always prime real estate."

I was drawn in by her eyes. Her hand was so soft and delicate. I drew circles on the back of it with my thumb. "I wasn't talking about what you do for a living. I know all that. I'd like to know more about you."

"I'm not all that interesting. Just a girl who works hard to pay the bills and indulge her pleasures." She held up the clutch to emphasize her point. "Like Aria and Declan, I have a house on the ocean, which I absolutely love. I'm constantly surrounded by people when I'm working, but I relish my time alone. My work also dictates that I socialize, so in my free time I enjoy the solitude. When I do go out for pleasure it's with our small group—you met most of them at Carter and Aimee's party. Aria's been my best friend since we were kids. When she married Declan, they were all part of the package. Now we're all friends." She squeezed my hand. "So, what about you? I'm sure your story is much more interesting than mine."

"You're good at that, you know?" I gave her a knowing look, noting she'd quickly changed the subject after a few sentences.

"Good at what?" She straightened as she removed her hand from mine and took a sip from her drink.

"Deflecting." I was sure my expression said that I was on to her. "You're very smooth. I want to know more about you, and you somehow get me talking about me."

"I'm not deflecting." She gave a slight chuckle. "I live a pretty boring life."

"You're not getting off that easy, sweetheart. I call bullshit—and don't try to pull that one on me again." I mimicked her action, straightened my spine, and gave her hard look. "Interrogation was one of my specialties in the military." Her expression turned serious, so I winked at her to ease the tension. It worked. She rolled her eyes at me and smiled, positioning her hands in her lap.

"Okay, Mr. Interrogator," she teased. "Fire away"

"What about your family? Do they live in Rehoboth?"

"No, but they're not too far away. Everyone lives in Maryland. Mom and Dad retired to Kent Island on the Eastern shore. They always loved it there, and still do. When I was young we lived in Baltimore but vacationed in Ocean City. I think we all love being by the water. My brother, Rick, lives in Maryland too. He has a waterfront home on the Magothy river, and in the summer spends most of his time on his boat. I thought I had him convinced to move to the ocean, but he says that he has the luxury of the river, the bay, and the ocean when he's on the boat. His family all love the water as much as he does. I have great memories of our childhood vacations. As a matter of fact, that's how I met Aria."

She paused for a moment, and I saw a glimpse of sadness. She disguised it very quickly. "The rest of the details are boring. I love to cook. I love to shop. I like to have my hair and nails done." She lifted her chin with a defiant tilt and gave me a cheeky smile. "Your turn."

I had to laugh. "It sounds like you have a great family. Not everyone can say that."

I could see she wanted me to elaborate, but our

food had arrived. I watched as she ate, enjoying and noting her expressions and mannerisms. When she took the first bite of her steak, I could tell she enjoyed the flavor. I watched with pleasure as she closed her eyes and savored the first bite.

"Mmm. This *is* good."

"Told you." I gave her a wink and turned my attention to what was on my plate.

We didn't say another word throughout the meal. Partly because we were hungry, but, on my end, I simply loved watching her. I was pleased she'd taken my advice about the preparation of the food. Even if she didn't realize it, in my work it showed a speck of bravery. It also showed that she trusted me, even if it was a small amount.

Once we finished our meal, we ordered coffee. I also took the liberty of ordering a chocolate dessert. Initially, she refused, but once I told her we could share it, she gave in. She took the first bite, sliding the fork over her plump lips as she pulled it from her mouth. I could have watched her do that for hours.

"This is delicious!"

"There you go, sweetheart. You can have it. It's all yours."

She frowned and lifted a forkful in the direction of my mouth. "Just one bite? Come on; you don't know what you're missing."

Determined. I like that. I grimaced but humored her by letting her place the bite in my mouth. It was much better than I expected. "I'm not a big fan of chocolate, but this is pretty good."

Her pleasure at my response made her glow. "See? You educated me about steak, and I did the same for you with chocolate."

Her satisfied look told me she, too, enjoyed small victories.

The rest of our time at the restaurant was filled with easy conversation. We lingered over the coffee and she opened up a bit more, talking about the people in our circle of connection. I enjoyed the sound of her voice. Her tone was soft, and her words were crisp and succinct. As she delighted me, I could imagine her charming potential buyers. She spoke a little more about her family. The slight lift of her chin told me they were good people, very supportive of her. Her demeanor only changed when I asked about the schools she'd attended. A look of defiance made her lips and jaw tighten. Her shoulders went back as her spine became more rigid. All of this she did in a slight way as she attempted to project an indifferent nonchalance.

"Just the usual, grade school, high school, college. What about you?"

Again with the deflecting. It was obvious to me

from the way she skimmed the details so quickly there was a story there. She gave me just enough of the facts to answer the question. No more, no less, but even though it was little information, I knew much more than I had before.

I decided not to mention Blake, Manny, or Marisol. Marisol never seemed to be a good topic for anyone, and from the history Carter had given me, Paige was no exception. If she knew they were in town she hadn't mention it, and I didn't want to be the one to bring it up and possibly ruin the evening.

Abandoning my thoughts, I concentrated on her. She had a beautiful face—especially her lips. They were full and plump with just the right amount of lipstick, elegant but not clownish. The dark red color she wore on them complimented her skin. Her eyes were very expressive, deep pools of rich brown, like the chocolate we'd had for dessert.

". . . never grows old when you have such a beautiful view. I wouldn't have expected it." She stopped talking and gave me a puzzled look. I'd tuned out her voice when I was distracted by her looks. "Fal?"

"Sorry." My apology was weak. After all, I was enjoying myself by staring at her.

Embarrassed, she looked down into her lap. "I think I should be the one who's sorry. I was rambling."

"No, no." I objected and reached out for her hand. "I was just lost in thought."

She looked up at me. "A good thought?"

I brushed against her palm with my fingers. "I was wondering how I'd get you to go out with me again."

"Oh . . ." she whispered. She gave me a coy look and spoke in a hushed tone. "I suppose you could ask me. That's always a good place to start."

"Sweetheart, you tell me when, and I'll surprise you with where."

Chapter 7

Paige

Falcon was so close I could feel his breath fall on my shoulder. And he smelled so good! I wanted to nuzzle him just to inhale his fragrance. It was a bracing scent with hints of cloves and pine. He walked me to my room. Once we arrived at my door, I retrieved the card key from my clutch.

"Do you want to come in?" I was enjoying the view as he leaned up against the doorframe looking all kinds of delicious.

"No, I think I'll let you catch up on some sleep tonight." He made me feel warm inside. His gaze was intense, and his tone was demanding.

"When can I take you out again?"

"I'll be in town for a month. I'm sure we'll have at

least one more opportunity." I teased, and he played along.

"A month, huh? How about tomorrow?"

His grin made me feel things I never had before. "I think I have plans with Elizabeth tomorrow, but maybe next week, okay? I should be free then."

"What about tomorrow?" he insisted.

I knew he'd heard my answer the first time but chose to ignore it. He took the key from my hand, opened the door and handed it back to me. I shivered from the rush of cold air that came from my room as he held the door ajar with his foot. He placed his arm around my waist and pulled me against him.

"Pretty confidant, huh?" I looked into his eyes. The heat in his gaze made me feel wanton as I anticipated his kiss. He didn't disappoint and pressed his mouth against mine. The kiss was soft, but his lips were firm and demanding. It stole my breath the moment we touched. My body reacted of its own accord, responding and returning with equally unbridled passion. His tongue pressed for entry, and I allowed him to explore. I was tingly with unexpected hunger, the sparks igniting from my lips to my core. He was dangerous. When, he pulled away, he left me breathless.

"Tomorrow?" His voice was husky and thick as he said the words against my ear.

"Tomorrow." I nodded.

He backed away and gestured toward the door with his chin. "Go on, now. I'll wait until you lock the door."

I disappeared into the room and turned the lock. Leaning my head against it I listened for his voice.

"Good girl. Get some rest. I'll see you tomorrow."

OH MY GOD . . .

I couldn't remember having such a good time on a date—but, then, when had I really gone on a date? Most of the men I met were just for drinks and a hookup. The possibility of anything more never entered my mind. Certainly not a relationship. But that was a date. Something I'd never had.

When I'd been a teenager I'd known enough about how to dress and do my makeup so I was pretty enough to get asked out. The problem was that the same girls who'd teased me in elementary and middle school now went to my high school. Anytime the little witches started their whispers I knew it was about me. I had no doubt they informed the boys *exactly* how much of a freak they thought I was. So, I decided to beat them at their own game and never went out on dates. I would talk to the boys in school, but never more than that. I refused to put myself in a situation where I would be pitied or ridiculed any more than I already was. The girls didn't bother me so much because they were more concerned with their social game than they were with me. They'd already done enough; why beat a dead horse?

After the second year of high school, I never gave it much thought. It became my normal. I did the same thing in college, concentrating on my grades and nothing more. I had more than enough time on my hands to develop my own style. *Thanks, Mom!* By the time I graduated, people took me seriously. Women wanted to be my friend, men wanted to date me, and my professors listened to what I had to say. It was the perfect testing ground for my future goals. I was listening to a finance lecture and the proctor said real estate very seldom lost its value; it almost always appreciated. I knew that was where I wanted to concentrate my efforts, not just selling it, but investing in it. If I was eager and hardworking, I could further my agenda of being financially independent. I didn't want to rely on anyone for anything. I imagined myself living a very solitary personal life, while having a very social professional one. But one date with Falcon made me wonder if I should take a chance.

I thought back to when I'd first met him. I'd become quite the actress over the years. Although I'd loved the idea of the party, I was feeling a bit claustro-phobic. When Falcon had asked me if I'd like to take a walk I jumped at the chance. All I'd expected was fresh air. Of course, I was polite to him, he was Carter's friend. I planned on doing my usual nodding courte-ously and feigning interest, but, even then, I knew Falcon was different.

I wasn't certain if it was his looks or the tone of his voice. He'd pointed things out along the way that I found beautiful, and I hadn't been reserved in telling him what I saw. An icicle wasn't just an icicle. When we'd come upon a bare bush encased in ice, I saw it as crystals melting in the sun. After a while, he'd begun to see things through my eyes. He'd lived there a long time and had become desensitized to the beauty I saw.

My breath had caught in my throat when I'd seen a red cardinal against the backdrop of untouched snow. He'd gotten very quiet, and we'd watched it until it flew away. Something had happened that afternoon, to me and to him. My life had become so black and white, going from home to work and back again. The same routine over and over. I'd forgotten to enjoy myself, and only did so when I went on vaca-tion. This was different. That afternoon had reminded me to take pleasure in the little things. I'd become so guarded my sight grew dim. I don't know what had changed that day other than me. We'd walked for the longest time, and I'd enjoyed every minute of it. Even the air had more clarity. Falcon had touched me, and my fingers had tingled when he'd taken my hand and led me to a fallen tree. We'd sat close, listening to the wind as it sang through the pines. The fragrance that had followed had been heavenly, and I'd closed my eyes to enjoy it. Then we heard a *crunch, crunch* sound. I'd squeezed his fingers when a fawn approached. I'd never expected to enjoy myself so much. My nose and toes were frozen, but I didn't care. Falcon had rubbed them to warm them up while we'd watched a squirrel outwit a fox. Nothing that day had been routine. Certainly not the way he'd behaved nor the way I'd responded. It had been . . . magical.

I hadn't given it much thought when the weekend was over. I'd known it would be just a memory I'd cherish. I'd thought my time with Falcon had been a one-time fluke. I hadn't expected anything more from it—until now.

Maybe it wasn't magic at all. Maybe it was him. I'd never liked anyone enough to want to know them, but I really liked him. The feelings I'd pushed away when the Christmas party was over resurfaced in one night with him. Even though the date tonight had been out of my comfort zone I couldn't help but dream about the things other women dreamed about. The more I was with him, the more I wanted to be with him. *So, how far do I let this go?*

Falcon was magnetic. I liked being with him, and that was my dilemma. I knew enough to know that appearance wasn't everything, unlike the popular saying. He liked what he saw because it was an illusion. If I saw him again, and I wanted to, how lightly could I tread without drowning? Eventually, I'd have to withdraw. Even though I risked having my feelings crushed, it would be for his own good, and my sanity. When I thought of hurting him I got an ache in my chest, but, then again, I was being presumptuous to think he felt enough for me to be hurt. The risk I was really taking was in letting myself go without calculating everything beforehand. It might be painful, but it would be painful for me no matter what. I'd been through worse than what I was anticipating. *So what's the problem?*

The problem was I didn't want to let him go. Yet.

Tonight was a repeat of the magic I'd thought I'd only experience once. I loved how special he made me feel. He'd only said he'd like to see me while he was in Vegas, so maybe that was the solution. Vegas. It was a temporary town. Things happened there that would never happen when someone returned to their normal life. It would probably be the same for us. He was as dedicated to his work as I was to mine, not to mention the logistics of where we each lived. It was a very sound and convenient excuse. We would probably talk on the phone a few times, and, little by little, "the relationship" would fade away—that is if one even developed. Now, I had a plan.

As I sat down on the couch, I realized I'd already fallen back into my old habit of working everything out ahead of time, but at least I felt content. The perfect scenario had presented itself and it didn't feel overwhelming. He wanted to go out again, and I'd go as many times as he asked, and I liked. I could enjoy as much of Falcon as I wanted while we were here.

I undressed and put my pajamas on. A million possibilities played out in my mind. As I climbed into bed, I felt lighter than I had in ages. The comforter enveloped me in its downy softness, and I closed my eyes to embrace the mental pictures. It had been a long time since I'd been this excited, so I enjoyed the lovely thoughts. Outside I could hear the hum of the roller coaster. It had as many twists and turns as the possibilities I entertained. One thing I was sure of, though, I was in for a thrilling ride.

Chapter 8

Falcon

I hadn't planned a month-long stay, but at dinner, Paige had mentioned she'd be there that long, so, I changed my plans and let my partners know I'd be marketing MarSin Falcon from here.

Paige was smart, interesting, and sexy, and I knew I'd be a fool if didn't take the chance to get to know her better. I enjoyed her company, which was quite a new experience for me. Normally, I shied away from entanglements, but this was something different, something big. We were like-minded on many topics, and she responded to my playfulness with good humor. I'd felt the same pull toward her on our first dinner date as I had when I'd first met her. There was only one thing that nagged at me: Blake.

Just seeing him reminded me of how much a pain in the ass he when I'd first met him. There were too many unknowns for me regarding Blake and Paige. Then, there was also his relationship with Manny Vallega. *What's up with the two of them?* My gut was telling me their being together was more than a chance meeting in Vegas.

Within MarSin Falcon, a service existed that went beyond normal security. That part dictated that it was my business to know everyone else's. The collection of intel was a multilayered task. Most people wouldn't think to go as deep as we do when the need arises. Having the security clearance that I had made it almost impossible to hide anything, that was if I was looking into a person's background. I was just as surprised as Carter when I found out Marisol and Manny were married. That was due to the fact neither of them had been on my radar, I'd left that to Carter. Chasing Marisol's past was cathartic for him, and I'd known better than anyone the feeling of satisfaction when bringing down someone who'd wronged you. But Carter hadn't gone deep enough when he'd investigated; he'd been blindsided when Marisol had been released. That was when I'd started doing a little digging of my own. I hadn't liked what I'd found.

Manny and Marisol. Not a good pairing. Both were narcissistic to the point of being sociopathic. The collateral damage they might leave behind would be an issue—especially if it involved people I cared about. There was only one-way to ease my mind; keep them under surveillance. When I'd first gotten to know Paige, my vigilance had faltered. Now that I know her better, I won't let that happen again.

I was good at reading people and knew Paige was just as interested in me as I was in her. I also knew her history with Marisol. She'd fallen through a window during the attack on Aria Sinclair. There was no way she'd be relaxed if she knew Marisol was in the hotel next to hers.

A smile filled my face when I thought of Paige being such a tough little cookie. Her recovery had been brutal. Being thrown through a window would have shattered someone of lesser grit, but she was still funny, sweet, and gorgeous. My kind of woman.

As I stripped and got into the shower, my mind ran risk calculations. It was a blessing and a curse having numbers constantly running through my head. As I leaned against the tiled wall, I tried to let the hot water pound out the tense muscles in my neck and shoulders. The story Carter had told me was no longer just a bunch of words over a few beers. I could clearly picture a haughty, superior Marisol gloating over an injured Paige. I didn't like what I saw.

Marisol was a heartless bitch. Manny Vallega's

heart was as black as pitch. I'd seen photos of the carnage he'd left behind when someone had crossed him. *What a match.* My heart clenched as I imagined Paige at their mercy. If the two of them considered Paige either a threat or expendable in any way, I had to keep an eye on her. *Not a problem.*

I let my mind wander to more pleasant thoughts. As she'd carried on conversation at dinner, the soft candlelight only enhanced how stunning she'd been. Her eyes had twinkled, her smile had been warm, and flickers of light had danced through her hair. The reaction my body had at the thought of her exposed how I felt. I knew I couldn't make a move on a girl like her that soon. Carter would kick my ass. So would Declan. Paige wasn't somebody I could play with and toss away. I closed my eyes and wrapped a tight fist around myself. The woman had left me with only one option, to relieve my pent-up frustration on my own. If she were anyone else, I would have had her on her back in my bed by now. I stroked harder as I pictured her face. I could get lost in those sweet, warm eyes. My heart squeezed in my chest and my hand imitated the same action as it moved faster. I surrendered to the explosive feelings thoughts of Paige gave me. I could take a bullet with less reaction—and it scared the shit out of me.

I reached for a towel as I opened the shower door. The bathroom was filled with steam. The walls sweated with it and it clung to the mirror. As I wrapped the towel around my waist I headed into the other room and sat down at the laptop. I looked up restaurants, clubs, and shows. If I was going to extend my stay in Vegas, I had to keep an eye on her without her sensing it, and if I wined and dined her, she wouldn't suspect I detected a threat against her.

With pen in hand I scribbled some keywords on a notepad. They could prove useful in a search on the Vallega's. I made one list for Manny and one for Marisol. As more uneasy thoughts came to mind, I also added a third person to investigate, Blake Matthews.

Something about that guy was raising red flags. Not that I gave two shits about the guy personally, but the weekend I'd met Paige he'd acted like he'd owned her. I would have put a fist in his face in a heartbeat if he'd tried to give her grief, but he'd given me dirty looks instead. No harm in that. He was just being selfish. This was different. Now that I knew the company he was keeping, he'd become as much a threat as the Vallega's.

Chapter 9

Blake

B lake was pissed. While waiting at the bar to meet Manny and Marisol, he'd seen Falcon Grey exit the lobby and get into a black Mercedes. He didn't like him and hadn't since the first time they'd met. He was a cocky, self-righteous son of a bitch with a misguided sense of entitlement. He could tell Grey was military when he'd met him. Blake wasn't short, but he guessed Falcon was half a foot taller than him. As Blake had played the gentlemen, Falcon's attention had been focused on Paige. It wasn't as though he'd made a secret of it either. Blake had ached to put a fist in Falcon's face, but, instead, had allowed his anger to steep all weekend, leaving a bitter taste in his mouth. Blake had tried to discourage him, narrowing his eyes in menacing looks every time they'd been in the same room. The stupid ass hadn't even seemed affected; he'd just looked Blake over as if he'd considered him a nuisance. Blake had seen red as compliments had dripped from Falcon's mouth, his eyes blatantly roaming over Paige from head to foot. Yet, whenever Blake had tried to get near her, Falcon had acted as if he were a pest and had blocked his attempts at engaging her. *Who the hell did he think he was?* Those were his friends! Nonetheless, he'd played the part of the professional businessman he'd been. He wouldn't let some government, over-trained gorilla eliminate him from the race, but that had been neither the time nor place. He'd been too busy being cordial with everyone else to play his game. It had been the longest damn weekend of his life, and he hadn't been about to let a soldier boy undo his efforts towards Paige.

Blake's anger was stoked by the burn of his fifth shot of whiskey—or was it his sixth? He belted the liquid down his throat and fixated on the fact that he'd been taking his time with Paige. He liked her, but she was hesitant, keeping him at a distance. It frustrated the hell out of him. He'd behaved like a gentleman because she hadn't seemed interested in anything more than friendship, but she was as attentive to Falcon as a shine brought notice to a fast car, and he'd thought he was slick because of it. What she'd failed to realize was that Blake hadn't reached that level in the industry by taking no for an answer. Rejection only made him more insistent. He'd played the good friend to her for more than two years, and he was sick of it! Blake had been working hard to get her attention, and he'd never had to work to get a woman to like him. As a modeling agent he had access to more than enough attractive girls. They were always willing to do whatever he wanted in order to get the prime shoots. Only two of the women in his stable had been spared, Aimee because Declan always had an eye on her, and Marisol.

He'd learned how to handle Marisol over the years. She'd been an easy pastime, but since Manny had been around, he'd left her alone. Marisol had threatened to tell Manny they'd had sex a few times. Normally, he wouldn't have taken the threat to heart, but he knew Manny excused everything she did, instead, placing the blame on those connected and making them pay for her transgressions That was a secret the little bitch had kept for years, that Manny was her husband.

He'd had no idea her drug connection had been affiliated with a drug cartel. There'd been rumors that Manny was the top guy, and Blake didn't want a reason to find out. He made nice with Marisol and, in turn, Manny and he got along. Blake needed Marisol. She acted as liaison between him and the other models she knew who wanted cocaine. She couldn't get her hands dirty because she was still closely watched, but it worked out to his advantage. The models had what he wanted, and they wanted what he had. They were more than happy to use other forms of currency as payment for their drug habits. He'd been able to use the term blow in a few contexts where they were concerned. It worked out for everyone except he'd had to be nice to Marisol.

She was his connection to Manny's drugs and the models who wanted them. It afforded Blake a bit of unexpected luck since both Manny and Marisol wanted to keep their images clean. It nauseated him.

He'd been with both of them when he'd seen Paige come out of her hotel. He'd quickly devised a plan to use her to make the trip more interesting and had been about to approach her when he'd seen Falcon exit the car. Anger had risen in him like an approaching storm when he'd seen Paige with him. She'd looked relaxed. The muscles in his jaw had tensed as they'd driven away. She wasn't in a league with Blake by any means, but she could do better than Falcon. *Bastard!*

Resentment had eaten at him like a cancer, and he'd obsessed about seeing them all the way back to his hotel. He'd have get on her good side, keeping an eye on her at the same time. The Aria was a more contemporary, hip hotel, and he could convince her to move over there. He could play the nice guy, picking up the tab for her entire stay. Eventually, he'd cash in on her gratitude. It wouldn't take long to win her over. He'd even throw in a few gifts so she'd feel obligated to thank him. Then he'd collect on the debt with a pound of flesh, literally. He was an expert at getting women on their knees, and she was one he'd spent too much time on. Salivating at the idea of knocking the smug attitude out of her, he was appeased. Timing was everything, and he would be vigilant to find the perfect opportunity—when she was alone.

The distinctive click of stilettos on tile warned him of Marisol's arrival.

"Are you ready to go to dinner?"

He glanced behind her and noticed Manny was absent. "Where's your husband?" Irritation darkened his timbre. She picked up on it immediately and threatened him with an equally hostile tone.

"He had a meeting." She grabbed his chin between her thumb and index finger. "I'd advise you to rethink how you talk to me." He angrily snapped his head away from her grasp, and, in response, she defiantly moved into his personal space. "Perhaps you should spit out the reason for your attitude."

He loathed her superior posture. "I just saw Falcon Grey."

Her eyebrows shot up. "Carter's dog? Why would he bother you?"

"He doesn't." Walking away from her, he attempted to disguise any telltale emotion. She stared after him, boring holes in his efforts.

"You're a liar."

Defiantly, he spun around., "And you're a bitch."

A sinister smile touched her lips, and she regarded him with a narrowed glare. "Touché."

Like a matador interprets the movement of a bull, she'd moved aside to allow his testosterone driven charge to pass. "Now, if your little temper tantrum is over, perhaps we can have a nice meal."

Blake responded with a smile, then led the way into the restaurant. Marisol was right; he was a liar. That was exactly the skill he needed to put his plan in motion.

Chapter 10

Paige

S nowflakes floated delicately and deliciously, high above the frosted lights. Their flavor was enormous as the tiny crystals burst into sparkles, igniting on my tongue and making light dazzle through my smile. They were sweet, like Amaretto, matched only by a hypnotizing texture. Soft and sticky, gold-trimmed batting stuck to my body in a sugary embrace. I rolled around in it. Hip to hip it cushioned me as I sailed high above the lights. The sky was cobalt and was decorated with tiny, white, buzzing lights. There were too many to count. They just buzzed, and buzzed . . .

. . . and buzzed!

. . .

MY BODY IGNITED, and my thoughts cleared as I shot from my dream. The sudden jolt up in bed made me dizzy. I fumbled for my cell, suddenly petrified something terrible had happened. No one would ever call me in the middle of the night unless it was bad news.

What time is it? Four in the morning!

I picked up the phone. An image of Declan and Aria lit up on the display. *Oh my God! Aria!* I pressed the answer button, hoping and praying everything was okay.

"Hello?" My voice was thick with worry.

"Paige? It's Declan."

He sounded . . . different. My heart immediately quickened, beating hard against my chest. His tone caused a rippled chill that traveled up the back of my neck. Declan's usually steady voice was quivering, and he sounded like he'd been crying. He was the steadiest person I knew. All at once, my mouth went dry, and my tongue grew sticky. I hopped out of bed in search of a bottle of water while I held the phone up to my ear.

"What's wrong?"

"Calm down." As soon as he heard the apprehension in my voice, his tone immediately became soothing. "Everything is fine. Aria and I . . . ." His voice cracked with emotion. "We have a little girl."

A little girl?

A LITTLE GIRL!

I reached for the bed pillows, propping them behind me so I could sit up.

I wanted to talk. I needed to talk. I wanted all the details.

Tears stung the back of my eyes. "Oh, Declan! I'm so happy for you! Congratulations!"

My mind bounced with emotions. Joy, fear, and concern collided, making me laugh and cry at the same time. This wasn't supposed to happen yet. When I'd left, Aria's pregnancy still had six weeks to go. I'd planned to be home for the baby's birth; I'd promised her. I'd even hosted her baby shower before I left so everything would fall nicely and neatly according to plan. I'd even told her I'd cancel my trip if she wanted me to, but she teased me, telling me it would take her nearly a month to put all the gifts away. We'd made plans to have manicures and pedicures as soon as I got back because she wanted to look pretty when she met her baby.

"I feel terrible I'm not there." Regret hung heavy in my voice. "Are they okay? This is too early, isn't it?"

"They're good." His tone had returned to calm, easing my concern a little more.

"Aria's going to need time to heal, but she's doing well. The placenta was beginning to detach, and she had to have a C-section. I'm not going to lie to you, it was very scary for a while. They were not only concerned about that but also about her womb tearing. When she began to have contractions, they told me to get her to the hospital as soon as possible. The damage that Marisol did to her womb when she stabbed her was the culprit. Although it was repaired after the attack, it weakened through the pregnancy. When I got her to the hospital the contractions were pretty strong. Of course, her recovery will take a little bit longer, and I may have to tie her to the bed to keep her down, but the doctors did what was necessary. They told me that the way they stitched her uterus back together corrected any deficiencies. Once she's healed they tell me that future pregnancies shouldn't be a problem."

"Future pregnancies?" I laughed. I imagined that wasn't the first thing on Aria's mind.

"Yes, well, I'll think about that another time. Right now, I want to concentrate on this sweet little girl!" His voice trembled, on the edge of emotion once again.

"Paige . . . this baby . . . she's the most beautiful little girl in all the world. She is absolute perfection—just like her momma."

His emotions were infectious. I cried a cascade of tears as I was engulfed by the affection in his voice. There was no denying the love he had for his wife and daughter. I was so thankful Aria had a husband who loved her more than life. His words of warmth fell on me like a fuzzy blanket.

"She has gorgeous, thick, dark hair—a headful—and the sweetest, tiniest, pink lips; they draw up into a heart shape when she's hungry or about to cry. And her eyes . . . Paige, she has the most beautiful eyes with the longest, darkest lashes I've ever seen on a child. She just stared at me when I went to the nursery to see her. They're big, and blue, just like Aria's.

"Other than her mother, she's the only girl I've ever fallen in love with at first sight."

I cried and laughed with every descriptive word. He was so happy and proud. I could almost picture her sweet face.

"You sound like a man in love. I can't wait to see her and hold her."

"I'll send pictures to your cell as soon as I hang up," he said proudly.

"Please do! I'll catch the first plane out of here, so I'll be home to help." I knew Elizabeth would understand, but I hated that I was leaving Falcon behind.

"No, Paige, please don't do that. It isn't necessary."

I was momentarily caught off guard and a little hurt.

"It isn't that I don't want you here, and I'm not trying to hurt your feelings, but we're covered. Aria is going to be staying in the hospital for a week or more.

The doctors want to keep an eye on her because they really want her to heal well. You know how she is. If she's home, she wants to be busy. The docs thought it best that she rest, and the baby is going to be in the NICU. We were lucky she was a little over five pounds, but she's still a preemie. The best I can hope for is that the two of them will come home the same day. I don't even want to think about having to leave the baby behind at the hospital. That would crush Aria. You stay. Finish your vacation. Aria's mom is here with me, and Carter and Aimee are driving down tomorrow. They're going to be staying at our house. By the time you get home everyone will be leaving. Then you can spend all the time you want with them—and Aria will tell you all the details, I'm sure." He paused. "And I'm not going to apologize for wanting to keep her under my thumb for a few weeks. I want her to rest as much as the doctors do."

I couldn't fault him for being overprotective. I felt the same way about Aria that he did. What he said made sense.

"Are you sure?" My emotions played with me because I wanted to see them, but if I stayed in Vegas there was a strong possibility I might be able to explore new emotions—and that was just as exciting as what was happening at home.

"I'm positive. Have a good time. Play a little. You

need the time off and, honestly, if you were here, it would be harder for me to make her rest. You know how the two of you are."

"True." I laughed because I could picture the look of pure exasperation on his face. He probably even rolled his eyes.

"Okay. You win. But be on the lookout for a huge bouquet of flowers." Then something hit me. "Oh, my gosh, Declan! I forgot to ask the baby's name!"

His tone dropped an octave and was cloaked with reverence. "Her name is Karas—Karas Rose Sinclair."

It was the names of two women who had been loved and lost far too soon. Karas was Lacey's middle name and Rose was the name of Declan's mother.

"It's perfect," I whispered. "Please give Aria my love. I'll call her in a few days."

"I will," he promised.

"And, please, give little Miss Karas lots of hugs and kisses for me."

After we finished our conversation, I laid back and tried to go to sleep, but it was impossible to close my eyes. Ripples of excitement coursed through me, more in one day than in my entire life. First from Falcon, then the new baby. All I could think of was shopping. I wanted to buy so many things to send home. Then, it occurred to me where I was. The stores never closed here! I would have called Elizabeth, but it was too early.

I could call Falcon! This would give me a glimpse of the man whose company I craved. Plus, he'd said he was an insomniac.

Excitedly, I called his cell. I couldn't contain my enthusiasm. I was taking a chance, for sure. If I woke him, he might be angry. Then I would apologize and tell him to go back to sleep. But if he was awake? I really wanted his company and to share the news.

And who didn't like shopping?

FALCON WAS A GOOD SPORT. He didn't get angry when I called. He picked me up, and after dragging him through many stores, I noticed his large hands were perfectly designed to hold many bags.

"Are you sure you're not angry? I know I dragged you out of bed, but you told me you had trouble sleeping!"

He gave me a sly, but playful, look. "If it was anyone else . . ."

"I'm so sorry!" I laughed. "I didn't want to wake Elizabeth—"

"So you woke me instead?" He interrupted and gave me an incredulous look, laughing at the irony.

"I would have woken up her whole family if I called—and I really wanted to go shopping! I'm going to FedEx everything home. It's a lot of stuff. Too much to take on the flight!"

He looked up one arm and down the other, and then held the armload of bags up in the air for effect. "Really? You could've fooled me!"

"I am sorry." I scrunched up my nose. "Are you really angry?" I bit my lip as insecurity gripped me.

He dropped his arms. "No. I'm just teasing you."

His expression was playful, so I smacked at his upper arm. The firmness hidden under his shirt nearly bruised my fingers, and I blushed.

"Not funny, Fal."

"I can't help it, beautiful." He laughed at my expense. "You're just too easy."

The look on his face assured me, and I smiled.

"Ah," he said returning my smile. "That's better. It's nine a.m. You want to grab breakfast?"

The truth was shopping had made me hungry, but fatigue was setting in as the excitement fizzled out. I was still reeling from what had happened the last time I was tired. Although I didn't feel the same angst I had that night, I was winding down and was a little fearful I'd fall victim to my weakness once again.

"I'd better go back," I explained. "I want to pack up all this stuff and get it out today. I'll just order something in my room." The look on his face told me he didn't like that idea and had one of his own.

"I'll tell you what. We'll eat breakfast at my hotel. I'll call room service. I can help you wrap while we're waiting for the food. Once we're finished, I can call someone to get the packing supplies and you can ship from the hotel."

"You don't mind?" My heart tripped over his thoughtfulness.

"Not at all." He winked at me. "And I'll have company for breakfast."

I hesitated, but his pleading made him boyishly irresistible. My stomach fluttered with butterflies. Dare I push the fatigue knowing what might lie ahead? Something inside told me it was safe to take the risk.

I shrugged and looped my arm inside of his. "Okay, why not?"

The corners of his mouth lifted in a victorious grin.

"You may regret inviting me," I warned. "Breakfast is my favorite meal of the day!"

Chapter 11

Paige

I was happier than I could ever remember being.

The days and weeks had passed by quickly, and I'd found I enjoyed Falcon's company more than I'd cared to admit. I wanted to allow myself the freedom to get close to him, but there was a gnawing hesitancy, ingrained in me from all the past hurts. Something about Falcon drew me in. I was so accustomed to planning everything out, but days with Falcon were refreshingly spontaneous. Unlike most men I'd met, I couldn't figure him out because he seemed to have no agenda. His only goal was to do things with me that we both enjoyed. He was kind, confident, and considerate. I spent more time on the phone with him in just a few days than I did my family in a month. Thinking about being in someone else's life daily usually made me feel strangely claustrophobic, but I didn't feel that way with Falcon. Conversations with him were stimulating, and when I talked, he heard every word. I had a preconceived notion that a man of his size and stature would be somewhat chauvinistic, but he never patronized me. He said he liked seeing me happy.

One day, when we were having coffee, the background music in the cafe was by Frankie Valli and the Four Seasons. My mom and dad loved their music and played it all the time. I hummed along with the tune while he watched, amused, leaning back in the chair. Three nights later, he asked if we could have an early dinner together, and at the end of our meal he surprised me by taking me to a showing of *Jersey Boys*.

Best. Night. Ever.

I found it necessary to extend my trip when a client of mine called. He'd phoned the office and learned I was in Las Vegas. He and his wife were planning to fly out and they wanted to look for a retirement community where they could purchase a home. I phoned home to check on Aria and the baby, and she assured me they were fine. Although I felt a little guilty, when I told Falcon I would be extending my stay, he did the same. I was happy at the prospect of spending more time with him. We'd been seeing each other nearly every day for several weeks. I flip-flopped between spending time with him and Elizabeth; I either had lunch with Liz and dinner with Fal, or vice versa.

Liz pressed me to meet him, but I kept putting it off. It wasn't because I didn't think she would like him, but because I selfishly wanted to keep him all to myself. I'd never done this before. It felt somehow dangerous to let Falcon through the wall of my inhibitions, but he fit so perfectly with my personality I couldn't help myself. He made me feel valued and beautiful. It was intoxicating. I so badly wanted to shed the barriers I'd built around myself, but day-by-day I was reminded this was temporary. The logistics of where we both lived would kill whatever was left of the relationship when our trip was over. I promised myself I could live with that. For now I would soak in what I could, enjoy the hell out of it, and figure out what to do about it later.

Elizabeth noticed the change in me and wanted to meet the man who was making me happy. I'd given in, and Falcon had made plans for the three of us. This was the night the two of them would meet, and I was nervous. It wasn't as if I hadn't apprised Elizabeth regularly on my dates with Falcon, but she'd pressed for more details, and I hadn't given her any. She could be as overprotective of me as Aria. The catalyst for this get-together was she'd threatened to crash our next date if I didn't let her meet him. Although I walked a thin line between apprehension and anxiety, I was glad she'd get to know him. He'd become my favorite, daily habit.

"Earth to Paige." Elizabeth's impatient tone interrupted my thoughts.

"What's on your mind? We were laughing a minute ago, and you zoned out."

"Sorry." I fumbled with the napkin then straightened and gave her my undivided attention.

"Is it him?"

I think I resented the question because her curiosity was maddening. She fixated on Falcon more than I did but, the truth was, she was right. I couldn't hide it. The answer was evident by my surfacing smile.

"I knew it!" she exclaimed. "I can't wait to meet this guy! Does he feel the same?"

"I don't know. Maybe. I don't think so . . . but maybe . . . I know it'll probably end when I leave. I helped him pass the time while he was here."

Her tone was firm, and her posture indignant.

"Don't discount yourself, chica. You're smart and beautiful. He'd be an ass to take a woman like you for granted."

"Please don't say anything when you meet him tonight," I pleaded. "Let's just have a good time, okay?"

She scrutinized my sudden change and gave me an exasperated look.

"I've never seen you act like this, Paige. You're excited one minute and hesitant the next. Where's all this coming from?"

I drowned my emotions in my glass of iced tea as I slipped my apprehension under the cracking ice. I wasn't sure how to answer her because I couldn't articulate exactly how I felt. Falcon was more than I'd hoped for because I'd never dared to hope. I didn't want Liz to see beneath the composure that hid my self-doubt.

Thankfully, she dropped the subject, although I knew it would be resurrected at some point, and instead she drew my attention to the sexy barista who was blatantly flirting with a customer. It was only a matter of hours before our date with Falcon.

For the remainder of our time together, Liz tried to lighten my mood with jokes and teasing—and she succeeded. I think the mood really lightened when she threatened to pull out all her Latina charm and make Falcon forget about me—*if* that was what I wanted. She batted her long lashes in my direction as she recounted the ways she could, and would, divert his attention. At one point she framed her beautiful, light-cocoa face with her fingers like in Madonna's *Vogue* video. Any other woman would have made me feel the sharp pangs of jealousy, but Liz's affection for me assured me she was playing. She reminded me not to take myself so seriously, and before I knew it my mood was more upbeat. Thank God for girlfriends! Women really do have the power to lift each other up or pull each other down. It was a choice.

I checked my watch. Though it had been only a short time since Liz and I finished lunch I saw that it was almost time to go to dinner. The dress I'd planned to wear was figure hugging and short, so I decided to add stilettos to complete the trifecta. I wanted to leave an impression that would make Falcon unable to forget me. Every time we went out I wanted to stamp a memory in his mind. Tonight was no exception.

I turned in the mirror, pleased that the dress I'd chosen showed off my assets and hid my deficits. Running my hands over my curves, I checked to make sure I looked as good in the front as I did in the back. I stepped closer to the mirror and popped gloss on my lips and combed my lashes to a killer length with mascara. My hair was super shiny, and I pulled it to the side. Falcon had commented several times that he liked that style, and it was easy for me. My earrings and bracelet sparkled. I couldn't help but remember the first time Falcon had made me feel beautiful.

". . . I think I'm looking at one of the most beautiful sights Vegas has to offer."

"I'm not going to be able to eat if you keep this up."

"Why? Because I think you're beautiful? I thought most women loved compliments."

Like then, this night promised that he would, again, make me feel like a princess—except that the villain in this fairy-tale was hidden beneath my clothes. At least, when this was over, he would remember me as beautiful. For me, that really *was* a happy ending.

Although Falcon had said he'd send Jorge with the car, I insisted Elizabeth and I would meet him. I used the excuse that I wanted to spend a little girl time with her before we met up with him. He didn't argue the point with me, but I could tell that he wasn't happy.

Men!

Just as I rounded the corner of the elevator, Liz met

me in the lobby. We'd just stepped outside when I noticed a familiar looking man across the street. It took a moment to focus but as I did I recognized him. *Mr. Dietz*. The moment of recognition cast a shadow on my mood. Our business dealings were brief. Unfortunately, our connection happened to be Manny Vallega and his wife Marisol, the owners of Vencedor Corporation. Mr. Dietz and I had been hired to liquidate all the real estate holdings that had been procured in the name of that company. Though clients didn't need to give us a reason why they choose to unload their properties, we were privy to this one. It was Manny's contention that his wife had purchased the properties during a severe manic episode of a, then undiagnosed, bipolar disorder.

I didn't believe that for a minute.

I was an expert at living through devious, black-hearted plans, but none could compare to the devastation Marisol had done in the life of my friend Aria. She'd nearly killed her but, thank God, she hadn't succeeded. She was a piranha, ripping and tearing at my social circle bit by bit, and wasn't happy unless she left them bleeding or dead. Her psychosis penetrated our lives with her depravity—and, at the time, Mr. Dietz and I couldn't wait to be clear of her. I'd concluded my part of the liquidation in record time, at Mr. Dietz's insistence. The whole deal had left him preoccupied and nervous. I did as he'd asked without question, listing every property they owned. Many of them had sold well below market value, but Mr. Dietz had been grateful for my help nonetheless. He'd confided that Manny had presented him with a power of attorney for Marisol and he'd been very anxious for any remnants of that particular time in her life to be put to rest. He'd been extremely anxious for her to move forward, saying it was necessary for her to heal.

I'd felt bad for Mr. Dietz. Manny and Marisol might have been able to dupe most people with that story, but I'd known better. My experience with Marisol was that she'd had a morbid and unnatural obsession with Declan. She'd erroneously believed Aria had stolen him from her. Of course, she'd conveniently left out a few facts, the biggest one being that she was married. She'd kept that little secret to herself, and Declan had assured all of us he'd never led her to believe anything existed between them. There'd never been any doubt as to who'd told the truth.

I'd never heard from Mr. Dietz after we'd concluded our business, and it suddenly occurred to me that if he'd continued to work for Manny, his opinion of me might have been jaded by any remarks the Vallega's may have made. Since I'd never run into him at home, it seemed fortuitous he was right across the street. It would only take a moment to say hello, so I thought I'd seize the opportunity. I touched Liz's arm.

"I'll be right back. I see someone I know."

She watched after me as I walked in Mr. Dietz's direction. I'd almost reached him when any thoughts of my good fortune scattered like dust in the wind. I quickly turned around and hurried back to Liz.

"Let's go."

She sensed my urgency and, although puzzled, followed without hesitation. The knot I'd had in my stomach now choked me with regret. I should have paid more attention; I hadn't noticed Mr. Dietz was walking with an entourage that included Manny, Marisol, and Blake Matthews.

I remembered how unnerved Mr. Dietz had been when he'd worked for Manny, so why were they together? I began to rationalize that it was reasonable for an attorney to be with a client in Vegas, especially one with Mr. Dietz's expertise in real estate. I mentally checked off sensible explanations. He was their real estate attorney, and Vegas was a hot spot.

There wasn't really anything suspect about him being with them, but I couldn't shake the ominous feeling in my gut. Something wasn't right. Why was Blake with them? Other than being Marisol's manager, they weren't friends, were they? But I couldn't shake the warning that ignited inside my brain.

At one time Blake had been a good friend, but his charm had waned each time I'd told him that's all I'd wanted to be—a friend. Blake was a conundrum. He had more personalities than I could count. At first, I'd thought he was a nice guy, but then I'd gotten to know him, and my opinion had changed.

After Aria and I had been released from the hospital, he'd repeatedly asked me out. With my desire to maintain personal distance, I hadn't thought it would be a good idea to encourage him when I'd known there was nothing there. The only thing we'd had in common was our mutual social circle, and I hadn't wanted anything to complicate that. Time after time I'd politely declined his invitations, but he'd been persistent and then, eventually, became pushy. If he and I were anywhere with our friends, he'd acted like we'd been there together. It had become obnoxious. All through the weekend at Aimee and Carter's Christmas party he'd been possessive. He'd always been used to getting what he'd wanted and, unfortunately, he'd wanted me. It had become awkward and embarrassing. Finally, I couldn't handle it anymore. I'd gone to Aria to tell her I didn't want to go anywhere with our crowd if Blake was going to be there, and I was counting on her to let me know if he would be. She'd refused to hear of it and had told her husband. Since Declan and Blake were friends and business colleagues, she'd asked him to intervene. Aria had told me everything had been taken care of. After that, Blake had backed off. He'd called me once afterwards and told me I didn't know what I was missing, that he could date anyone he wanted. I'd told him he was behaving like an ass and to get over himself. We hadn't spoken since then.

Liz and I were almost around the corner when I heard him. He was calling my name. I ignored him, but he only became louder.

"Paige!"

The sound of his voice sickened me. I walked a little faster.

"Paige!" His shouting embarrassed and alarmed me.

Liz tried to turn around but saw my reaction. I held tightly to her arm.

"Keep walking." I felt the blood leave my head, making me spin.

"Paige!"

The scene he was creating left no escape.

I took a deep breath, then let it out slowly. Liz looked confused, and her eyes darted back and forth between Blake and me. He was nearly on top of us when I turned. A forced smile transformed my face.

"Hello, Blake."

I prayed Liz could sense my discomfort and help me make a quick exit. She only knew Blake as "the guy who was being a pain in the ass." I'd never mentioned his name when I'd said that someone was getting on my nerves, but she was a smart cookie. I knew it wouldn't take long for her to connect the dots.

"Didn't you hear me?" It was evident by his condescending tone he resented being ignored by me. He tried to mask his irritation by putting on his best, fake, overly whitened, smile. "Why didn't you stop when I called?"

Unconsciously, I stiffened. Liz read me instantly and was on high alert. Ever the professional, I morphed into my capable business persona.

"I'm sorry. I didn't hear you. My friend and I were talking." I quickly changed the subject to his favorite topic, himself. "What are you doing in Vegas?"

He eyed me skeptically but behaved himself in front of Liz. "A little relaxation, a little gambling." He turned toward her and extended his hand.

"Blake Matthews. And you are?"

Her eyes flared at his flippant tone. "Elizabeth Santiago. Paige and I go way back."

"Really?" He looked at me, straightening his shoulders. "I don't remember her mentioning you." His stare was intense. "I haven't seen you for a while. We should have dinner while I'm here."

Liz quickly resented his misguided sense of authority, and intervened. "I'm afraid I've monopolized her calendar while she's in town."

He didn't look at her, behaving as if she weren't there. "I'm sure not all of her time is taken," he countered, giving me a defiant look.

"Lunch, then."

Liz took a step forward, and I thought for a minute she might slap him. I stilled her by touching the back of her hand. "I'm afraid I have plans."

He grinned spitefully. He issued a challenge with his slimy expression as he looked between Liz and me. "Well, then, I'll be sure to catch up with you when you get home."

His arrogance bristled my nerves. I couldn't wait to get away from him. "I'm sorry but we have to go. We're meeting someone."

As we walked away I could still feel his eyes as they burned a hole in my composure. I didn't say a word, moving quickly toward the intersection of the street to put as much distance between us as I could. While we waited for the light to change, Liz touched my arm. I'd been so intent on getting away from Blake that I jumped.

"Breathe." Liz said the word softy as she tried to calm me down.

My shoulders slumped. As if the prospect of an evening with Falcon and Liz hadn't peppered me with enough edginess, running into Blake had fully flavored my nerves. My shoulders slumped from the weighted tension, but Liz's soft command brought me back to reality. I took a deep breath. Whenever I was near Blake my chest tightened like I'd worn a sweater made of armor, but it was lightening with each breath. I was dizzy from trying to maintain my composure, so Liz led me over to a street vendor bought some cold water. She opened, then handed me an icy bottle, and I took a long, slow drink. She said nothing, not pressing, giving me some space. Once we began to walk again, her concerned expression turned questioning.

"He's the guy I met through Aria's husband," I began slowly. "The 'pain in the ass' guy I told you about. He keeps pressing, like he wants to go out, but I just don't like him. I don't understand why he doesn't get it. He doesn't need me—and I don't want him. He's around models all the time. He's also one of those guys who's a little into himself. I mean, he's good looking enough that he could be a model himself, but I'm not interested. I just wish he'd leave me alone."

Liz's brow furrowed, and her jaw clenched. "I don't think I've ever seen you like that. Don't get me wrong, you were certainly polite enough, but I could tell you were just going through the motions. I think you're wrong, he does get it; he doesn't want to accept it."

I shook my head in disagreement. "I don't know. He acts like he's made up his mind there's more and because I act nice to him he thinks that's proof."

"Or maybe he knows there isn't more to it, but he doesn't like it," she countered. "This guy seems like a narcissistic ass. He's used to getting what he wants, and he thinks he's entitled to you because he wants you. You're a challenge, and, from what I saw, I think he's a little unstable."

"He's unpredictable, Liz, but he's harmless. I just want him to leave me alone."

Her hand folded over mine, and she patted it in a sweet and protective way.

"Just be careful, chica. I'm not getting a good feeling from him." She gave me a very cheeky smile. "Now enough of this! Let's go meet your man."

Chapter 12

Paige

We. Were. Drunk.
Seriously drunk.

I clung to Falcon's hand. I'd self-medicated my jumpiness with alcohol but I couldn't remember what I'd been nervous about. Dinner with Liz had been completely uneventful. As usual, I overreacted while anticipating the get together. She'd been as sweet and sassy with Falcon as she'd been with me. Nonetheless, I felt it necessary to calm my frayed nerves. I couldn't remember all the bars we'd gone to, but I distinctly remembered we laughed so hard all night that my face hurt. Our last stop must have been very close because we were walking. Liz, however, was enjoying a ride to her house. I remembered Falcon and Jorge after going to the clubs, but details escaped me like effervescent bubbles. Both men had helped me get out of the car while making her stay inside of it. Liz had leaned her head out the window. Once she'd thanked him for a great night she'd given him a big kiss on the cheek. Falcon had patted the top of the car and told Jorge to get her home.

My high heels dangled in my fingers and bounced with each step. The concrete beneath my feet connected me with reality while my head swam in the warm waters of simple emotions. Falcon was so close beside me I could feel his body heat. He held my hand, steadying me with each stumbled step. His touch was blistering my plans for being casual. With a blowtorch of pent-up desires, I leaned into him, savoring the burn while he walked me all the way to my room.

"Do you want to come in?" I shivered with boldness only to be instantly flamed by a fire of liquid confidence. Each word that tumbled from my lips was laced with need.

"Yes." A chuckle came from deep in his chest. "But I'm not going to. Not tonight."

"You don't have to go. You can stay here with me." I pouted and slid my arms around his neck. He claimed me with a kiss before I knew what was happening. It was hot, wet, and demanding—and better than I'd ever expected. My head grew woozier, and my knees went weak. He teased my lips as his tongue ran over them. I wanted more. Need and heat bubbled through my core, threatening to boil over.

"Stay with me," I pleaded.

"Don't tempt me." The vibrations of his voice strummed my starving sexuality. I stood on my toes to purr into his ear.

"I'm not tempting. I'm asking. Nicely."

He reached around me and fed the key into the slot. My arms were clasped around his neck when he opened the door, and we practically fell into the room as I lost my balance. When he tried to catch us both, our momentum carried us, slamming our bodies into the wall. He fell against me, pinning me with his body and his heat. My hands slid from his shoulders while my fingers enjoyed the ride over the masculine ridges of raw power beneath his shirt. The need in me grew as his muscles rippled beneath my fingertips. Our eyes locked, and I fell into a sea of green lust. He wanted me. His hips pressed into my belly as I threaded my fingers through his hair. Barely a breath separated us as he held me tightly against him. The hard evidence I felt between us clearly defined the depths of his craving for me, and the knowledge was heady. I breathed hard against his lips.

"Stay, Fal. Please. You know you want to and . . . I

want you," I whispered, and followed his lead by lightly licking the rim of his bottom lip.

"Woman . . . you're killing me!"

His groan resonated through me like an obsessed embrace. His hands slid down my body, while his cock possessively ground against my core. Our clothes were the only thing preventing a skin to skin connection, but the temperature between us was palpable. The wall at my back chilled me while the front of him torched my hunger. He crushed his mouth over mine and expertly claimed it with his tongue. The intensity delivered a shattering explosion of need to my core. It was so intense, I barely breathed. I wanted to feel every inch of him in the dark. A woman blind to all else except the detonating intimacy of touch.

My need for him grew with each breath and drove me to be careless with my own rules. I wanted him to want me, to strip my insecurities and lay bare my hurts. My appetite for him was gluttonous and pulsated deep inside me. I knew he was struggling. He groaned as he came up for air.

"I want you, beautiful, but . . ." He pushed away. His hands flexed into fists as he fought to regain control. His eyes never left mine as he backed himself toward the door. I narrowed my eyes wickedly, seductively motioning for him to come back with my finger, but it was no use. He reached behind him for the door handle and turned it, the click of the latch severing my hopes with a brutal blade. His lips curled into an agonized smile, the painful evidence of his sacrifice straining beneath his zipper as he labored to speak.

"I'll see you in the morning, beautiful."

Damn it!

Frustrated, I flopped on the bed as the hunger inside me dissipated into a black death. I had extended an invitation for him to take what he wanted from me, and, still, he was the gentleman, and I wondered about the rumors that said he was a man whore. Strangely, I was baffled, but happy. If they were true, it meant I really was special to him. Waves of joy and disappointment alternated, swelling and diminishing as fresh memories of the night consumed me.

I don't know how much time had passed because I was still savoring them when I heard a faint knock. Excited, I pushed off the bed. I pictured him kicking himself for leaving and coming to his senses. I felt a wide grin begin to form on my lips as I anticipated teasing him. I curled my fingers around the knob and flung the door open, fully prepared to mock him.

"Soooo . . . change your mind?"

Though I said the words under my breath they wrapped around my throat and choked me. I froze. Adrenaline rushed through me, sending every nerve into overdrive. Blake leered at me as he leaned against the doorframe. Instantaneously, I sobered as fear morphed hope into despair. I grabbed the door and tried to close it. His eyes blackened, and he pushed back. I stumbled as he barged into the room.

"Aw. You don't seem happy to see me." Sarcasm dripped with each word. He was drunk.

I tried to stay calm but teetered between fear and anger. "What are you doing here?"

"What? No hug and kiss?" His words were slurred, and his snicker was filled with evil intent. He grabbed my arm, painfully squeezing as he tried to pull me toward him. I shoved at his chest as hard as I could and lost my footing.

"Get out!" I tried to sound in control, but the panic in my voice rose to a dangerous level. My knees shook as I pointed toward the door.

An evil sneer painted his face. My demand had the opposite effect, and he laughed at me, lunging. I tried to move, but his fingers closed around my throat. I struggled to breathe and used both hands trying to break free. I sunk my nails deep into his hands, drawing blood, and he slammed my head against the wall. My fear quickly transformed into terror.

He pulled one hand away and looked at the blood. His face was tight with rage, and I flinched as he raised his fist to me. "You think you can play games with me?" He growled as I pulled oxygen into my lungs. He licked my face like a mad dog, his tongue burning my skin as it slithered down my neck. "You know you want this." His words burned like acid. I fought like a trapped animal.

"Get off of me!" I spat out the words through gritted teeth as my mind scrambled for an escape route. I was fighting two battles—Blake and the suffocating panic. "Let me go!" I screamed and brought my knee up, hard, but he blocked me. He laughed at my effort like a demon possessed. I barely threw him off balance, but it was enough to break free. I jolted to the door. Blake got there first. With nowhere else to go, I scrambled to the other side of the room.

"It's okay, baby," he chuckled. "I like it rough." His eyes were emotionless. With all my might I strangled my tears, but my heartbeat thundered against my chest. He was an animal, and I was his prey. His frustration and anger over the many times I'd kept him at arm's length collected like a powder keg and his anger struck like flint. At any moment he would lose control completely and hurt me. I sobered as an icy sanity rushed through my veins. If I could just stay calm, I could use it to my benefit.

"C'mere, bitch! We're just getting started." He snarled, and his expression contorted. He was breathing hard when he lunged forward, but, in his plastered condition, his foot caught the edge of the bed.

He crashed to the floor. I ran to take the only advantage I might have to escape. I flew over the bed and headed straight for the door in a tsunamic frenzy. I'd just gripped the handle with fingers damp with sweat when I was yanked backward. I screamed as Blake gripped my hair. My neck snapped back as my scalp cried in agony. He wrapped my hair around his arm like recoiling a whip, pulling my face to his.

"You wanna play hellcat, bitch?" His breath reeked and assaulted my face while his spittle seared my skin. I weakened under his powerful hands. I tried to push against him, but my petite shoulders were no match for him. He gripped my waist in a painful grasp and tossed me to the floor like I was a ragdoll. I crawled backward as I looked in his eyes. My only hope was to try and reason with him. With a rapid resolve I focused my energy on calming my voice.

"Blake, we're friends. You don't want to do this."

"Oh, but I do." His eyes burned with fury. Like a raging bull, his nostrils flared, and the realization that I might not leave this room alive slapped me in the face.

"Blake, please. You're drunk," I said calmly. "Just leave. Go back to your hotel and sleep it off. We'll forget this ever happened."

His gaze dropped to the floor. A flicker of hope sparked and led me to believe that reason was slicing through the madness. I could only hope I was getting through to him and, if I wasn't, all I had to do was keep him calm enough so I could run out of the room.

As I stood, I inched my way toward the door. He raised his chin watching my every move. I was nearly there when he shrugged his shoulders. He rotated his head to the left and right like he was releasing tension. Pops and cracks from the motion filled the momentary stillness.

"Maybe you're right." An eerie air of calm washed over him, and I froze as he walked past me. He reached for the door handle, and I prayed he'd leave. All I had to do was keep him calm and wait for him to step out into the hall, and then I could throw the lock. I barely breathed as his fingers tickled the metal. His eyes caught mine, and he smirked.

"But I don't think so."

He swung around so fast I didn't realize what was happening, and, as he pivoted, his fist connected with my jaw. My vision splintered into fragments as I crashed, face first, into the mirror. My reflection exploded into a thousand shattered grains of silver, and my world upended. He tore at my hair, and once he had a handful in his fist he pulled back with a ferocity that guaranteed my surrender. I screamed as a nightmare of black terror swallowed me. He pulled my neck back brutally. I landed against his chest with a thud so hard it winded me like a punch to the gut. Blake's forearm tightened around my neck until it was so constricted I couldn't breathe. Life drained out of me in puddles of terror as he bit the back of my neck, sinking his teeth in ravenously until I felt the tender skin give way to blood that trickled from my violated flesh.

He was a madman, and there was no one to hear me cry. I had two choices. Surrender or fight. In desperation, I whipped my body back and forth in a tragic dance, hoping to break his hold. My vision was so distorted I couldn't focus. Deep in the bowels of desperation, I blindly bit and clawed at anything on him I could reach. Still, he refused to let me go, using my head as a battering ram. The fortress of my sanity began to splinter, yet I held tightly to any rational thoughts I could muster. I shook so hard I thought fear would break my bones, but it wasn't strong enough to break his grip. The carpet raked my skin when he threw me on the floor. He kicked me, and I felt the contents of my stomach rise in my throat. One more kick, and I rolled to my side, praying I was quick enough to keep my bones from being broken.

"You're nothing but a goddamn cock tease." He spat at me, the slimy excretion landing on my throat as I coughed and gagged from his brutality. The unmistakable sound of a descending zipper ripped me apart with misery as I heaved scattered memories on the floor. I'd been betrayed by his friendship, deluded by his normalcy, and violated by his inhumanity. Of all my tormentors, he would be the one to break my body and set my soul free.

Tears stung my eyes, and a knot formed in my stomach when I thought of the people I loved. When I'd last seen them I'd never that it would be the last time. I might not make it out of this room in anything other than pieces. At best I'd be raped, at worst I would die, but I knew that no matter what happened I would never be the same. I couldn't help but feel that, if I should die, those who loved me would suffer as collateral damage to a madman.

Blake bent over and made two ropes of my hair. He used them as a painful hoist to raise me to my knees and then he pulled my face to his crotch. His legs were spread, and his hardness repulsed me. I tried to turn away, but he held me tightly in his grip.

"Open your mouth, damn it!"

For one hopeful moment clarity presented itself. I realized that my hands were free. I thrust my hands up between his legs and, using my fingers, I grabbed his sack in a death grip and twisted with all my strength. An ungodly scream escaped him. He let go of my hair and pushed at my head with his fists.

As he doubled over and fell to the floor I scampered back until I'd gathered the strength to stand. I tried to hop over him, but he caught my ankle in midair. I kicked at him with my other foot, but, even injured, he was stronger than me. He pulled me down and rolled me under him while he slithered over me like a snake. His hips were even with mine once he'd subdued me. He straddled me and slapped me so hard my ears rang. Two hits—forehand and backhand.

"You're going to pay for that!" He growled against my ear. With the last of my energy I bucked my hips but I couldn't move. Violently, he ripped the delicate material of my dress and bra, and I was smothered by the reality of my circumstances. With a meaty hand, he pulled downward, and the ravaged material fluttered over my breast. Sadistically, he exposed me, unveiling a lifetime of disguise with one, brutal motion. Staring at my uncovered flesh, he paused. His mouth twisted, and a sadistic sneer appeared.

"Well, aren't you just full of surprises."

His words stabbed at me with a thick and impaired tongue, but he poked at my tender skin with a pointed finger. I felt my throat close as fresh emotion choked me. I began to sob.

"Blake. Please . . ."

He sat back on his haunches, laughing in great rolls while he harshly jabbed my scars.

"You're fucking hideous!" He cackled while a tar pit of dark memories suffocated me with sticky fingers.

It stole any breath of sweetness that lingered, that struggled to stay alive. His laughter at my expense was a familiar asphyxiation as hurt upon hurt reemerged, only to anchor around my feet. I felt myself pulling away. It was over. I'd fought the thickness of cruelty for so many years there was little left inside of me. Although I'd fought to stay afloat, so much time had passed I was out of practice. I felt myself sinking.

"You son of a bitch! I'll kill you."

A sob of relief caught in my throat as I recognized the unmistakable reverberation of Falcon's roar. My eyes were blinded with tears as the pressure lifted from my chest, and I watched Blake go airborne. Falcon's fist was a blur of motion as it sailed through the air and Blake's face crumbled. His aggression toward me was dwarfed by the ferocity of Falcon's fury.

I tried to move.

My mind told me to stop them.

My body refused to listen.

Falcon dragged Blake out into the hall, and the door would have slammed behind them if not for my shoe. It had come off sometime during the attack, but I just stared at the red sole blocking the entrance. Threads of anxiety pricked me and pulled at my skin in a toxic needlepoint. My vision grew cloudy, and my hearing became muffled. Tears washed my face in the salty wetness that then dripped from my chin and bathed my chest. My mind screamed at the surreal quality of the situation, while the rational part of me was kidnapped by the insecure girl inside of me.

I looked down at the marks Blake's violence had left behind. They joined with my scars. The memory of a few moments ago wedded with memories of long ago, and the cruelty of both blended to form a macabre marriage. The favors they gave to me, their only guest, was disgust. I wasn't strong enough to fight. My physical strength was gone. My mental state weakened.

SHE'S COME BACK.

This isn't my fault.

You're not me.

Oh, but I am.

Please go away.

Not a chance.

SHE POUNCED on the fortuitous opportunity. I floated above as I watched her. She tried to hide, but the spotlight shined painfully through the Swiss cheese insecurity that was thicker than the scars. The resolve I'd so bravely developed through the years came crashing down horribly. Blake's attack had fractured the spirit of the girl who lived inside me, and she'd come forth to exact her revenge. He was worse than the juvenile torturers. Theirs were only vicious words. His fists had stroked the immature accusations and stabbed the broken girl until she'd screamed to be set free from her cage within my scarred flesh. What was left of my senses and me were shut down and mangled, leaving me fractured into two separate victims.

I couldn't help the one.

I couldn't fight the other.

Chapter 13

Falcon

I examined my fist as I rode up the elevator to Paige's floor. The blood on it wasn't mine. After getting in a few good punches to Blake's much too pretty face, I'd taken him downstairs to the hotel security office. Once the police had arrived I could only supply them with a brief rundown of events because I wasn't aware of all the facts. When it was over, all I could think about was getting back to Paige.

I hated she'd been left by herself, but, at the time, there was no other option. The minute I'd gotten asshole Blake into the elevator, the enclosed space had filled with the smell of alcohol. He'd reeked of it. I didn't care that he'd been drunk. What I'd cared about was that he'd put his hands on Paige. Son of a bitch got what he deserved. Nothing would excuse the fact he'd hurt her. Then, all I could think about was getting back to her. Blake could spend the night in jail until Paige went down and pressed charges against his sorry ass. For now, I'll insist she let me take her to the hospital.

As I approached her room I saw one of her shoes. Kicking it aside, I pushed the door open. In an instant my heart slammed to a stop.

The sight of Paige crumpled over cracked my heart open. In front of her, the contents of her stomach were spilled out on the floor. I looked back from the vile puddle to her. She seemed to be in a trance.

Facing the corner of the room, Paige stared blankly at the wall. I could see half of her body reflected in the mirror on the wall. On her knees, her arms were wrapped around her middle as she slowly rocked back and forth. I moved in closer to her for a better look. When I did, the crack in my heart widened. I moved and stood in front of her. Her stare was vacant. Though her eyes appeared to be looking at the wall, I could tell her focus was turned to somewhere inside herself. She was locked in some kind of isolated torment. I looked to her right where a soft pile of crème and coffee colored threads lay feathered in a nest on the floor—her hair.

The altercation between Blake and myself had burned off any lingering effect of the alcohol I'd consumed earlier, but if there'd been any residual drunkenness in me, seeing Paige like this would have sobered me completely. I've seen it before in men who'd served with me, but nothing could have prepared me for this: a gorgeous, sweet woman lost in a PTSD nightmare. She looked so fragile. So broken. And she was unraveling right before my eyes. *Damn that son of a bitch!*

The sight of her cheeks wet with silent tears broke my heart. I stood stunned, unable to move. Even fractured she was beautiful. My soul ached as I watched her being tortured by an unseen demon. In a trancelike state, her long fingers threaded through the waves of hair that were pulled to the side, lying over her shoulder and down her breast. Over and over, she repeatedly ran her hands through the tresses, her fingers separating them as a makeshift comb. When she isolated one strand, she pulled.

I stared, daze for a time. A few moments? A few minutes? I didn't know. I watched as she decimated a few follicles. Once she ripped a strand of hair from her scalp she held out her hand and let it fall gracefully into the pile below. I scanned her body for injuries only to find various pieces of hair that had gone rogue. They lay against the surface of her skin, kissing her breast, stomach, and thigh on their way to the multistrand grave on the floor.

I had to wait her out. My experience in dealing with the PTSD soldiers experienced had limits, but I knew enough not to startle her. Her clarity was lost within her emotional pain. I wanted to touch her gently to let her know I was there, and as I did so, I saw a scar.

Red semi-circles marred her skin. Her pain had not been limited to tonight's event. Slowly, I pulled back and watched for some sign of when I should break her concentration. Hopefully, I could guide her safely back to reality.

As I waited, all I felt was a protectiveness that was foreign to me. I wanted to pull her into my arms and slay whatever dragon gave her such torment. Her expression was one of anguish and loss. I restrained myself from touching her until, finally, she let out an exhausted sigh. Her gaze went to the pile beside her. I stooped down to her level and placed my lips an inch from her ear.

"Paige."

She jumped. My voice startled her, and at the sound of it her hands froze as her body stiffened. It took her a moment to realize that it was me and not Blake. The part of her that I could see in the mirror confessed much as I watched. Her shoulders slumped. Her expression crumbled. A defeated look arrested her features. Shame etched her eyes as she realized I was witness to her torment. I kneeled on the floor, anchoring my chest to her back

"I've got you."

She didn't move.

I placed my hands on her shoulders as delicately as one would touch a butterfly's wing. She was so cold. I warmed her by lightly brushing my fingers across her skin. The strokes, slow and tender, soothed her. I allowed myself to apply a heavier touch as my hands traveled up and down her arms. When I finally felt her muscles relax, I entwined our fingers, my hands over the back of hers. She surrendered. Her breathing reduced to a more even, calmer pace. I held her tightly, pulling her into my embrace. Her head drooped, heavy from exhaustion. I held her for several minutes. When a sigh escaped her lips, I moved away from her, leaning her against the wall for support.

Her eyes were closed as I went into the bathroom. I kept an eye on her as I wet two washcloths. I returned and moved so that I could wipe the vomit from around her mouth with a warm one and wiped the fine film of perspiration off her face with a cooler one.

"I want to get you out of these clothes. Can you help me to do that?"

I spoke in a hushed tone. Paige complied but moved with the hesitancy of someone in pain. Robotically she did what she could to assist me. It was as if all energy had drained from her. She didn't seem to have the strength to lift her arms. She still wore the dress that bastard Blake had torn, and I removed it. A tiny rush of relief washed over me when I realized her underwear was intact. I tried to move her hair away from her neck to wipe the cool rag over it as well, but she stayed my hand.

"Don't."

I wasn't sure if it was because of the chilled cloth or because I had brushed over a scar, but the word strangled in the air. She moved her hand to cover the marred flesh. I caught her as she swayed, apparently weakened by the night's events. I touched her, guiding her to the bed. Her footsteps were labored as she blindly followed my lead. I sat on the bed, leaning my back against the pillows in front of the headboard, and pulled her into a sitting position between my legs. She was broken. I cradled her, tucking her head beneath my chin. She wilted lifelessly into the embrace. With gentle fingertips I lifted her chin, rotating her head until her eyes met mine. My heart skipped a beat when I saw the raw depletion there.

"Rest."

I prayed she'd obey my order and was relieved when her lids dropped. She was beautiful even in her pain. I hugged her against me and pressed a kiss into her hair. Tiny goosebumps erupted on her skin, and I pulled the covers up and around her shoulders. She soon fell asleep in my arms.

I was convinced there was more to the attack than an unfortunate run-in with Blake. Although, what little I did see of that encounter would have been enough to push anyone over the edge. Conflicted and curious, I lifted the blanket to get a better view of the scar.

White, shiny, and tight, it looked like it was a healed burn. As I slightly raised the cover, I followed the trail down her chest and saw where the scar spilled onto her breast. In shades of whitish pink, it decorated her milky skin, then disappeared beneath the ripped bra. I wanted to see where it ended and shifted us both to get a better view. She turned, and I froze. I didn't want to wake her with my movements. Once she stilled and fell back to sleep, I was provided the opportunity to satisfy my curiosity when the covers fell back and exposed another scar. The way that Paige had positioned herself gave me a view of the injuries in their entirety. There were more of them than I was prepared to see, but not one of them looked fresh. Whatever happened to her had happened long ago. They explained why she always dressed so conservatively—she was in hiding.

The thought sobered me. I sank further into the pillows and pulled her tighter. Stroking her hair absentmindedly, I twisted it so I could lay it over her shoulder. My fingers hit something sticky and I pulled them away. A painful lump formed in my throat when I looked at an area of missing hair. *What the fuck?*

I couldn't wrap my head around what could have happened to her, and with more questions than answers, I slid into my own exhaustion. As I wrapped her in my arms, fatigue set in. Before I knew it the remnants of her perfume had lulled me to sleep.

PAIGE STIFFENED IN MY ARMS, and I woke up immediately. One look at the clock told me we'd been out for hours. Her attack replayed in my mind. The police could only hold Blake so long without formal charges. I had to impress upon her the importance of charging him with her assault. If he'd already been released, I had the connections and technology to find him. My only concerns were for Paige and her safety. If stress was the trigger for the condition I'd found her in, I'd have to tread lightly. The last thing I wanted was to catapult her into another episode.

"Good morning."

She knew I was awake, and she lay very still. Intuition told me she was aware her secret had been exposed. I'd never been accused of beating around the bush and addressed the matter head-on.

"Tell me what that was, and how you got the scars. I want to know."

I tightened my arms around her. She broke our connection, moving until we were laying side by side. As quiet as the whisper of a breeze, she began.

"You know . . . it doesn't happen all the time. As far as the scars? It's a long story."

I stroked the delicate line of her jaw, and she turned toward me. There was a storm of emotion brewing behind her eyes.

"I'm not exactly sure what to think or feel now that you've seen me at my worst, and my scars at their best. No one, outside of my parents, knows I harm myself. You're the only one." Her voice held a tremble. Then she paused and bit her lip, uncertainty tightening the corners of her eyes. "I'd think you'd want to run far away now that you've seen what I look like and know what I do." She lowered her chin and her voice. "I would if I were you. I truly would; it's all disgusting."

I heard her, but she'd said so much more with her unspoken words. Her eyes glazed with tears, and her body stiffened as she prepared herself for my response. All I could do was admire her for trusting me with her fractured reality.

I didn't speak just then. Instead, I reacted. Call it the irrational act of a rational man, but I couldn't help myself. By admitting the truth, her honesty had humbled me. Her transparency made her even more desirable than she'd been before. Her lashes fluttered, and her breath hitched as light filtered through the curtains. Soft rays of sun caught the twinkling of tears in her eyes. I stroked my finger across her cheekbone as a lone tear escaped. It trailed down her face, creeping over her nose to comingle with more tears. They trailed down her face, moistening her lips where it landed. I craved her mouth and pressed my lips to hers, tasting the salt that pooled there. She responded to my demanding tongue as it claimed her mouth. I could have feasted on her willingness but pulled back instead.

"Paige . . ."

Her name caught in my throat. She shivered as the weightless touch of my desire transmitted electricity to her sensitive flesh. She couldn't see herself as I did because I saw her as the closest thing I would ever know as a princess. I thought so the first time I saw her, yet I hadn't fully defined the thought at the time. She stood straight and tall in Carter and Aimee's house. Fully regal, fierce, brave, and beautiful. I wanted her at that moment, and though I thought she was out of my league, I went for it anyway. This was my second chance. I wasn't going to blow it. I raised the back of her hand, pressing her fingers to my lips, and gave them a light kiss.

"Disgust? Never." I looked deep into her eyes. "I don't know much about what's perfect, but I think *you* come pretty damn close."

Her tense muscles liquefied in my arms, and a soft look filled her eyes.

"Thank you."

In that moment I knew I didn't deserve her but wanted all of her.

Chapter 14

Paige

Twenty-one hours. One thousand two hundred sixty minutes. I marked the biggest change in my life by the ticking of time. Two hours at dinner, three hours of dancing, countless minutes of assault, and a lifetime of hiding exposed.

I was about to reveal all when the buzzing from my cell phone interrupted the connection between Falcon and me. Liz's bright and cheery voice filled my ear.

"Paige? Are you okay?"

I hesitated. "Why wouldn't I be?"

"Because you told me to meet you at Il Fornaio, and I've been waiting here an hour. I think I've had about four cups of coffee."

"What are you talking about?" I was puzzled. "We're supposed to meet tomorrow."

"What are you talking about? The night we went out with your beefcake boy, you told me to meet you at Il Fornaio."

"Right! On Wednesday. Did you get your days mixed up?" Liz could be a little forgetful. In fact, she said her nickname was Dory, like the forgetful fish in *Finding Nemo*.

"Right. Wednesday. Today *is* Wednesday."

I pulled the phone away from my ear and looked at the display. Right there, in backlit letters, was Wednesday and, right there, in my calendar, it said I was meeting her for breakfast. I laid my head back on the pillow and put my forearm across my eyes. I had been pushing through work, stress, shopping, Falcon, and an attack. I was normally so vigilant about my health and rest. Trips to Las Vegas were a respite for me. This time, not so much. I'd let everything go and had paid the price. I'd lost a whole damn day!

Behind me Falcon yawned and cleared his throat.

"Is that Falcon?" She bubbled with a brew of teasing and inquisitiveness. "Did he stay the night?"

I looked over my shoulder. Falcon peered at me through narrow slits. It was so quiet in the room he could hear everything she said without eavesdropping. He seemed amused at my uncomfortable situation and raised his eyebrows as he, too, waited for my response. Neither one of them was going to be satisfied because I decided that, for the time being, the best response was no response.

I looked back at him playfully while I spoke into the phone.

"I don't think I'm going to make it this morning, babe." He gave me a stern look and put his arms behind his head. "I'll meet you later. Sorry about breakfast." I rolled my eyes to emphasize my agitation.

"Oh, I can't wait to hear this!"

Elizabeth's sarcasm gushed through the phone. I hung up to the sound of her laughter and tossed the cell to the bottom of the bed. A low chuckle escaped Falcon, and he patted my leg.

"Was that the cellular equivalent of a walk of shame?"

"Sure." My voice was muffled by the pillow I now had over my head as I hid my face under a light dew of mortification. "I'm so glad you find this amusing."

"Do you remember anything that happened?" His tone changed from playful to serious.

"Some, but I'm sure I'll remember more once I have some coffee and the fog lifts from my brain."

I mentally sorted the night's images by going through the events. The pleasant ones faded away while the one of Blake coming to my room clarified. I pushed the covers down. The moment I saw the bruises the pain registered. A panic attack hit when I touched the black and blue skin.

"Oh my God! I shouldn't have gotten so drunk."

"And I shouldn't have left you alone." The remorse in his voice was palpable.

"What are you talking about? It wasn't your fault. I thought it was you at the door. I didn't look through the peep hole, even though I know better."

Rising up on his elbow he pulled the pillow away from my midsection and looked at the bruises himself. Once his eyes raked over me his gaze was harsh.

"Blake spent a night in jail and deserves a lot more. He attacked you. Are you seriously blaming yourself?"

Shit! He spent the night in jail? Falcon arranged that, I'm sure. I just hope everyone at home doesn't know.

"Well, it was my fault," I countered. "I just opened the door without even asking who it was. That was a very stupid move on my part."

"Are you kidding me? I'll agree you should have looked through the door to see who it was, but Blake's the one at fault here. He's obsessed with you!"

"He was drunk." My eyes dropped, and I turned away.

"Jesus, Paige! Are you defending him? Being drunk is not an excuse! Go look at yourself in the mirror. You took a brutal beating from him. There are bruises all over you and a bite mark on your neck."

As soon as he spoke the words my body reminded me of exactly what Blake had done and how he'd done it. I ached where he'd hit me, but the fresh memories of how he'd reacted assaulted me even more.

"You can't let him get away with what he did. You have to press charges." His voice was commanding, not suggestive.

"He was drunk, Fal. That's not an excuse, it's a reason. You're right. He should pay for what he did, but maybe he didn't mean to do it. Criminal charges could cost him his career. He may be a giant pain in the ass, but I've got to, at least, give him the benefit of the doubt. I'd hope he wouldn't have hurt me if he'd been thinking straight." I understood his anger. Internally I was enraged. Falcon couldn't possibly understand because I didn't truly understand it myself. I just wanted to move forward. Put what had happened behind me. What happened was horrible, but even more horrible would be reliving it by recounting the whole thing. I didn't want to think about it anymore, and the last thing I wanted to do was bring more attention to myself.

"Do you hear yourself? Why are you defending him? He attacked you!" Falcon tore the sheets off him and jumped out of bed. The look on his face was one of complete disgust and disbelief. He ran his hands over his face and through his hair.

"I'm not defending him! All I'm saying is that I don't want to ruin the man's life." I spat. "It's over. Let it go. I'll probably never see him again once he realizes what he's done."

He flattened his knuckles at his temples and paced the floor.

"Paige. Listen to me. If he was drunk and killed someone he would still be responsible for the murder; he'd have to be held accountable. You can't let him get away with this! That's just nuts!"

I knew that no matter how I tried to explain it to Falcon, he still wouldn't understand. I'd been through this type of scenario too many times to count when I was a kid. I was the victim and they always got away with it. It was always my word against theirs and this was no different. Even though Falcon had come to my rescue, what exactly could he say? What he saw? Blake could say it was consensual and that Falcon walked in at the wrong time. I was a nobody, but Blake . . . well, he wasn't. The tabloids would jump on this. They were always looking for a good story and nothing said "Read Me" more than an agent with a prestigious modeling agency having a Fifty Shades of Grey moment in Sin City. I could just see the headlines in the grocery store! I knew enough that, if I pressed charges against Blake, it would definitely make the gossip papers. And then what? He would tell them I was a freak who'd tried to get him into bed by playing sex games? He wouldn't lose his job, but other people—my friends—would suffer. Some unwarranted guilt by association. Friendships would suffer. Declan would suffer, he and Blake had been friends for years. It would be unbelievably awkward at holidays and cookouts if I did this. I couldn't be responsible for hurting people just because Blake had been a drunken ass. It was just better for everyone to let him live with the one night he'd spent in jail. It'd probably scared the hell out of him. For a man like him, who was used to the best amenities, it would be a warning to leave me alone. Falcon would just have to live with it.

"I won't do it. I can't."

"You're making a mistake, Paige. He's a son of a bitch with a misguided sense of entitlement. He thinks he can do whatever he wants and get away with it. And you're letting him." Falcon stared disbelieving at me. His fists were tight with anger.

I looked up at him with sad eyes and felt like someone had sucked way all the oxygen in the room. Although I was afraid of him, I wouldn't give Blake the opportunity to hurt me again. If I ignored this, he'd be afraid I'd tell everyone what he'd done. I'd have the power.

"I know what I'm doing, Fal. Please. Leave it alone."

It was obvious he was angry. I didn't expect him to recognize it. In this situation, I was the one with more experience. I hoped that would be the end of it, but my refusal to act, and his resulting anger were a volatile mix. He exploded.

"How can you be so naïve? This is bullshit!" Defiantly, he stood before me. His chest was a heaving wall of muscle. The veins in his neck bulged with his controlled rage. He stepped toward me, his jaw set defiantly, and I reacted by recoiling and taking a step back. He misunderstood my action and glared at me.

"What's wrong with you? I'd never hurt you!" He waited a moment and then shook his head in disbelief. "I don't know what I was thinking," he muttered and finished putting the last piece of his clothing on by pulling his shirt over his head. I touched his shoulder, and he hesitated.

"Fal, please trust me. I know how to handle this."

"Yeah. It looked like it. You handled it so well that you pulled your hair out."

Scenes of other hurtful words rattled me as the memories from Marisol's, and now Blake's, attack played in my mind. The Band-Aid had ripped clean off, leaving me raw and exposed. I followed him as he marched to the door.

"So run away! You don't agree with me, you're pissed off. I get it." My hands were set defiantly on my hips, and I got up in his face. "I know Blake can be a bastard, and he's clearly self-absorbed, but he's a pathological flirt. He just went too far!"

He spun around and eyed me indignantly. "Really?" His head tilted to the side, and his eyes were as dark as death. "It looked to me like he wanted to fuck more than flirt."

I felt like I'd been slapped across the face. The weight of his words left an acrid taste in my mouth, and the truth in his statement deflated me. My defiance evaporated just as quickly as his patience. He was right, and I knew it; I just didn't want to admit it. It was easier to kid myself into thinking I was taking the high road when, in reality, I was running away from confrontation. Appropriate action *did* need to be taken, but the argument I'd given Falcon was the same one that had worked for me all my life. *So how did he see through it and know it was all bullshit?* His way was absolute and final, but I had more experience in this area than he did. I had suffered more torture at the hands of childhood bullies than he probably had from enemies in war.

Devastation crumbled in on me like an avalanche as he stormed out the door, and, once I was alone, I was buried in the darkness of my emotions. The scene played in a continuous loop over and over in my head. Here I was worried that my scars disgusted him, but the truth was that my reasoning was the thing he found repulsive.

Shit! Shit! Shit!

I chastised myself. I sat on the bed fisting the covers while I fixated on the look on his face. He'd seen right through me, and that made me nervous. My heart raced, and I felt like I wanted to run, but, honestly, if I did, I didn't know where I'd go. Anxiety and panic crept in on me with icy fingers. Like a plague it spread up the back of my neck, and I knew that if I didn't get out of my room, I'd be an unwilling guest at my own pity party.

Frustrated, I ripped the bra from my shoulders and threw it to the floor. I did the same thing with my panties and stomped into the bathroom, angrier with myself than with him. I put the water on so hot I prayed it would scald away my self-loathing. After I stood there long enough for my skin to redden I began to gain perspective. The burning spray sorted my thoughts and washed away my conflicts. The inner debate between fact and speculation swirled away with the soapy water, but no matter how hard I tried, I couldn't wash away the fact that if Falcon hadn't shown up when he had, I would have been raped—or worse.

As the filthy memories of Blake touching me were cleansed and clarified, an appetite for justice surfaced. I didn't know how I would do it, but Falcon was right. It was time to confront my fears. He didn't know everything I'd been through and in order for him to understand my reaction I had to tell him. I was apprehensive. My track record of dealing with vicious people was not the best. I had to find him and talk to him. His stalwart opinion about Blake's accountability could be the strength and conviction I needed to tap into so I could face Blake. I only hoped he would help.

Elizabeth wasn't smiling; she was staring. At least I'd covered the bruises. I had one on my jaw from where Blake had punched me, but none had surfaced from the slap. If she'd seen them, she would be interrogating me, instead, she stared.

I nursed a cup of coffee to ease the ache in my head. Even contemplating a confrontation with Blake had opened a painful door inside of me. I was consumed by a cyclone of thoughts and, as my friend, Liz deserved an explanation in exchange for her concern.

"What do you want to know?"

Furrowed brows and pursed lips etched her face with worry.

"I thought you were having such a good time. Was Falcon a jerk after I left?"

I stiffened and wrapped both hands around the warm cup like it was a security blanket.

"Falcon was great. I had a wonderful time, in fact, but . . . but it got very interesting when Blake showed up." As I looked up, Liz's eyebrows rose, and her mouth quirked. "I'm going to give you the short version. Blake came to my room, tried to rape me, and, apparently, Falcon kicked his ass."

Liz was no longer smiling. She looked like she was going to hit something. "Why would that guy ever think you were into him?"

I shrugged. "I don't know or, at least, I don't think I know. I've had to do this balancing act with him between being his friend and discouraging his advances. I've told him repeatedly that we're just friends. For the longest time, he either didn't get the hint or just ignored it. One time he went over the top and I told Aria. Of course she told Declan, who wasn't happy about it, and he told Blake to back off. Since then I've kept my distance."

"Apparently, he didn't keep his," she chimed in.

"Anyway, Falcon walked in when Blake was . . ." I fumbled for words. I didn't want to say anymore until after I'd spoken with Falcon. "Blake was taken to the police station, and Falcon stayed with me."

"The police station? What happened?"

"I don't want to go into it, Liz." I inhaled deeply as another panic attack threatened. "Falcon took care of it . . . and then he took care of me."

"That was nice, right?" She wore a hopeful expression.

"Sure, if you don't mind a guy cleaning vomit off you . . ." My voice shook, and I swallowed the lump tickling the back of my throat. "And seeing your scars and other, horrible things." Feelings of worthlessness and dejection stung my eyes with sorrowful tears, and the fresh memories conjured an anxiety filled despair.

"Paige, it's okay." Liz's voice was comforting, like a soft piece of worn flannel.

I shook my head. "No, I don't think so. He wanted me to press charges against Blake, and I made every excuse I could think of not to. Between what he saw of my scars and how I acted, I think he's written me off."

She placed her hand on top of mine and spoke in a reassuring tone. "I think you're wrong. He doesn't strike me as being shallow. Look at what he did for me! I was drunk last night, too, but he made sure I got home okay—*and* he put up with us all night in every club and bar. Hell, we were crazier and sillier than we've been in a long time, and he didn't ditch us. That doesn't sound shallow to me."

"He's really pissed off at me."

"What the hell happened?"

My shoulders tensed as I told her what had transpired. There were a few times I saw murder in her eyes but, even though I hadn't planned to tell her, I felt better as I purged the details. When I'd finished, I saw concern and worry on her face.

"Paige, I'm afraid for you. What are you going to do?"

"I've decided to do what Falcon suggested. I'm going to press charges."

"Wow!" Her eyes widened. "Did you tell him yet?"

I shook my head. "No. But I'm going over to his hotel—and ask him to help me do it. I don't think I can do it by myself."

She nodded. On some level she understood my hesitation, but no one could really know how I felt, but, in that moment, I just felt sad.

"You do realize you're beautiful inside and out, right?" The hopeful expression she wore exposed the sincerity of her words. Unfortunately, my cynicism took over.

"That's a crock, Liz, and you know it." I opened my arms and emphasized our surroundings. "Look where we are! Women are half naked at every hotel pool, at every casino. With how I'm mangled, there's no comparison."

"Stop it, Paige! There are men—and Falcon may be one of them—who aren't into just the flesh. Some guys think a woman is sexier by what she *doesn't* show, and by what she has inside."

"Whatever." I took a deep breath, closed my eyes, and composed myself. "I don't think I can take on Blake by myself. I honestly don't know if Falcon will ever speak to me again."

"Oh, I don't know about that. He's got to talk to you sometime." As she snickered, an impish grin appeared.

"What makes you so sure?" She tapped on my hand. When I looked down I saw a thin gold band. Suddenly, a scene replayed in my mind. A wicked trifecta—alcohol, a dare, and an Elvis impersonator. I groaned.

"Oh hell."

Chapter 15

Falcon

I went back to my room, my footsteps thundering in my wake. Outrage poured off me in sheets.

What was she thinking?

I couldn't get her crestfallen expression out of my mind. It killed me that I'd hit her with such a low blow, but if I hadn't left when I had, more wounding words would have followed. The last thing I wanted to do to Paige was hurt her, but it seemed impossible to me that she'd let Blake get away with what he did. *Why wouldn't she want to make him pay?*

It was very black and white to me, break the law, pay the price. Blake was an overconfident, arrogant prick and to let him get away with hurting her only made it easier for him to attack her again. *That's bullshit!*

I walked over to the bar and poured myself a stiff scotch, then knocked it back with such force it numbed my throat on contact. I only wished it would numb my mind. It was bad enough I'd had to see Matthews nearly naked and on top of her, but it'd been nothing compared to how broken she was when I'd returned to her room. The whole damn situation had thrown her into a tailspin.

I turned to lean against the wall and pondered the situation. I considered myself a tough man. I'd been through a lot of shit and was so desensitized by war, and the inhumanity it bred, that not much bothered me anymore. But no matter how tough I thought I was, seeing Paige so wounded had shaken me. It was now branded into my memory.

She was in shock. I was convinced of that fact, especially when I'd seen her self-mutilating. When I'd seen the scars I realized Blake's attack had triggered some type of post-traumatic event. And I was especially certain it was some form of PTSD. Something horrific lingered below the marks on her body. Maybe the appearance of them would have mattered to another man, but all I'd wanted to do when I'd seen them was protect her from whatever was torturing her then. Though I'd been curious to understand what had caused Paige's pain, all it had made me want to do was hold her and never let anything ever hurt her again.

Because, I love her.

My eyes widened as the realization came over me. It was so sudden it felt like a punch to the gut. I'd known by our second date that I felt differently about her than I had any other woman. She made me feel something more than I ever had before. For too many years, women were the needles providing my sexual high. Before Paige I'd had so many hits that I was numb. Paige wasn't like any of the others. She was a priceless treasure, and I was the raiding bastard who had found her. No matter how much time I spent with her, it was never enough. The biggest difference between her and any other woman I'd know was that she was the crown jewel. Not the kind that was cursed —she was the precious kind.

As I pictured her in my mind's eye, I began to crave her. I was never bored when I was with her. No matter where we were, what we were doing, or how many times we'd done it, time spent with Paige only made me appreciate her more. She made me see everything through different eyes.

So why couldn't she see Blake through my eyes?

Matthews was the worst kind of man. A leech. He bastardized his position, using it to get himself laid. There wasn't a speck of honor in him. His egotism showed him to be as self-centered as the sun. He infused his clients with bright buzzwords and shiny gifts that would assure a good flow from their pockets to his. Maybe, at one time, he was a good guy, but not anymore. Now he was an overconfident douchebag—and if he touched Paige again, he'd be dead.

I felt myself grin as admiration flooded me. Paige was a fighter, no doubt about that. Her scars proved a source of inner strength I admired. That kind of power called out to a place inside me that stirred me on more levels than I could count. She was a warrior. Though she may never have seen herself that way, I'd felt that strength—and it was long before I ever saw her scars. *So why is she so weak when it comes to demanding the justice she deserves?*

I banged my head back against the wall and stared. No amount of scotch would quench my thirst for justice. What Paige needed was for someone to sit her ass down and educate her about where the line was drawn between someone being an asshole and a criminal. My guts twisted in rage contemplating whether or not I should be that person. What she would hear from me was the truth about perfection—it doesn't exist. Perfectionism was pride. At least imperfection had enough room for love to fill in where one was broken.

I took a deep breath, fighting back the urge to march over to her room. I knew what she needed was time, at least I could give her that. I was still too pissed off to trust what I would say to her. Considering the state of mind I was in, I'd probably call her out and confront her with the truth of last night. Rage burned inside of me. The more I thought of Paige giving Blake a free pass the more my anger grew. There was no excuse for his behavior, and sure as hell no excuse for his. Both of them were wrong but only one of them suffered because of it. The more I thought about the situation, the more pissed off I became. Until I calmed down enough to do that in the right way, all I could do was bide my time, savoring the sweeter memories of the evening, both before and after Blake.

My fifth scotch helped me to do just that.

Chapter 16

Paige

After my insightful conversation with Liz, I was somewhat convinced it would be better to talk to Falcon than to believe the damning voices in my head. I knew she was right, but I wasn't ready to talk to him. My acting skills were good, but, somehow, I knew he'd see right through me if I wasn't honest. So, I went back to my room. I spent hours contemplating my next move. I revisited everything that had happened, not just from that night, but all the time we'd spent together. My plan to remain aloof and noncommittal had, obviously, crashed and burned. The realization of how deep I'd gone into myself thoroughly exhausted me, and I slept most of the day.

After several hours of restful slumber, I focused on

the future. I knew I'd been a victim long enough. My brain had finally calmed down enough for me to think rationally. I had to talk to Falcon. I had to explain—really explain—about everything. He deserved that much. I wasn't going to worry about him wanting to see me after Vegas. I'd told myself that almost everything that had happened between us was superficial or make-believe, even if it was the most real relationship I'd ever had. I just wanted the chance to clarify that my experiences with facing up to people like Blake had made me jaded.

The scenario from the day before had never been part of my plans. I'd had something completely different in mind, especially since I blatantly tried to seduce him. I'd had it all planned before we even went out. I'd even had a brilliant thought that, if he stayed the night, I'd have the memory I wanted, and he wouldn't notice the marks on me as long as I kept the lights turned off. Either he would leave, or I'd get dressed before morning. It would've been a win-win, or so I'd thought.

I'd wanted it to *feel* differently. For just one night of my life, I'd wanted more than human contact, I'd wanted the fairytale. I'd earned it. *Hadn't I?*

Then Blake had happened. I didn't know what I'd been thinking. I'd never been destined for a fairytale. Princesses were the beautiful ones, and I, most certainly, was not. I'd been lying to myself because it made me feel better. Then Falcon had come to the rescue. He really was a white knight and he deserved much better than what I could give to him. I thought—I hoped—that if I could justify my actions or enlighten him as to what my true reasons were for letting Blake get away with what he'd done to me, maybe Falcon and I could at least walk away as friends.

My heart ached from wanting more than that, and I remembered the pain of wanting to be like the other girls. Those other girls could have survived a man like Falcon. He was more than just a warm body. That night he'd been my savior and protector, a combination that proved to be dangerous to my carefully guarded heart. I'd been kidding myself hoping for a three-dimensional memory to comfort me when I returned to my two-dimensional life. I'd somehow gotten caught up in my own fantasy and I was hurting for it. Feelings I'd never felt had fused with my happiness. I was still utterly conflicted by the emotions he'd awakened in me. I shouldn't have let my guard down, but he made falling in love with him too easy because he made me feel beautiful.

I had to talk to him. At the very least, he deserved an explanation before it got messy and before we went home. I couldn't let my hopeful mistake complicate the relationships we had back there. So I prepared. I showered and put on my favorite disguise: a competent woman who had it all under control.

I walked from my hotel to his. I needed the air to prepare. All through the lobby and while riding the elevator, my mind swirled with what I'd wanted to say. I was so preoccupied I didn't remember noticing any of the surrounding details of the distance I'd traveled. Before I knew it, I'd arrived. As I stood in front of his door, I took several deep breaths and then knocked.

Perspiration bit my skin with prickly teeth, and I struggled for oxygen, which, because of my anxiety, seemed to be in short supply. I moved to the side of the door so he wouldn't see me if he looked out. It felt like an eternity, and I counted the seconds off to the beating of my heart. I tried to steady my hands when I heard a click and then saw the handle turn.

When he opened the door my breath caught in my throat. Just the sight of him sliced through my façade and vaporized the character I'd prepared. The determination I'd arrived with melted away. His eyes widened slightly when he saw me. It was painfully obvious I was the last person he'd expected to see. I heard the tinkling of my heart as it shattered into a million pieces.

He left the door open in silent invitation. When I followed him into the room, I lusted after the man I desired but couldn't touch. His jeans hung provocatively low, and he wasn't wearing a shirt. His room was stunning, and the lighting showcased tanned skin and broad shoulders. His arms were thick and hard, and I very much wanted to be held by them. He turned toward me, and I froze. He may have thought it was because I was uncomfortable, but it was really because I wanted to remember how beautiful he was. I couldn't keep my eyes from roaming his solid chest and chiseled torso. The only thing about him that didn't look right was his expression. It was hard and tight, and I knew it was me that had caused it. I looked down. My gaze caught the arched lines of the V that traveled from his hips down into the fabric, and I ached because I would never be able to touch him. No other man had ever affected me the way Falcon did, and I vehemently hated how my body betrayed me. He just stood there, observing me. Somehow, I managed a weak smile.

"Can we please talk?" My voice was low and hoarse, and my mouth was dry. I stood nervously in the uncomfortable silence and wondered if he could hear my stomach turning. Finally, he motioned with his head for me to sit while he disappeared into another room. I had nothing else to distract my racing mind except to enjoy the exquisite decor.

It was massive, which made me feel very small. The floor was a heavily veined marble tile. The rugs that complimented them were so plush they looked as deep as the ocean color they were dyed. The furniture was bold and heavy and blended in complimentary colors of the blackest blue and gray. A huge, mirrored bar, framed in thick mahogany, anchored the room. It was well stocked, and I suddenly wished Falcon would offer me a drink to wet my mouth and wash away my suddenly decomposed confidence. If I hadn't been so miserable I would have enjoyed its sophistication, but instead I decided to use it as fodder to break the ice for the serious conversation I hoped to have with him. My attention was drawn to the bedroom door as he returned, fully dressed.

"This is beautiful."

"Thanks."

His tone was stiff. He was making me pay a heavy price by being cold to me when all I wanted to do was repent for my shortsightedness and move on. He sat down across from me and, after what seemed like an eternity, leaned in.

"What are you doing here, Paige?" His voice was neither compassionate nor accusing, simply monotone, and I wondered if his feelings for me were as flat as his voice. I shifted uneasily in the chair.

"Wow." The word came out with a rush of air. I looked him dead in the face. "You're not going to make this easy, are you?" He answered with silence. That said more than words ever could. "I wanted to thank you for last night." His raised brows mocked me. It was obvious he doubted my sincerity. "You deserve an explanation." His eyes never left me, but he relaxed a little and eased back in the chair. "Fal . . . look . . . I know what Blake did wasn't right. I also know he would have done a whole lot more damage if you hadn't shown up. You could have left when you saw me . . . saw the condition I was in when I was alone in the room, but you didn't. Instead you took care of me. I can't imagine what you think of me because I know what you saw, my scars and my hair pulling. I wish you hadn't, but you did." My throat was thick with embarrassment and shame.

His expression softened. I took a deep breath and stared at the floor.

"Lots of people have scars, Paige. Inside and out."

I waited for him to say more and was surprised when he didn't. I couldn't tell if he was genuine. *What is he doing? Trying to be nice by acting like it was no big deal?* I had a personal memory bank catalogued with reactions from various people, so I knew he thought something. What did he have to gain by acting like it didn't matter? Things were already tense between us, and I didn't need him sugarcoating the issue. Whatever thoughts he had couldn't be any more corrosive than what I'd heard all my life.

"I know what my scars look like. I see them every day. I don't even have to open my eyes to see them;

their images are burned into my brain. Just spit it out. I can take it." A thin wash of indignation washed through my voice.

He studied me intently before shaking his head. His expression was one of disbelief. He brought both hands up and covered his face before he wiped over it. A look of concern etched his handsome features.

"You know, Paige, if you were anyone else, I'd think you were fishing for someone to coddle you, but I can tell you really do believe your scars, and whatever caused them, should make a difference to me. Well, they do, but not in the way you think. What you see is totally different from what I do. From what you say, I can tell you see yourself as a victim, but I see you as a survivor. They're just marks; it's just skin. Whatever the story behind them is, it's yours to tell—and you don't have to share it with me. As a matter of fact, I don't want you to tell me simply because it matters more to you than it does to me. What's worse is that you're willing to let some bastard get away with hurting you because you think that by hiding it the whole thing will go away. You don't need to hide. What's on the inside of you makes you who you are, not how you look or what you wear. By presuming that I—or anybody else—would care more about how you look than your wellbeing, you're pretty much accusing me of being shallow. That really pisses me off because, the truth is, I didn't think less of you when I saw them, I thought more."

I was speechless. For the second time in two days, I'd been slapped by his words. I didn't know what was harder to take, people making fun of me because the scars mattered or Falcon chastising me because they didn't. I stared at him as he got out of the chair.

"I'd ask you to stay, but . . ."

I was being dismissed. He walked over to the door and opened it, indicating he wanted me to leave. It appeared the conversation was over.

"I . . . Fal, I'm . . ." I stammered. I was confused. I walked up to him and looked into his eyes. They were sad and heavy with hurt. I touched his face.

"I'm sorry."

My thoughts were fragmented. If he was telling the truth, if he *really* saw me differently, I wanted to know why. Why would appearance matter to so many people but not to him? I grasped at whatever opportunity I had left. "Would you like to go to dinner? Please. I'd really like to—"

"I don't think that would be a good idea, Paige," he interrupted. "Besides . . . I'm flying home in a few hours." The chill in his tone formed a chasm between us, and his hurt expression consumed me.

"Oh. Some other time then."

He struggled with a grin. "Sure."

I managed to smile as I walked out the door. My heart was heavy. I'd screwed it up. I wouldn't have the chance to salvage anything. Maybe I was living in a bubble that was made from my warped physical perception, but wasn't that what I'd been taught? First impressions are lasting impressions, appearance is everything, and put your best foot forward were some of the first sayings I'd learned once I was old enough to go to school. They were proven to me the first time I'd been bullied, and I still put them into practice to guide the appearance side of my business. So, if they weren't the truth, what was?

Mindlessly, I walked down the hall. Falcon had detonated the stories I'd told myself in my, leaving me with the revealing truth behind my wall of lies. In the brief solitude offered by the elevator ride, I realized my presumptions and beliefs had, inadvertently, caused pain to someone whom I never wanted to hurt. I struggled with the notion that it could have been possible for someone to love me more than I loved myself and I never entertained giving it a chance—giving us a chance. As the elevator doors opened, I stepped out in a fog.

"Well, well, well."

A heavily accented voice greeted me. The tone was laced with the poison of sarcasm and ripped off the

Band-Aid I'd quickly put on my emotions when I'd walked out of Falcon's suite.

Marisol glared at me. The woman whose haughty imbalance I'd suffered from and despised addressed me with her signature contempt.

"I didn't think a girl like you could afford to stay in such a nice hotel."

"Why not?" I countered without missing a beat. "Your husband paid me very well to fix your mistakes." She hadn't expected such a quick comeback and eyed me cautiously. Women cowered before her, but I refused to be one of them. It took her a moment, but she recovered.

"That's right. I suppose that would make you my employee since you sold my properties. I'd like to tell you I'm sorry for that, and, also, for what I did to you and your little friend, but I can't. Because I'm not."

What a lunatic! She's screwing with the wrong woman today! I wanted to unleash on the bitch in front of me. Had she lost her mind? I wasn't afraid of her. I'd been dealing with females like her my whole life and I'd learned quite a lesson: mean girls only know how to strike, not kill. They crush the tenderhearted, especially while there're young, but what they really did was make us stronger. We grew up to be their worst nightmare. How effective! She expected me to cower, but I wasn't in the mood for her superior bullshit.

She narrowed her eyes. "So . . . how *is* our little Aria?"

"Like you care." Sarcasm dripped through my every word. She acted so superior I hoped she fall off her pedestal and hang herself. "Aria is fine. As a matter of fact, despite your effort to kill her, she is alive and well and just became a new mother. She and Declan couldn't be happier."

The smile fell from her lips, and I tasted the sweetness of this one bite of victory.

"You're a shark and you swim in shallow waters, Marisol. One day I hope you'll drown in them."

I walked away from her, infused with a taste of triumph. She'd tried to dish out her superior attitude, but I'd given it back to her in one, diseased bite. I didn't look back.

"What lovely news. Please give them my best." I loathed her voice.

I kept walking and heard her haughty cackle as I exited the hotel. First Falcon, then Marisol. I felt so burdened, I couldn't wait to go back to my room and collapse.

"Excuse me. Ms. Paige?"

A man's voice startled me.

My body relaxed when I saw who it was. "Hi, Jorge."

"Ms. Paige, Mr. Grey asked me to take you wherever you wish."

He held the car door open as an invitation. I was touched. Although Falcon was very angry, he was also very considerate. It gave me a sliver of hope.

"Thank you, Jorge. I'd really like to go back to my hotel."

I slid into the cool, crushed leather, and Jorge closed the door behind me. Nothing had gone as planned. My relationship with Falcon was fractured, and Marisol frayed what was left of my nerves. Falcon had one thing right; it was time to go home.

Chapter 17

Paige

A few months later . . .

Princesses came in all shapes, sizes, and colors. Today, at the local church, was the christening day of Karas Rose Sinclair, my own little princess. I was so happy and thrilled to be her godmother. I'd been emotional when Aria and Declan had asked me to stand for their daughter. Since I'd left Vegas I'd had nothing in my life other than work. Aria was as close as a sister to me, but I tried very hard to respect her personal time. Her life with a husband and new baby was very full, but, because she'd been through so much with me, I think she felt like she was somehow abandoning me. Although I was touched, I assured her I was okay. Aria had noticed, since my return, I hadn't been trying to make much of an effort to enjoy a social life. I'd always preferred to keep my social circle very small, but for the last few months I'd been mostly keeping to myself. Since feeling that connection with Falcon I'd learned I wanted one with meaning, not volume.

Katherine, Declan's assistant, and I had been getting together every few weeks for dinner and girl time. Aria's mother, Jeannie, was my second mom and had also insisted on dinner at least once a month. Since I'd been making an effort to be more engaged, I'd felt my walls slip down even more when I was around them. I'd be seeing all of them today, including Aimee.

We'd been friends since we'd met, and she used to be like the pesky kid sister I'd never had. She had matured since she moved to the Lake. I wouldn't have confided in Aimee when she lived closer to me because she was a meddler. I'd been privy to her antics when she'd plotted to get Aria and Declan back together after a breakup.

When Aimee had moved to Western Maryland she was still very spunky, and a bit of a busybody, but she'd become the victim of a horrible attack one night when she'd been walking through the woods. After that, she became much more serious. When I returned from my trip, Aimee had begun to call me more regularly. At first, I was suspicious Falcon might have somehow been involved, but she assured me he wasn't. I loved Aimee. Carter was ever so protective of her, and that touched my heart. Falcon's eye-opening comments had done me a favor, and when I returned home I really spent time thinking about my life and had begun to count my blessings. One night, after hours of introspection about an area of my character that he'd brought to my attention, I realized I was a hypocrite. I'd always lent an ear to the women in my small circle, but I'd refused to impose on them for the same. Since that night, I'd made more of an effort to open myself for more than superficial relationships and had come to believe I had just as much to give to them as I received. I think that was why I missed Falcon so much. He made me see myself in the mirror of his observations. I ached for something real with him but was uncertain how badly I'd damaged what could have been.

All my friends would be together today, and the festivities promised to be a little bittersweet. In the past months I'd made very little progress in repairing my relationship with Falcon. Nonetheless, a seed of hope remained because even a little progress was still something. I'd waited for him to contact me. I'd hoped he would once he got over being angry. First, a month went by, then six weeks, and still I'd heard nothing. I hadn't received a call, text, or e-mail. Thoughts of him began to distract me. The more I mulled over the last time we were together the more I examined myself. I'd been wrong, and I wanted to tell him. He was right; I'd let Blake get away with his behavior that night because of an old pattern. For years, I'd protected myself by putting a steel coat over my feelings. I'd let people get away with throwing whatever they wanted at me. I'd pretended to ignore their actions, but it dragged me down emotionally. I'd thought the sheath was an effective barrier, but the weight of wearing it was breaking me. The saddest part? I'd thought by not reacting, I'd made myself stronger; by taking the high road, I wasn't stooping to their level. I'd concentrated on his comments, and once I'd really seen myself through Falcon's eyes I made a decision: I went for counseling. By seeking help, I'd learned it wasn't a steel garment that covered me, it was more a sponge because I was still absorbing every hurtful word. When I'd finally been so full I'd become saturated in the criticism of people who shouldn't have mattered, I'd wrung myself dry by pulling out my hair.

Aria had warned me that Falcon would be here today. Although I was hoping for the best, I wasn't sure how it would go. I was so thankful for the distraction that Karas provided. It was hard to stay in an overly anxious state of mind when in the presence of that sweet baby. I'd never thought I could love so unconditionally, but she'd stolen my heart from the moment I first saw her precious face. When I held her in my arms, she was magic. She rocked my world and everyone else's with her tiny hand. All she had to do was place it on my cheek, and everything else melted away.

Today was no exception. Beautifully flawless, seldom crying, and perfectly content wherever she was, Karas sat in her daintily decorated perch observing everything about the day. She cooed and made baby talk to the mobile of butterflies that floated on the handle of her infant seat. She was almost singing to them as they danced above her head. Declan adored her and, just as her mother did, she had him lovingly wrapped around her little finger. There was no mistaking that the affection was mutual because whenever Declan held her she lit up by smiling and kicking her feet ecstatically. Whenever I watched the three of them together my heart swelled—making the hole I'd had in it since I'd left Las Vegas even more noticeable.

"Do you want to hold her?" Aria walked toward me as she lightly bounced her little bundle.

"Absolutely."

I held out my arms, and she filled them with my little love. Her eyelids fluttered as she fought sleep. I kept up the gentle pattern Aria had started, and, within moments, she drifted off. Although she was as gentle as a star-filled night, she had the power to chase away my monsters. All through the day I'd been plagued with clouded thoughts, but it was impossible to stay in a dark state of mind when little Miss Sunshine was near.

"Aria, open the gift I brought for her. It's next to my purse." I spoke softly and tilted my chin in the direction of Karas's present.

She retrieved the small, pink bag and removed the decorative tissue. Inside was a blue velvet box.

"What did you do?" As she opened the box she gave a small gasp. "Paige . . . it's beautiful." She removed the necklace and held it up.

"I'd really like her to wear it today if that's okay. Something from her godmother," I whispered so as not to wake the baby.

"Leave it to her Aunt Paige to accessorize her," she answered with a nod.

I held Karas up, so she could fasten the gold cross and chain around her neck. There was a diamond in the middle that sparkled as it caught the light shining through the beautiful stained glass window depicting the Virgin Mary holding baby Jesus. It looked so pretty on her. My friends always teased me about my love for accessories, and, for Karas's big day, I couldn't help myself. Every girl should have an arsenal of accessories, even sweet, petite ones.

I waved Aria off to greet friends and family while I

stole a peek around the church. I had a twinge of uneasy anticipation. Almost all the guests had arrived, yet there was still no sign of Falcon. *Would he come? Would he act like nothing happened, or would he avoid me?* My mind was working overtime. The reality was that, legally, we had an issue that needed to be dealt with. His anger toward me was lessening. I still got the impression he wanted to put the matter behind us, but he held himself back. I hoped today would be promising, that I could tell him face to face about all that had happened and that he'd been on my mind. Hopefully, once I told him I'd realized he was right, we would be able to move forward. Although we'd spoken at his hotel, I never had the opportunity to tell him how much I'd appreciated what he'd done for me that night. That I hadn't realized the value of it until I'd started counseling. My therapist confirmed it was a blessing in disguise. Falcon's disapproval and the loss of his friendship had been the catalyst for my self-examination. I'd discovered he was the first person that made me face myself. I was drawn to him because he refused to hear my excuses. I missed him. Our first conversation after Las Vegas had been awkward.

"FALCON? IT'S PAIGE." The only thing I heard was the sound of my nervously rapid pulse. "Are you there?"

"I'm here." His tone was flat, revealing no hint of emotion.

"How are you?"

"I'm fine."

This wasn't working out the way I'd hoped. My nerves were on edge, and he wasn't making it easy, so I got to the point.

"I don't want to bother you, so I'll make it quick. I wanted to let you know that I'm having papers drawn up for our annulment. You'll be receiving them soon."

"Fine." The chill in his voice cut deeply.

"Fine." I waited, but he said nothing more. If he didn't want to talk then neither did I. "I guess that's it. I hope you enjoyed Vegas. Take care of yourself." I was about to end the call when he spoke.

"Really, Paige? That's it? Like nothing happened? Because no matter how I try to wrap my head around it I still don't understand you. I've tried to make sense out of what happened but no matter how I try I still can't figure you out. After all the shit you went through with Marisol, you gave the police everything they needed to deal with her. So, why? Explain to me how you could let Blake get away with the shit he pulled on you? He's a menace, and I tried to tell you that, but my opinion meant jack. You kicked my concerns to the curb. I know I can be a cold-hearted bastard but you . . . I wanted to *protect you. I thought we had something. Was it all an act?"*

His honesty caught me off guard, but he'd never understand. "It's just me. Don't take it personally."

"Don't take it personally? Maybe I wouldn't have if it hadn't been me who dragged that bastard off you. I wanted to kill him. I was the one who held you while you fell apart. I couldn't help but take it personally, but you shut me down when I wanted you to hold him accountable."

I heard the hurt in his voice, and it stabbed me in the heart. Maybe this wasn't a good idea. Maybe I wasn't ready to talk to him. He made me feel like crying, and I didn't want to do that. I almost hung up on him.

"Shit!" he interrupted. "I didn't mean to be a prick and go off on you like that."

"It's okay." My voice was barely a whisper.

"You made your decision. I'm living with it, but I still don't understand it. All I wanted to do was . . ." He paused. "I mean, I can understand it a little bit if he means more to you than I thought he did—but, even then, I still think letting him get away with it was wrong."

"He didn't mean more to me—and he still doesn't." I sighed deeply. No matter how uncomfortable this discussion made me, it needed to be dealt with. "Can we talk?"

"It's been a shitty week." His tone was strained. I could hear his shoes scuffling on the hardwood as he paced.

"I'm not asking you to accept how I handled it, but at least give me a chance to explain."

"Today's not a good day."

My heart dropped. I had just about given up when he started again.

"But how about I call you tomorrow?"

THE FIRST FEW conversations after that had been tentative. At first, we'd both acted like we were walking on eggshells but, eventually, we'd relaxed a little. I'd told him about work and the baby, and he'd shared with me about going fishing on the lake and the business. Each time we'd talked after that, it had gotten easier. Usually, I'd been stressed because I'd had more show-ings than I'd had agents, but no matter how tense I'd been, he'd popped my anxiety filled balloon. Before I'd known it, our calls had become more and more frequent, and less and less uptight. I'd felt the shift as we'd relaxed into each other's routine. Today would be the first time we'd seen each other since Vegas. I had no idea how it would go but I ached for what we'd had. I couldn't wait to see him. I hoped for the best, but expected the worst, and not because of Falcon—Blake was coming as well.

I hadn't told anyone about what had happened, but now I was second-guessing that decision. While Karas slept in my arms, I mulled over the reasons but, just the same as I'd concluded back then, I didn't know how much of it had been Blake and how much had been the alcohol. I hadn't heard anything from him, which I hoped was because he'd been too ashamed and embarrassed to talk to me. The only other option was he'd felt no remorse at all. If that was the case, and I told Declan and Aria what he'd done, it would completely ruin his friendship with them. If I was wrong, and he had no regrets, I would expose him to them, but today wasn't the day to do that. My friends had gone through so much to have this little girl, and they didn't need to have someone like Blake around their daughter. For today I desperately wanted to help them make wonderful memories. Right now my biggest fear was having Falcon and Blake in the same room. I might be able to ignore Blake, but that would be impossible for Falcon.

Low voices echoed in the sanctuary. I pressed my lips to Karas's forehead and inhaled her soft, baby scent.

"She is sweet, isn't she?" Aria laid her hand on Karas's chest. At the sound of her mother's voice, she woke up and looped her little hand around her mother's fingers. "It's hard to believe she's mine."

"And mine." The hushed, baritone confession came from her proud father. Declan stood almost reverently behind his wife. He kissed her head as they both looked at their daughter. Aria tucked her head under his chin and leaned into him. He spoke so lowly that only the two of us could hear.

"Everyone's here, babe. We're going to get started."

Aria and I walked around to the baptismal font as the priest welcomed everyone to the ceremony. I cradled Karas in my arms while Declan's brother, Carter, joined me so we could stand together as her godparents. The ceremony was as beautiful as the baby and flowed seamlessly as we committed ourselves, and Karas was baptized into the faith. She didn't even cry when Father Metzger introduced the newest addition to the church body. The church erupted into applause and Aria and Declan exited to the vestibule. Everyone greeted them to offer their well wishes and congratulations. The crowd thinned out quickly as everyone headed to the Sinclair home for the festivities.

Chapter 18

Paige

Although the weatherman had predicted rain, the day couldn't have been more beautiful. Under a warm sky, a gentle sea breeze played at the hem of my dress as I walked up to the door. Once again, Declan had allowed his home to be transformed for this milestone celebration. It was the place that had come to be a home, where their friendships had originated, and where everyone who cared for them felt loved and accepted. The last time a big occasion had taken place here was for the wedding. The house was an island floating within a soft blanket of creamy, white sand overlooking the ocean. In the afternoon sun, the house was infused with light. Inside, the gauzy, sheer curtains danced in the light breeze. The party planner

Declan and Aria had hired reflected their personalities perfectly and had done a beautiful job with the food and decorations. There was one distinctive fingerprint that was recognized by everyone and that was the cake. Declan had had the baker make an edible storybook castle for his perfect, little princess.

While they got everyone started with food and drinks, I was left with our sweet girl. I had tucked myself away in a quiet corner and had rocked the baby to sleep.

"Hey." Declan came up beside me and spoke quietly. "I'm going to take her from you and lay her down so you can mingle with everyone." He saw my reluctance but wouldn't take no for an answer. "C'mon now. Don't argue with me. You've been helping us all day." He took Karas from me, cradling her in his arms as he kissed her.

"God, she's a sweetheart." It was obvious as he gazed at his daughter's face that he was smitten. His expression was filled with such adoration it brought to mind something Aria had told me: unless you see it and feel it for yourself, it's nearly impossible to describe the love a parent feels for their child. I could only hope that one day I'd find out firsthand.

As Declan disappeared into the bedroom with the baby, I made my way outside to the porch. It was my favorite part of their house. I couldn't shake the foreboding I was feeling about the day. I immediately relaxed at the sound of a flock of seagulls. As they ran in and out with the remnant edges of the waves, they took a little of my worry with them. The sounds of the seashore calmed me. They soothed my inner spirit. Although I also lived on the ocean, there was something special about this particular view from their home. I was reminded of the story that Declan had told of the first time he'd seen Aria. He'd shared it many times. He'd said he would always remember how beautiful she was that day as she'd let the waves crash over her feet—time had stood still. It was a hopelessly romantic story that I hadn't appreciated at the time, but my feelings for Falcon had made me realize there was still a spark of a romantic inside me. I was thinking of him as I breathed in the pungent salt air.

"Nice party for a baby, wouldn't you say?"

I cringed as I felt his hot breath against my neck. Memories of him came back in a deluge. His voice grated my nerves and my ears, and a sickening anxiety made me nauseous. My focus on the screne scene evaporated in the nearness of Blake's evil presence. For months I'd tried to give him the benefit of the doubt, but that had vanished the moment he'd opened his mouth. He was the same leech he was when he'd attacked me.

"You're looking as gorgeous as ever." He pressed

his cheek near the back of my head, and I stiffened. I felt dirty as he inhaled long and deep. "Mmm, you smell good, too." I turned around, ready to slap him.

"I would have thought you'd seen enough of me in Vegas to divert your interest to other, less *freakish*, sights. Or did you forget about that?"

He was stunned by my quiet aggression. His memory of that night may have been tested, but mine was perfectly clear. He flashed a wicked smile.

"All the more reason for me to show you how sorry I am."

I was disgusted by his cavalier attitude and began to walk into the house and rejoin the party but, as I went by him, he grabbed my upper arm. Instantly furious, I tried to yank myself away from his slimy fingers.

"Get your hands off me before I scream!" I spat the words through gritted teeth. He wasn't disturbed at all and grinned while he pulled me closer. There was an underlying threat in his tone.

"Now, Paige. You don't want to make a scene, do you?"

An almost eerie calm came over me, and I and narrowed my eyes at him.

"Get. Your. Damn. Hands. Off. Me."

I raised my hand to slap him in the face, but I barely had time to draw my arm back before a hand, much larger than mine, flew in front of me and clamped Blake's wrist. As I was released, he bent over in pain. Stunned, I looked up to see the face of my rescuer.

Falcon.

He cocked his head toward me. "You okay?"

I nodded. He turned his attention back to Blake.

"Seems you have a problem with your hands, Matthews." He twisted Blake's hand into a painfully backward position, forcing him down to his knee. Although I could tell he was furious, I saw a hint of satisfaction in his eyes.

Just then a crowd broke into laughter inside the house, and I was reminded of where I was.

"Please." I looked up at Falcon with pleading eyes. "I don't want to ruin their day."

"I'm sure he was counting on that." He looked back at Blake. "What were you trying to do? Kiss and make up after you tried to rape her?"

Falcon's expression didn't soften. He didn't take his eyes off Blake and made him cry out. He bent Blake's hand back until it looked like it would break. Blake's cry was only masked by the laughter inside.

"Go back in the house, Paige. Now!"

Obediently I did as instructed, mostly because I wanted to divert attention from the two of them.

As I walked inside I slipped into a comfortable smile. I used my body to block the scene and keep everyone's attention inside while Falcon contained the commotion outside. My peripheral vision allowed me to keep an eye on Falcon. He was explosive. He'd released Blake, but his jaw was tight as he glared at him. I watched as he escorted him off the porch and around the house. Then a sudden motion from inside caught my attention. Carter was going toward the porch and he looked furious. I quickly intercepted him.

"Carter, please. It's under control—I promise." He looked between me and the two men quickly disappearing along the side of the house. I placed my hand on his forearm to assure him everything was okay. He stilled, and we both watched Blake's car as it took off down the street.

Most of the guests were too engrossed in conversation to notice what was happening outside, but Aimee wasn't one of them. As a delayed reaction of nausea rolled my stomach, she made her way over to us. The impact of Blake's aggressive behavior hit me, and I felt the blood leave my face. I quickly navigated through the crowd to get into the bathroom; Aimee followed me. Although I went in alone, my mind was at ease knowing she was just outside the door.

I welcomed the brief solitude. Taking a few deep breaths, I fought the commotion that trampled my insides. I ran my hands and wrists under cold water and I placed them against my flushed cheeks. For the second time, Falcon had averted yet another assault on my behalf. I didn't expect him to come back. He'd been livid when he'd left, and I knew him well enough to know he wouldn't let his personal feelings disrupt the party.

"Are you okay in there?" Aimee's soft knock and concerned voice traveled through the wood. I opened the door enough to peek out.

"I'm good."

She gave me a look that said she wasn't convinced. "Do you want to talk about it?"

I shook my head. "No, I'm good, Aim. Really."

A few minutes had ticked by when I came out. As we walked into the living room, I could feel her eyes on me. People surrounded us, but I was the one Aimee kept in her sight. I looked around to see if Falcon had returned, but he hadn't, and I felt dejected.

"What's up, buttercup?" Aria put her arm around my shoulder.

"I'm really tired. Would you mind if I slipped out?"

"Of course I don't mind." She looked at me inquisitively. "Did something happen? You look upset."

"No," I lied. "I'm just ready to call it a day. My stomach's acting up."

"Do you want me to get Declan to drive you home? The party will be over soon, and it looks like it's starting to rain."

"No. I'm okay to drive." I assured her with a hug. "I'll call you when I get home."

Concern washed over her as she watched me walk to my car. My heart was heavy. Of all the scenarios I'd let run through my mind, I'd never imagined what had transpired today, and my thoughts were muddled because of it. All I wanted to do was go home and get into comfortable clothes. I knew once I got there, my friends Ben and Jerry would keep me company.

Chapter 19

Blake

T he sound of heavy droplets smacked the windshield in concert with the image playing out in his head. Blake's thoughts were as grey and clouded as the sky, and it was all because of Falcon Grey. He wanted nothing more than to slam his fist right in that bastard's smug face.

He jerked the car into a parking space and threw it into park. His condo was in a secured building, and he quickly punched in the access code. Fueled by anger, he bounded up the steps two at a time and slammed the door behind him when he was inside. Once again, Falcon had interfered in a matter that was between him and Paige. The more he replayed the scene in his mind, the more he wanted to hurl something in an incapacitating rage.

He paced in front of the window. The spectacular view of the Atlantic Ocean was a reminder to him of all he'd achieved. Compared to him, Falcon was a piece of shit. Indignation shadowed his mood. There was no way he was letting him get away with this.

He paced the confines of the place, rounding the floor of the living room for what seemed the hundredth time.

"Son of a bitch!"

He threw himself down on the sofa. Crossing one leg over the other his foot shook violently as his ankle teetered on his knee. The door clicked, alerting him to someone's presence. Only one person had accompanied him to the beach.

"Where the hell have you been?"

Marisol regarded the barked question with a murderous glare. She set her shopping bag down gently on the glass-topped table. Her expression was full of contempt. If looks truly could kill, her gaze would have annihilated him. She strolled toward him. The sound of her Louboutin's graduated from a hearty click to a dull thud as she went from marble to carpet. When she stopped, she stood in front of him.

"Blake. Dear." Her words were encased in an icy

threat. "I would caution you not to use that tone with me. It might prove hazardous to your health."

She looked him over, roaming from head to foot. There was only one reason for his reckless tone, and, because of it, she extended a bit of leniency.

"Knowing what your plans were for the afternoon, I can imagine what or who put you in such a foul mood. Perhaps we should wait to talk until you're in a better frame of mind."

She bent over the coffee table and lifted the top off the crystal dish sitting there. A small, silver spoon lay nestled in the sparkling white dust. She emptied a measurement of it onto the glass mirror underneath and replaced the lid. Right next to the crystal dish sat an oak box . It was polished so beautifully the depth of the grain was showcased. Marisol lifted the lid. Inside were a razor blade and a rolled one-hundred-dollar bill. She carefully scraped the powder into a thin line. When she turned around she held the tightly wound currency out to Blake. A wicked smile crossed her lips.

"Here you go," she said sweetly. "This will put you in a better mood."

Blake studied her. He knew she was right. He also knew he was lucky enough to get the best quality blow because of her. While he hated her superior attitude, he hated how he felt even more. The coke always took the edge off.

He grabbed the bill from her hands and rested the tube on the edge of the glass just beneath the snowy line. While he kept an eye on her, he put his head down. He dropped his gaze only long enough to snort the powder.

Blake threw the money on the table, sat back, and closed his eyes. The drug kicked in on contact, filling the synapses with redemptive bliss. He tumbled into its sweet effects as it cascaded the residual happiness through his entire body. His shoulders relaxed, and his fist unclenched.

Marisol maintained a vigilant superiority as she watched the whole scene with interest. His addiction profited her in many more ways than just money. The one she liked best was control.

"There, now." She crossed her arms across her chest with a smile of satisfaction. "That should help you to be a bit more civil."

Like a queen on a throne she took a seat in the thick leather chair. She placed her hands on the rounded arms, her feet flat on the floor. The only thing that was missing from this scene was her scepter and crown. She bided the time patiently as she waited for Blake to become more pleasant and relished the few moments of peace. He'd become quite an annoyance lately, but she tolerated him because he was useful to her and Manny. So far, his belligerence had been easy to fix. As long as his habit didn't reach too deeply into her pocket, and he continued to be an asset, she'd keep him supplied.

"Feeling better?" She mocked.

His eyes opened to narrow slits. In the blanketing, crystalline haze he'd forgotten she was there. Straightening up, he made a noble attempt at lucidity.

"I just needed a minute." He leaned forward, ran a hand through his hair, and then rested his arms on his thighs. "What were you saying?"

"I was saying that someone must have made you angry, and, apparently, you thought you could share your irritation with me. You questioned where I was, which, might I remind you, is none of your business."

"Oh, yeah." For a moment, clarity sliced through the miasma. "Sorry about that. I went to Declan's and I was asked to leave the party."

She smirked, enjoying the juicy tidbit. "Declan threw you out of his house? I didn't see that coming."

"*He* didn't throw me out. It was that prick, Falcon." Indignation cut through his numbing haze.

"Falcon? Carter's friend?" She was surprised and amused. "What did you do to him?"

"I didn't do shit to him!" Blake's euphoria was peppered with violence. "I was talking to Paige, and the bastard cut in on me."

She burst into laughter.

He shot to his feet. "Shut the hell up, Marisol!"

A rekindled hatred boiled in his veins, making him careless, while the verbal slap earned him a dangerous look.

"What did you say to me?" Her tone was ferocious.

Blake rambled indignantly. "He doesn't have exclusive rights to her! He's ruining all the work I've put into that uppity bitch! I'm the one that gets to fuck her, not him."

Marisol suddenly grew quiet and confused. She had no idea what he was talking about. As far as she knew Blake had gone to a christening. She couldn't imagine why, of all places, he was trying to have sex at Declan's house.

"I don't know what you're talking about. You're acting like an idiot."

He dismissed her with a look. "Paige—and I didn't try anything at Declan's house. I tried in Las Vegas."

Her shocked look mirrored his arrogance.

"Yeah, that's right, I tried to fuck her. She played games with me and I tried to collect. I was ready for a good time. As a matter of fact, I'd just dusted up. I was almost inside her. If I hadn't been so sidetracked by all those disgusting scars . . . then he showed up."

He confused her with two words—Paige and scars. She was rabid for clarification.

"What scars. Paige has scars?"

He sneered. "Yeah. Disgusting ones. All over her."

She shuddered with excitement. *Paige scarred?* The thought was too delicious, but Marisol savored it. If what he'd said was true, her disfigurement was probably a result of being cut by the glass when she pushed Paige through the window.

"Tell me about these scars."

He smiled at her morbid curiosity. "They're ugly. I went soft as soon as I saw them, I mean, who wants to touch that shit?"

Marisol closed her eyes and relished the news. There was no other explanation. She was responsible for Paige's scars. It was more than she could have hoped for. Although her initial goal had been to eliminate the happy little group of friends, it seemed destroying them gave her more satisfaction. One by one she was obliterating the little circle that had dared cross her. She'd pushed Declan into moving traffic, sliced Aria's flesh, and was party to Lacey's death and Aimee's rape.

As she assessed the collective destruction she drowned in malevolent satisfaction. She always knew she was smarter than them. Maybe they'd think twice before dismissing her.

As Blake rambled on about the indignation he'd suffered and how he planned to retaliate, she tuned him out and offered him another line of coke; it might even feed his delusional invincibility. She was counting on it because, eventually, he would also be held accountable. He was, or used to be, one of the people in that little circle. Even though, now, he was useful, he would have to be dealt with one day.

After rambling on, Blake finally fell asleep. Marisol left the room to make a cup of tea. Soon they'd be returning to New York. She had to play this carefully. It would serve her purpose if Manny knew what Blake had done in Las Vegas. Since her release, he'd been adamant about them keeping a low profile. Any behavior that drew attention to the activities in his business was dealt with swiftly, harshly, and permanently. She would assure her husband she was looking out for his best interest by telling him about the incident and reassuring him she'd keep an eye on Blake. When Blake no longer served her purposes, she would tell Manny he'd become problematic. It would work out beautifully; she would pull the strings and Manny would pull the trigger.

Manny pushed the noise of the casino out of his head and, instead, concentrated on the information from his wife. What he'd just learned was unacceptable. His merchandise moved quickly and smoothly. Blake's actions could be a problem—and he didn't like problems.

The cartel did business discreetly, and Blake was becoming anything but. In an attempt to reposition Marisol at Bella Matrix Modeling, he'd hesitantly agreed to let Blake feed cocaine to his connections in the business. Paris, Italy, and New York had a large and diverse fashion industry and Blake had many colleagues who indulged in recreational drug use. The vein of business that Blake tapped into was extremely lucrative, but risks to the organization would not be tolerated. Now that customers had been established it would be very easy to recruit a replacement when the time came. It was a disappointment because Blake had proven to be an asset until lately. Once he'd begun using himself, his behavior had become erratic. Now his competence was in question, and it complicated things. Drugs always complicated things.

Mari was a smart girl. He counted himself lucky because she knew all about the nature of his business, and she knew what it took to protect it. Her father had run it well. It was fortuitous that Manny and Marisol had met. They understood each other. When she called him and relayed the information about Blake it pleased him because, of all people, it was her loyalty he craved most. It would be most unfortunate should she ever prove disloyal.

In this instance her instincts were correct. This new development required delicacy. There was no question as to Blake's fate, but timing was a factor as well as location. His elimination would not be in Ocean City or New York. Both were too obvious and reeked of Mari. Of course, anything linked to Mari was indirectly tied him, so, much care would be given to the details. They had an upcoming trip to Las Vegas planned. That trip could prove to be beneficial in this instance. Even Blake wouldn't be suspicious. He'd gone to Vegas with them before so inviting him again wouldn't raise suspicions. There, he could more effectively deal with the offense. Permanently.

Manny motioned for his man to come over to him.

"Eduardo, I need you to get a driver for Mrs. Vallega. She'll be returning from the beach, and Blake Matthews will be accompanying her. I suspect we may have a problem with Mr. Matthews so I'm relying on your discretion. We don't want to attract any unnecessary attention to my wife."

The man nodded, indicating he understood. "Anything else?"

"Yes." Manny looked at his watch. "Please tell my wife I wish to have dinner with her. It's been a while since I've seen her. Tell her I want to . . . reconnect."

Chapter 20

Falcon

My tires crunched on the gravel as I turned off the back road to Paige's house. I pulled my car behind hers. A jumble of thoughts assaulted me. It had been like that ever since I'd left Las Vegas. Thoughts of Paige would appear out of nowhere, and I couldn't think straight for hours. I was glad we'd gotten comfortable with each other again, but, then, that was over the phone. Today my mind and body had reacted to seeing her and reminded me I was in love with her. Just thinking about her made me want her. Seeing her today had compounded the matter. I'd taken a drive down Coastal Highway. It had been long enough for me to take a breather and compose my thoughts.

Carter had pointed me in the direction of Paige

when I'd arrived at the party. The long drive from Western Maryland had given me plenty of time to think about her. Although, when I'd first gotten back from the trip to Vegas I'd been angry. Over time, I'd come to admit I wanted to mend my relationship with Paige. It would be difficult because we were polar opposites when it came to confrontation. I dealt with it head-on and Paige avoided it at any cost. If I had my way, that was going to change.

I suspected there was one big factor in her makeup that was part of her disorder—stress. She didn't deal with it well. Shoving all that shit down deep inside was a big part of what made her implode. Her trichotillomania was a combination of stress and PTSD. I'd thought it through and was prepared to tell her I'd do whatever was necessary to help her sort it all out. I wanted this relationship to work. Today would, hopefully, mark the first step of that journey.

I'd sucked it up to attend the christening for Declan's daughter. I'd known Blake would be there. I'd known when I saw the bastard I'd want to punch him out, and I would have if I hadn't known it would distress Paige. The last thing I'd wanted to do was upset her. Unfortunately, when I did enter the room, I saw Blake looming over her out on the porch. I cast aside all my good intentions and practically dragged him from the party. When I got him out of sight, I gave him one final warning: touch Paige again and that would be the last time he used his fingers.

"I DON'T KNOW *why you think there's something between the two of you, because she assures me there's not. Stay away from her. If you so much as look at her the wrong way, I'll find you—and you won't like it when I do."*

"*Get your hands off me, you prick! You don't own her!"*

"*You see that's where you're wrong. In a way I do, because she's my wife—and I'll kill anybody that touches what's mine!"*

Now THAT I'VE taken care of Blake, all I had left to do was straighten things out with Paige.

RAINDROPS PELTED me as I walked up the steps. I could only hope it wasn't an ominous sign. She answered my knock, opening the door, and, when she did, I sucked in a breath. I couldn't have prepared for how I felt after our many months apart. She stood there in the doorway wearing sweats and a T-shirt, and, still, a jolt of desire ran though me. We stared at each other for what seemed like forever, but as the few raindrops grew into a downpour, I regained my composure.

"Can I come in?" The words sounded tentative.

"Sure."

Her tone was stiff as she moved to the side. I stopped beside her, closing the space between us. "Do you think I can get a towel?"

She eyed me cautiously and then headed down the hallway. When she returned she roughly placed the towel in my hands. I dried my head as I took a quick glance around the room. Paige took a seat on the sofa, and my eyes followed her trail. "Nice place you've got here."

"Thanks. What are you doing here?"

Distaste dripped from the question. I sat across from her and extended my hand. "Okay. Let's get this over with." I grinned. "I'm Falcon Grey. It's nice to meet you. I hear your husband's an asshole."

Her lips pursed as a smirk formed on them. "Well, that was the last thing I expected you to say."

That smirk was my lifeline. It gave me a glint of hope that Paige wasn't completely pissed off.

"And you're right; my husband *is* an asshole. He's also stubborn. I think we're headed toward a divorce."

I cocked to the side and studied her. The question

had to be asked, so I jumped in. "Is that what you want?"

"What I want is to not talk about it right now." She reached over and patted the top of my hand. "Besides, there are other things that need to be said."

"Yeah?"

"Yeah."

Paige had told me she was going to therapy, but I'd never pressed for details. She smiled.

"It's been helping," she said, as if reading my mind. "We've discussed what happened with Blake . . . and a lot of other things. Stuff I was holding on to." She looked me straight in the eye with a determined look, but her voice waivered. "I'm sorry I was so stubborn. I had my reasons."

Once she stopped talking, she tried to compose herself. I knew it had taken much for her to open up to me. Her body language spoke volumes. She licked at dry lips, slowly wringing her hands as she looked down at her lap. I said nothing. Paige, obviously uncomfortable, stood and went into another room. When she returned, she had two drinks in her hands. She handed one to me before she sat. A shadow of a smile played on her face, while a lone teardrop kissed her lips. My heart clenched in my chest. She had no idea how brave and strong I believed her to be. I wanted her to feel more at ease with me there, so I changed the subject.

"The christening was nice. Did you have a good time today?"

She shrugged, averting her gaze. "It was nice. It was much better arrived."

"Paige . . ." Her eyes met mine. I reached out, touching her cheek. "I want to cut through the awkward bullshit, so let me get to the point. I've missed you. I hope you could tell when we spoke on the phone."

Her fingers were blanched from the chokehold she had on the glass in her hand. She inhaled deeply, then breathed it out, and sat the glass on the table beside her, the ice making a tinkling sound as the tumbler came to rest on the wooden top. Her hands shook ever so slightly. If I hadn't been so acutely aware of her every move, I wouldn't have noticed. Paige eyed me cautiously, took a deep breath once again, and then her expression changed as she adopted a look of determination.

"Okay, fine. Let's cut through the bullshit." Her chin rose defiantly. "I'm not a woman who's going to play games with you, and I'm not one of those women who's clingy, but these past few months apart have proven to me I don't like being without you." She rolled her eyes. "There. I've said it." Her shoulders relaxed as she cleared the hurdle of words. Resigned, she looked at me. "I've lived my life behind smoke and mirrors, letting people see only what I wanted them to see. I've only taken what I felt I deserved, and I've worked damn hard for it. I've shied away from relationships because I never wanted anyone to see what you've seen because, if they did, they might try to make me feel less than I was once they saw what was underneath the designer clothes. I don't want to put any more time and effort into this, Fal—whatever *this* is—until you understand. About me, that is. I've learned a lot about myself in counseling, and one of the biggest things I've learned is that I'm not sorry for what happened in Vegas."

He raised his brow. "Which thing in particular? A lot happened in Vegas."

"Blake and what you saw after you pulled him off me. See, the thing is, it doesn't have anything to do with you or Blake. It has everything to do with me. If that night hadn't happened, I wouldn't have gone to get help. There's a whole lot more you need to know about me before we can decide where we go from here. After you know the whole story, you might go running for the door. But, if you don't, I want you to know that I was never happier than when we started reconnected."

I nodded. "I'm glad you're learning about yourself in counseling, but you need to know this about me— I'm not a man who scares easily."

"Maybe it was good it worked out this way." She tipped her chin as her brows pinched together. "I got to know you at the same time I was getting to know myself. When I came home from Vegas, I missed you. Missing you spooked me—*you* spooked me. I knew how I felt about you, but I wasn't sure if I liked feeling the way I did. For the first time I didn't have to ask myself if I was happy, I just was. Then Blake pulled his bull-shit, and you came to the rescue. I both loved it and resented it. I didn't want to *need* to be rescued and I sure as hell didn't want to *need* you to be my rescuer. But let me be clear, because I'm going for full disclosure here, I didn't know how to react when you saw me at my worst. Pulling my hair out isn't something I want anyone to know, much less see. You didn't freak out. I did."

"But there's a reason for it. Sweetheart, I'm a ratio-nalizer by nature. I might not understand it, but I accept it."

"I don't like it when I get that way, but I own it. I'm proud of my life—what I've accomplished—but every-thing I'm ashamed of, you saw that night. I was having a pity party in my private hell, and you walked in on it. I've dealt with this in my own way for a long time, but I've always managed it alone. Having you see the crazy part of my life scared me. I knew it would change how you felt about me. I liked that you made me feel what I've never felt before, loved and desired. I was terrified of how you'd treat me once you saw how imperfect I really was. And after I went to your hotel? I told myself I should never have been so stupid and being with you wasn't an option."

She took a breath as tears welled in her eyes. Her honesty was so raw it hurt my chest. It took balls to admit all that and I felt her courage. It only made me think more of her, not less.

"Falcon, I went to your room to apologize, but you were so cold. Reality smacked me in the face. I've never had a serious relationship, and the way you acted made me think having one with you was off the table. In that moment I thought the best I could hope for was to salvage our friendship. Right now, talking to you like this, I'm scared shitless. But I have to get this out. I want to move forward with my life, not live in the past."

How in the hell did we get here? Not long ago I was dead set against being with one woman only, but after nearly a month of Paige and I having a good time together, and really getting to know her, I couldn't think of being with anyone else.

I wrapped my arm around her waist and pulled her in close. My eyes locked with hers. "I missed you too."

Paige's eyes widened and shined with tears. "Everyone has battle scars, Paige. No one's getting out of here without a scratch. If you don't believe anything else, I want you to believe this—nothing I saw that night made me think less of you. The shit I saw you dealing with? It didn't scare me away, it made me want to help."

She looked down at her hands in her lap. I could tell she struggled to believe me.

"When we first met, I thought you were this sweet, fragile girl. It didn't take me long to see that you were tougher than most people thought. I don't want to fix you. I know you don't need my help, but I want to be there if you do. I've seen guys deal with PTSD. They have to overcome some pretty bad shit. *But* there's a reason why they can deal with it better once they're home. It's because they're with people who love them." I tipped her chin to force her to look at me. "Let me be there for you."

Her attempt to show me how strong she was faltered as her voice shook. "The baggage I've got . . . it might scare you away."

A deep laugh rushed out of me with a rumble. "I'm touched by your concern for me, beautiful, but I don't scare easily."

She smiled, and it fractured my heart. For months the image of her had only danced in my memory. I lowered my head and kissed her. Her mouth was as sweet as I remembered. Though stunned and momentarily stiff, she quickly became more than receptive. Paige was a long, cool drink for my thirsty soul, and I greedily took as much as she gave. Though I'd thought our connection might be fragile once we were together, when she pulled back her eyes were hopeful. I could lose myself in them and cascade into the depth of her soul. But I couldn't pursue the type of relationship I wanted until I was certain she felt the same way. There was only one way to find out how much she trusted me. It was time for full disclosure.

"I want you to tell me what happened to you."

The tenderness in my tone encouraged her. She gently nodded. The promising aspect was that I became part of the holy trinity of her inner circle of men: her father, her brother, and now me. It seemed the person she trusted least was herself.

She stared into empty space. Bracing herself, she took a deep breath and leaned against my side. With my arms around her, I saw the inner struggle and pulled her a little closer. A protective feeling engulfed me as she sank against my ribs. I knew I was about to be privy to a darkness that she rarely shared.

"I was a little girl when it happened. Just a baby, really. But not so young that I would forget." She looked up at me with a faltering smile. "Children are naturally brave, and I was a child who wasn't afraid of anything. You'd have to have been hurt to understand pain. I'd never had been, except for maybe a scraped knee or a needle at the doctor's office. The little booboos I'd experienced, my mom had kissed away. I'm the youngest. Everyone always looked out for me. Even if a scary show came on television, my brother would hold my hand while both of us would put our other hands up to hide our faces."

"It was a hot day when the accident happened. Weather in Baltimore is very unpredictable. My mom made us stay inside because they were calling for a bad storm. My brother, Ricky, and I were bored. We were acting like crazy kids, running around in the house playing tag. My mom was making dinner in the kitchen."

"We were as rowdy as kids can get, I suppose. I hid from my brother under the dining room table. It was the best hiding place in the whole house—at least for someone who was as little as me. Ricky couldn't find me because I'd squeezed into a tiny spot between the chair legs. It wasn't visible unless you got down on the floor. I was so excited when he leaned up against the table. I saw his feet and reached out to tickle his ankle. He jumped, as if a spider was crawling on him. I took off running while he swatted the nonexistent bug. I was frantically looking for a new hiding place when my mom yelled that we'd better knock it off. But I was winning, and I didn't want him to catch me. I didn't pay attention to what I was doing. I ran into the kitchen. I'd been thrilled to discover that underneath tables was the perfect place for me to hide, so I grabbed a spot under the one in the kitchen. My mom wasn't in there. She was off somewhere else in the house trying to corral us. I wouldn't move. I wasn't coming out of there until someone made me."

Paige inhaled and breathed out a sigh. "Mom had dinner cooking on the countertop in one of those electric skillets. I could hear the sizzle of the fried chicken she was making for dinner. I stayed put but could hear her in the other room with my brother. She was still giving him a good talking to when the storm picked up. A crack of lightning and thunder like I'd never seen or heard before split the sky. It was a very close strike; it shook and lit up our whole house."

Paige paused and stiffened. When she continued, her voice waivered. "The window in our kitchen was big. It was called a 'picture window.' When the lightning struck, I was blinded by it—and I was terrified."

"Something like that would have scared any little kid," I assured her. She turned and looked at me with fresh pain in her eyes.

"The accident was my fault. I wasn't paying attention, I just wanted my momma."

I brushed a tear from her cheek. The muscles in my chest tightened. I had an idea how this story was going to end. Though, I couldn't know how scared she'd been back then, it killed me to see the anguish she was going through now.

"I busted out from under that table so fast I knocked the chair over! When I did, I was so unnerved I fell into the cabinets. I grabbed at whatever I could to break my fall. The cord to the skillet . . ."

My jaw tightened. I swallowed the lump in my throat and held her tighter.

Paige choked out words in a whisper. "The grease . . . it was hot . . . it spilled everywhere. And I . . ."

Laughter drifted through the air, as invisible as dust particles floating in sunlight. Paige's long, brown hair bounced and swayed in concert as she ran through the house. A lyrical note of giggles glided behind her. Her mother loved the sweet sound of this little one's laugh.

Three was an odd number, but never more so than in relation to Paige. There was a special term for her— "three-tween." She was three going on thirteen. It was a term that Kyla coined to describe her youngest child. She was an effervescent bubble of charm, but this little girl could quickly exhaust her mother's patience. She behaved as innocently as her years yet was fiercely independent beyond them.

Today, her older brother was the instigator of her

happiness. He chased her around the house, inciting her sailing shrieks of excitement as he surprised her by doing goofy brother pranks like peeking around a corner, or jumping in the air and landing in front of her as she entered the room unaware. Ricky enjoyed the game. His eyes were as brown as melted chocolate, the small specs of gold accentuating a mischievous sparkle. As a baby, Kyla had rocked him, gazing into his eyes endlessly, the gold flecks fascinating her. They gently reminded her that her little boy was as priceless as the metal itself.

Kyla was thankful her children enjoyed a good sibling kinship. Her friends assured her the closeness was rare. Despite their age difference Ricky, or Rick as he preferred to be called, now that he was in fourth grade, was extremely protective of his little sister. When Kyla was a little girl she'd shared a similar bond with her own brother.

"Hi-yah!" Ricky yelled as he extended his leg to demonstrate a karate kick. It was an attempt to intimidate his sister. His efforts were in vain. Paige rolled her eyes to prove the point. This wasn't the first time he tried to impress her. She was neither delighted nor bored with his imitation of a kung fu master. His next move made him fall over the arm of the worn, brown, corduroy sofa. Paige barely escaped his projectile limb as it flew through the air.

"Stop it, Ricky!" she giggled.

"*Make me, punk!*"

Accepting the challenge, she pushed his foot out of her way. Her tiny giggle graduated to laughter when she realized she'd pushed so hard he'd lost his balance.

Spinning his body in a poorly executed roundhouse kick, his confidence faltered when his foot landed in the hollow of Paige's collarbone.

Her bottom lip puckered as her eyes filled with tears.

"*Why'd you do that?*"

"*I didn't mean to hurt you.*" *His shoulders slumped in defeat.* "*I was just having fun.*"

"*Mommy!*"

Paige ran to the kitchen and gripped her mother's leg for protection. She watched for her brother.

THUD*!*

He landed right in front of them. The old kitchen floor rebounded from the unwelcome force. The sound jarred her from her thoughts, making Kyla jump. All that was left of Paige was a peek of her curls as she ran into the next room. The kids are in full force today! Wiping her hand on a dishtowel, she went after them, shouting loudly enough for them to hear her.

"*I'm warning you! Slow down, or you're going to go to your rooms!*"

The threat had no effect. They whizzed by her, and she grew increasingly more exasperated as they ignored her. She shook her head and returned to the kitchen. All the craziness was stressing her out and short-circuiting her nerves. Right now their only outlet was running around, playing games, and acting like wildlings. She decided to ignore it one last time. While the kids took off in the opposite direction, she went back into the kitchen to prepare tonight's dinner.

Under normal circumstances Paige and Rick would have been outside playing, but a hot and humid Baltimore day threatened thunderstorms. The sky had waxed and waned with dark colors since morning. Adding insult to injury was the rotten smell from the neighborhood garbage. The metal trashcans stood all over the vicinity like putrid sentries. On the radio the announcer said pick-up delays were a result of the weather. The sanitation workers couldn't come soon enough for her. When she'd walked a bag out to the curb, the pungent combination of household waste and the sweltering heat had made her nauseous.

Summer days were notorious for hot humidity on the East Coast. It was a unique mugginess that drenched you in perspiration as soon as you stepped outside. Today was no exception; in fact, it was one of the hottest days on record so far that year. The air reeked and was so oppressive even air conditioning seemed inadequate. The poor window cooling systems had been working overtime, but everything was still sticky to the touch. She hoped the weather forecast was correct and that a cool, soaking rain would arrive to ward off the scorching temperatures.

Rick and Paige had given her a temporary, peaceful reprieve it seemed. Her decision to turn on the television had paid off and when she glanced in the other room, both of them were sucked into a show. Up until then, the entire day had been an exercise in tolerance. Any weather that forced the kids to stay inside made her forfeit her sanity, but she reminded herself they were just kids and didn't want to be inside any more than she did.

As a damp tendril of hair fell across her cheek she pushed it out of her face and tucked it back into her ponytail. Any effort she made to fix her hair and makeup was in vain. The weather wasn't conducive to looking pretty. If the coming rain was a shower and not a downpour, she could take the kids outside to jump in puddles. A good, rumbling shower could be a kid's best friend. Kyla loved a good thunderstorm. As a child, she and her mom would take an umbrella outside and walk barefoot during a downpour. Now that she was an adult she was always glad when the opportunity presented itself to recreate the memory.

She silently tiptoed to the doorway, looking from the kitchen into the family room. Rick was sitting in his father's overstuffed chair, engrossed as he watched

Captain Chesapeake. Paige had wiggled in beside him and was leaning her head on his shoulder. It was almost time to put her down for a nap, but she knew it would be difficult. Her little girl was terribly afraid of storms, but a good children's book could work miracles if Paige fell asleep while Kyla read it to her. Ricky would be happy watching something on television, and she would have a little quiet time before her husband came home.

Her mind swirled. Kids. Storms. Dinner. Making a mental list, Kyla realized she needed to get moving. Once she had the chicken sizzling in the pan she washed the dishes and cleaned up the kitchen before dinner. It was the calm before the storm, both literally and figuratively. Looking out the kitchen window she saw large black clouds moving in the direction of the house. Thunder had started to boom while she wiped down the counter and static electricity filled the air. As if on cue, a loud smack sounded against the window. She shook her head. After the loud noise it would be a battle to get Paige to lie down. She grabbed the novel she had been reading. Maybe, just maybe, she'd be able to get in a page or two of reading.

"I'll bet you can't catch me!" It appeared Paige had lost interest in the TV show and was goading her brother into playing tag.

"You wanna bet?"

The children were once again running through the

house. Paige's voice percolated between laughter and squeals. Much to their mother's dismay they darted behind, around, and in front of furniture, evading each other's grip. It was only a matter of time before something was broken or someone was hurt. They ran relentlessly from room to room, bumping into walls with loud threats and screaming laughter. The excitement escalated, and Paige seized the opportunity to hide under the dining room table.

"Where are you?"

Ricky's voice resounded through the house, the shuffling sound of his feet trailing him as he investigated his sister's normal hiding places. Paige refused to answer him, reveling in her perfect refuge under the table. Crouching low like a kitten, she smiled while she tried to hold in her giggles. The tablecloth draped far enough over the sides to give her a sense of security. Watching his feet, she slapped her hand over her mouth. She tried not to make any noise as Ricky crept silently around the room. He came closer to the table, his footsteps hesitant. She barely breathed when he leaned against the table. It was too much excitement for a three-year-old.

"Tickle, tickle, tickle."

Paige's fingers teased his foot, and Ricky fell to the floor, banging his knee in the ruckus.

"Tag! You're it!"

Even the most patient mother had her limits, and

Kyla had hit hers. While the kids were running around, the storm had started. The wind was howling, the rain coming down in sheets, and her nerves were shot. Exasperated, she threw the book angrily on the table.

"That's it!" she yelled.

The proverbial straw had broken the camel's back. She stomped quickly into the family room where the television still blared. Ricky froze in place. She pinned him with a stare, her expression forecasting he was in very deep trouble.

"You!" She pointed at him with a rigid finger. "Sit! Now!"

He obeyed immediately. Opening his mouth to speak, he quickly closed it in the hope he wouldn't get into more trouble than he already was. Kyla surveyed the room looking for Paige before returning her attention to her son.

"Where's your sister?" Her demanding tone giving him a healthy dose of fear. He shifted his eyes from right to left and then looked down to the floor. She raised her voice louder.

"Where is she—NOW!"

"I don't know, Mom! The last time I saw her she was running!"

He shrugged his shoulders, his hand folding in an innocent posture on his lap. Ricky never took his eyes off his mother, watching silently as she pivoted toward another room in her quest to find Paige.

"Paige! Get your little butt in here!"

Kyla's footsteps were heavy with irritation as she went in search of her daughter. In the days that followed, she would remember the exact moment she took a step toward Paige's bedroom because blinding lightning ripped through the house. It cracked the sky so violently that the vibration shook the house.

An explosion of thunder boomed through the air making the windows rattle. Ricky hurled himself to the floor in fear and threw his arms protectively over his head. Kyla's stress level heightened to panic, and her clenched hand flew to her chest. The downpour that immediately followed produced grenade-like drops detonated when they came in contact with the panes of glass. The two of them had barely caught their breath when the front door flew open and hit the wall behind it. In the doorway, Kyla's wet husband stood soaked and heaving for breath. He wrestled with the wind to close the door behind him. Finally succeeding he stood in the living room, dripping from the rain and heaving from the exertion.

Ricky wasted no time running over to his father and throwing his arms around the large man's waist. His little face disappeared beneath the wet trench coat, his shoulders relaxing once he realized he was safe in his *father's arms. Kyla's own composure disintegrated beneath the sounds outside, but then she, too, took a sigh of relief when she noted her husband was home safe and she needn't worry about him. For a split-second Paige was an afterthought. Everyone froze when sounds of banging and clanging metal came crashing to the floor, the next sound striking terror in all three of them.*

"Aaaiiieee!"

An outburst followed by eerie silence.

Flooded with a feeling of helplessness, Kyla rushed to her daughter. Paige lay on the floor, her small body wrenched by unspeakable torment. The entire scenario seemed to take place in slow motion. As she cradled her daughter, Paige's father and brother approached. Once there a sucker punch was delivered to them both, stripping them of oxygen. Paige stared at the ceiling, her tiny, rosebud mouth open. Pain had ripped through her body and stolen her voice, leaving in its wake a child whose life would forever be changed.

I CLOSED my eyes and drowned in the strain of her emotions. As Paige had begun to recant the story of her injury to me she had begun to tremble. It took a few minutes for her to continue. When she did, her mouth was dry, and her voice was hoarse.

"Memories grow sketchy as to what exactly

happened. It's probably my mind protecting me. I remember it hurt, but I don't remember the pain. I remember the ambulance, but I drifted in and out of consciousness. My family refused to leave me. It killed them to see how much pain I was in. Every time I woke up either my mom or dad was with me. They insisted that Ricky be allowed in my room because they knew he would comfort me. He's still my best friend. After that he never antagonized me. A lot changed between us. Though he didn't tease me like he did before, he couldn't cuddle me either. I cried. A lot. When they changed the bandages I screamed because it hurt so badly. Being so young, I didn't understand why my momma and daddy were letting them hurt me. Over the next several years I had many surgeries to repair the damage. What remains are . . . well, you've seen the scars."

I reached for a handful of Kleenex and placed it in her hand. A sob escaped her. Picking her up, I turned her so she sat on my lap. She weighed barely nothing. I placed my hand on her head and guided it until it rested against my shoulder. She cried bitter tears. I thought the story was over, but I was wrong.

With a stuffy nose and a ragged voice, she held the tissue in a tight fist as she spoke.

"I was in the third grade when the teasing began; kids can be cruel. I had to keep my skin covered to protect it against infection. There was a group of little girls . . . they called me names, like mummy amongst other things. The healing skin was thin, and I got cold easily. My grandmother crocheted a little shrug that went around my shoulders and buttoned. That earned me another list of creative names. I was the same girl on the inside; I just looked different on the outside. Now that I'm older, I guess the kids didn't understand the extent of what had happened any more than I did. Instead of being compassionate, they were cruel. I was a tenderhearted little girl. I couldn't understand why no one wanted to be my friend. No matter how I tried to get them to like me, they never did. They acted like I had a disease, and as a result I began to isolate myself."

Paige sat up and took a handful of hair, moving it to reveal the back of her head. "There's a spot right here." She circled an area with her finger, and I leaned in to look. "A huge dollop of grease hit there before it trickled down my neck. No hair will grow there because the hot grease killed the follicles.

She tugged the hair in the area she had designated a moment before. "This is a hairpiece.

When I was little, I met Aria on vacation. She was my only, and best, girlfriend. She told me that when she grew up she was going to fix my hair so pretty that nobody would ever make fun of me again. She didn't go back on her word. She went to vocational high school.

She studied hard and got a cosmetology license. When she graduated, she delved into the area of hairpieces for special needs. She learned how to apply falls with skin safe adhesives, and she taught me how to do it myself. I can usually wear one for a week or two before I have to change it."

"I thought Aria ran a home improvement business?"

"She does, but that's her second career. She did hair before that. Before she ever went to high school I'd try to cover the spot with my other hair. The spot was tender for the longest time and I had to massage it to ease the soreness. The motion soothed the pain physically and emotionally. It eventually became a nervous habit, like a tic. When I was upset I would rub it in circles. It felt good. In counseling I've been told it was a form of self-soothing. I managed it just fine until I was in my senior year of high school. Then the darling little girls became demons. They knew about my scars, but they didn't know about my hair because I hid it well. They still teased me, but not as much, until one day after gym class." She raised her head to look at me. Hurt and anger swirled in her eyes, darkening their beauty with their fury.

"I don't know what set them off, but one day they called me names all through PE. I'd tried to stay under their radar. As usual, when class was over, I lagged behind the other girls, giving them time to clear out of the showers. I jumped in and out of the shower as quickly as I could so I could make it to my next class. Usually, they were so self-absorbed with fixing their hair and talking about boys I'd go unnoticed. But that day they'd waited for me. I walked out of the shower room wrapped in a towel and found myself in the middle of this arc of mean girls. My hair was soaking wet and plastered to my shoulders. When I tried to go around them, they all saw the spot on my head. Then I earned some new names: baldie, moon head, spot."

I swallowed the lump in my throat as an image formed in my head. Paige shrugged her shoulders and sat straight as if, with the motion, she'd dusted away the pain.

"Anyway, I couldn't wait to get home. I ran into my room and slammed the door. I rocked back and forth while I rubbed the spot. Before I knew what I was doing, I'd pulled out a few hairs—and, weirdly, it felt good. I only did a little bit that day, but there were more times after that. With each stressful event, I pulled a little more. The more I pulled the better I felt."

I don't know what I'd been expecting when Paige had begun this confession, but I hadn't expect this. "Jesus, Paige. What did your parents say?" Pieces of my heart broke for her with every new revelation. She shrugged.

"What could they say? I'd been pulling for six months or so before my mom walked in and caught me. I think she blamed herself. She cried, and so did I. I was ashamed. I felt like I'd let my parents down after they'd done so much to help me. My mom made an appointment with a dermatologist. Both she and my dad went with me. I was diagnosed with Trichotillomania, and the doctor referred me to a psychiatrist for additional help. Both physicians said that stress was the trigger. My parents thought it was a delayed reaction from the accident. I never told them what the girls in school did because I didn't want them to worry. The doctor put me on an anti-depressant."

Her eyes were dark and rimmed with runny, tear-moistened mascara. "I flushed the pills down the toilet because I didn't like the way they made me feel. Again, something else I never told my parents."

Her pain crushed me, and her anguish sliced my heart. I'd had no idea, until that moment, how brave this woman truly was. I handed her a few more tissues. As she wiped her eyes and blew her nose, she gave me a weak smile.

"I had a few more surgeries when I was in college—plastic surgeries. The doctors tell me that this is the best I can hope for. Aria, Elizabeth, and now you, are the only people that know about the accident. I haven't told anyone else. And as far as the pulling? Other than my parents and Aria, you're the only one who knows."

Exhaustion washed over her, and suddenly she slid down into a more comfortable position, leaning her head against my chest. The emotional burden she'd carried alone for so long had won this latest battle and succeeded in overtaking her. As I digested her confession something stirred inside of me. I'd come here to smooth things over with her, but this went deeper than mutual attraction. I had a newfound respect for this woman and couldn't have been prouder of her than I was in that moment. She was as strong as any soldier I'd ever known.

As she rested, I offered silent comfort, alternating strokes to her back and hair. She'd hidden it so well. No one would ever suspect the battle she fought daily. Paige's outward appearance was always the essence of self-confidence and poise; she was a master of disguise. Pleasure washed through me knowing I was one of the select few to know the woman behind the mask. She performed the role perfectly—almost too perfectly.

Chapter 21

Paige

I lifted my head to look into Falcon's eyes. I kissed him gently on the cheek, and my fingers strayed to brushed against his hair. I rested my forehead to his. When I looked down I saw the makeup stains on my shirt. The remnants of the mascara-stained tears smeared when I tried to brush them away. "Looks like I made a mess." My voice sounded nasally from a stuffy nose, and I was sure my eyes were red. "I'll be right back. I need to clean up."

I went into the bedroom, stopping in the bathroom before I changed my shirt. I caught a glimpse of Falcon over my shoulder. He'd trailed behind me and leaned against the doorframe as I changed my top. Normally, I would have been self-conscious. In previous encounters with men I'd insisted that intimacy only happened in the dark and I kept some clothes on. But that changed as I saw myself through Falcon's eyes. From the smile on his face, I could tell he was admiring the view. The magnetic force that drew us together was undeniable. My vulnerabilities had been exposed, but Falcon had a way of soothing my fears away with love.

Taking a few short steps to close the distance between us, he crushed me to him. Without my high heels, I was forced to stand on tiptoes to meet his lips. We were barely a breath apart, but one brief, brush against his lower lip, and I remembered the taste. In an instant I became addicted to him all over again. His cologne drugged me with hints of spicy cinnamon and patchouli. I wanted more. I craved every inch of him as his fingers went through my hair. He cupped the back of my head as his kissed me. I opened my mouth to permit his tongue entry and lapped at the velvety skin. A sigh escaped me as our kiss deepened. His hand roamed down my neck and over the curve of my breast. I enjoyed the sweet sensation of his touch after having been denied it for so long. Pressing my body against his, I encouraged him to explore.

There was no mistaking that Falcon wanted me as much as I did him. His behavior was that of a man half starved. His kisses traveled down my neck as his lips seared my skin with molten heat. When he reached the hollow of my throat, I could feel the rapid beat of my pulse against his tongue. His hands lingered on my skin, his touch raising goosebumps as he slid the straps of my tank top and bra over my shoulders. When his hands reach the clasp at my back, the lacy garment tumbled to the floor. My nipples demanded his attention, and I took pleasure in the feel as he teased them with his thumbs. My head fell back as quickened gasps of excitement escaped my throat. My back arched as he dug his fingers into my hips. I wanted him so badly, but Falcon refused to be rushed. Although I'd had sex many times, I was confident this time with Falcon would be the first time I'd ever made love. This—what we had—was worth fighting for, and I was determined that my demons wouldn't stand a chance against us both.

Falcon's expression made something inside of me change. I felt like a goddess in the night's glow. He kneaded my breasts with eager hands and adoringly kissed them. One was perfect, and one was scarred. Any self-consciousness I might have felt disappeared as he loved them equally, laving each tight point. My gasps turned to moans, the graduation of my voice arousing him further.

Hooking his thumbs inside the band of my panties, he slid the sheer material slowly over the curve of my hips. He teased my thighs with feather-like strokes and kissed all the way down my legs to my ankles. Pausing only long enough to measure the passion in my expression, he continued, this time burning me with kisses as his lips traveled all the way back up again.

I sucked in a breath as his lips touched the skin below my navel. His touch was controlled, the pressure of his fingers and mouth waxing and waning as he worshipped me. Falcon's breath fell on the inside of my thigh as he tasted me. My fingers sought his hair, but he captured my wrists. His expression was one of warning. I sensed he wanted me to watch as he explored.

As he continued his survey, Falcon touched the marred flesh of my scars and watched me to gauge my reactions. With each kiss from his lips to my skin I relinquished more and more of my bruised and battered heart. My body was an open book to him, responding to the questions of his touch with lust-filled passion. Words would be inadequate, so my body spoke its own language. It gave him the answers he sought, and I knew in my heart that just as my body had healed, so would my heart. Like magic, Falcon had a way of taking my negative, doubtful thoughts prisoner. With one glance he made me feel beautiful. His eyes spoke of a desire I ached to satisfy. "Please. I want to touch you."

Lust clouded my vision, my voice near breathless. He released my wrists. His expression said he was eager to feel my hands on his body. His lip curled up on one side, forming a crinkle in the corner of his eye. I pulled at the bottom of his shirt until it came free of his pants. With both hands I journeyed beneath the material until they rested over his heart. He placed his own over mine and pressed them harder into his chest. Our pulses beat in perfect synchronicity. I couldn't help myself and branded his flesh with my lips, placing loving kisses all the way from his chest to his stomach. He closed his eyes, and when I pushed him on the bed, he surprised me by pulling me down with him.

With one hand I snaked my fingers down his body, undoing the leather belt at his waist. He watched me as I made a show of flipping the leather and the buckle side to side. He dug his fingers into my hips. With a shake of my head, my hair fell over my shoulders and breasts. I looked down and noticed the brunette waves framing the tips of my nipples. My body both whispered and shouted what I needed, what I wanted.

Falcon's hardness strained against the zipper as I slowly pulled it down. With a bold move I revealed my own desire as his flesh sprang free. My perfectly manicured fingers closed around his shaft, and as he sucked in a breath, excitement lit up his eyes. Like a match to dynamite, I felt an explosion of blood as it rushed to his cock. The pulsation in my hand connected to my core like a lightning bolt and my sex clenched hard and tight.

I reveled in the effect I had on him. I baited and teased as he felt my longing and sensed my desire. I needed him to fill me. Together we lay naked in the ghost of the afternoon rainstorm, clothed only in shades of shadows. Our bodies danced to the music of measured breaths, keeping tempo with the thundering waves.

He kissed each scar, and I trembled. As his fingers moved against my skin they left goose bumps in their wake. His lovemaking was a melody of sensation. It crescendoed in a symphony of eroticism as he rocked against me with a hard, steady rhythm. My hips bucked beneath his to the tune of his touch. As our flesh met tip to heat, my heart pounded a drumbeat in my chest. The look in his eyes told me he savored each inch as he entered, and I responded by wrapping my legs around him. My heels dug into his ass, urging him closer as my body took in his full length. He tortured me with strokes that entered hard and powerful, while the withdrawal dragged inside me, against sensitive nerves. I began to lose myself as I entered the sweetest bliss. All I wanted him to do was take me, claim me, and mark me.

"Falcon . . ."

With bated breath I called his name as I clenched

him tightly from within. As moans caught in my throat, his thrusts grew more powerful. My voice collapsed under a whispered moan as I surrendered completely and splintered over the edge. He rode the crest of my undoing, driving harder as he sought his own release. A growl ripped from his chest as he emptied himself inside me. The sound was my undoing. I shattered completely.

I COULDN'T TAKE my eyes off him. For all his rugged, rough appearance, Falcon was more beautiful a man than I could have imagined falling in love with. As he held me close, I barely breathed. Physically, we were still connected, and I was desperate to stay that way. A fine coating of perspiration clung to our skin, and he brushed the damp hair away from my face. With a tender touch, his fingers followed the line where my neck curved into my shoulder. The way he pressed his hand to my cheek humbled me. All over me I felt the warmth of a rosy glow, and it made me happy knowing Falcon had put it there. He ran his fingers through my hair, then along the line of my jaw to skim over my lips. I never imagined my heart could feel so full, but old hurts haunted me. I didn't want to spend another day without him.

"Falcon, I . . ." I bit back the words, but he knew what I was going to say. It was almost as if he'd read the fear in my eyes. I was afraid to be the first to say them. Bitter memories made me afraid of rejection.

"I know."

Oxygen caught in my throat, but his eyes only looked at me with reverence. Though I was his wife, would he truly want me to be his woman? Tears tickled against my eyelashes and I fought to hold them back.

"I love you, my beautiful girl."

His lips met mine, and he kissed me long and deep. I couldn't control the tears that bathed my cheeks. When he released my lips, our eyes locked. All I saw was truth, and I knew I would never go another day without knowing I was loved.

Chapter 22

Paige

The morning was oddly normal. I relaxed as I listened to the squawks of a flock of seagulls after an afternoon rain. The sound of the surf washed over me, eroding and consoling my concerns. I enjoyed inhaling the pungency of clean salt air while lying in Falcon's arms. It soothed me. I was obliviously lost in my thoughts. So much had happened in such a short span of time. *Did that really matter when everything felt so right?*

I laid my head on his chest and allowed myself the luxury of listening to his heartbeat. The steady rhythm was so intricate, and it made me feel a strange sort of peace. Falcon had divulged in Vegas he'd never been in a close relationship with a woman. It made me happy to know he'd shared this tenderness with no one else.

I skipped my hand lightly over his chest, barely touching the firm muscle. It gave me a sense of satisfaction to know he was mine. My love life had always been superficial, and though he wasn't my first in many ways, he was my first in all the ways that counted. This was the what I'd been missing, the love I'd craved.

Mine.

Finally, I understood what I'd always seen between my parents. Logical or not, I loved this man. Other people might have taken years to feel what I feel now, but I wouldn't waste time analyzing; it was there, and that was all that mattered. It was something I'd been afraid to hope for, and I promised myself I'd never be so vulnerable I couldn't accept joy. Hurt and I were too well acquainted.

"Good morning, beautiful."

His gravelly, morning voice was something I could get used to; it echoed deep in his chest.

"Good morning." I lifted my head to look into his eyes.

"How'd you sleep?" He played with my hair, alternating between stroking my head and playing with the curls between his fingers.

"Good. You?" He answered by pulling me up for a kiss.

He released me and cleared his throat. "Coffee?"

"I'll go make some." I got out of bed and wrapped my robe around me. He kissed me on the back of the neck as he made his way into the bathroom.

I went into the kitchen and picked up my cell. I must have set it on the counter last night. The display showed that Aria called. I listened to the message. She wanted to know if I was okay and wanted me to stop by before Carter and Aimee left. I was about to return her call when Falcon came in. My thoughts instantly went carnal as I savored the sight of him naked.

"I need to go to Aria and Declan's today. Do you want to go?"

He nodded and stepped behind me. He wrapped his arms around my waist and nuzzled my neck. "I want to feed you first. You didn't eat much yesterday, did you?"

I shook my head. "I can make breakfast."

"We both can," he said, against my ear.

I turned in his arms and wrapped mine around his waist. He radiated heat, and I leaned against him. My fingertips grazed his naked flesh. He pushed me backward, pinning me between the granite top and his hips. His growing hardness made me feel wanton and bold.

"If you keep this up we're going to be late." He pushed my robe off my shoulders. It fell to the floor where it puddled at my feet. Nipping the sensitive spot where my neck and shoulder met, his lusty voice teased my ear.

"Punctuality is overrated."

AIMEE ANSWERED the door at Aria and Declan's house. As she and Carter had come down from Deep Creek Lake to assist Declan and Aria with the party, I was happy to see that they were enjoying some family time. "Hey, girl. Are you feeling better?"

I nodded. Falcon stood close behind me.

"Good. I was worried about you." She gave me a quick hug. Carter came down the steps from the upstairs guest room and joined her. The four of us walked into the living room.

"I'm sorry I haven't called," I apologized. "Between work, and our sweet, little sunshine girl in there, life keeps me busy."

Aimee agreed, and then offered her own explanation. "I'm the one who should be apologizing. I have no excuse for not keeping in touch. I have plenty of time, especially when Carter is busy with work." She held out her hands, which were obviously lacking a manicure. "I've been doing some furniture makeover projects, but I always have time for a phone call. I just lose track of time, but I'm really enjoying our visit. It gives us all a chance to catch up." She looked at the two of us and smiled. "Were you ever going to tell us?"

I was momentarily at a loss for words, but Falcon didn't suffer the same issue. He reassuringly squeezed my hand.

"We didn't tell anybody but we spent a lot of time together in Vegas." He looked into my eyes while still talking to her, and I calmed instantly. He had everything under control. "We wanted to keep it to ourselves for a while."

They seemed pleasantly surprised. As Aimee beamed like she'd just won a scavenger hunt, Carter grinned. "I don't know what the hell happened there, but he was a grumpy pain in the ass when he got back. We thought it might have had something to do with you."

"Me?" I looked at Falcon and teased. "I have nothing to do with his mood."

"Yeah. Like I believe that." Carter cocked his head. Declan and Aria approached from the direction of Karas's bedroom, obviously engrossed in their daughter's laugh. "Do they know yet?" he asked, his voice a hushed tone.

"No." We both answered at the same time. Falcon put his arm around my waist and winked at me. "But they're about to."

Chapter 23

Falcon

Carter slapped me on the shoulder as the four of us walked out onto the porch. Declan and Aria remained in the kitchen tending to the baby's breakfast. The atmosphere was thick with excitement at the news that Paige and I were a couple. "You could've told me, brother." He shook his head with a feigned disbelief.

"Yeah, well, some things are better left unsaid." I gave Paige a playful look. "And others speak for themselves."

"You said you'd spent time together in Vegas, but I'm curious, did this start at the Christmas party?" Aimee pressed us for details.

I pulled Paige to me as I leaned against the post. "It

did start at the party. The day we went for a walk in the woods." Paige tilted her chin up and looked into my eyes. I loved that they twinkled with mischief. "I thought she might have been somebody else's little snow bunny."

Carter laughed. "Paige? A snow bunny? No way." He raised an eyebrow as he looked at us both. "She must love you. Normally, she would have busted someone's balls for that remark."

"Seriously, at the time, I thought she was attached. I'd noticed Blake's possessiveness whenever I got near her. If he comes near her again, it won't be pretty." I felt her stiffen at the mention of Blake's name. I responded by holding her tighter and pressing a kiss to the top of her head. "It didn't take long for me to learn the truth. While the two of us were in Vegas, she assured me there was nothing."

Aimee noticed the change in Paige's demeanor. "Are you okay?"

I fielded the comment, looking over Paige's shoulder to answer Aimee's question. "I think my woman is getting a little weak. She hasn't eaten yet today."

"C'mon girl." Aimee walked over to us and looped her arm with Paige's. She nodded toward the dining room. Declan came toward us with the baby in his arms while Aria carried a plastic wrapped tray of sandwiches and sweets. "Aria is putting out the leftover food from yesterday. Let's get something in your belly."

THE BROTHERS BEGAN A CONVERSATION, but I fell back as they bantered. I kept an inconspicuous eye on Paige. She stood in the doorway of the kitchen sipping a cup of tea as Aria finished readying the table. Aimee walked toward the men but stopped where I was standing.

"Aria said lunch is ready." She nodded toward Carter and Declan who were nearer to the porch than me. "I'm going to get the guys."

I walked over to Paige and extended my hand. When she placed hers in mine we walked together to the table. She was pale. "Why don't you sit down in the living room? I can make a plate and bring it to you."

She smiled and complied. Maybe all that had happened between us had finally caught up with her. Our friends now had no doubt we were a couple, but before the end of the day they would know we were married. Even though I had no doubt Paige loved me and didn't regret our marriage. When we'd discussed revealing it to everyone we'd prepared ourselves for mixed reactions.

As I approached the table, I looked at her while

pointing to the different selections that were being served. I waited by each one to see which met her approval. I chuckled at our unspoken conversation. Food that I would have eaten, Paige scrunched her nose at, and I would have bypassed the healthier fare she selected. *Is this the same girl who downed alcohol with a medium rare steak?* Apparently, she'd left that girl in Vegas. Just like everyone else, the rules didn't apply to her while on vacation.

I brought the plate to her. "Eat," I ordered. She rolled her eyes at me but took the food. I left her for a moment and returned with a glass of wine and a beer. "There's a thin line between excitement and anxiousness, and a lot has happened in two days. If you're a bit nervous about telling everyone we're married, the wine might help—and you need to get something in your stomach."

She took a sip then narrowed her eyes. "I'm not nervous."

"Of course, you aren't." I put my arm around her. "Food making you feel better?"

"Yes." She scooted closer to me and spoke in quiet voice. "I was afraid Blake would ruin everything for them yesterday. What if he shows up today?"

"He won't bother you again. Not if he has any smarts."

"Yesterday we were lucky. I don't know if Aria and

Declan even noticed what was going on. They shouldn't be dragged into Blake's issues regarding me. I don't want anyone to get hurt, especially because of me."

"First, you have nothing to do with ruining anything. Blake's issues are his own, sweetheart. Second, no one will get hurt as long as he keeps his distance. Trust me on this one, okay? I thought you were apprehensive about telling everyone we're married." I placed a reassuring kiss on top of her head. As I did, I noticed a surprised Aria walk in on the scene. She looked between the both of us, a puzzled expression appearing on her face. Then she looked to me.

"Declan said to tell you to come out on the porch. The guys are going to have cigars."

Though she spoke to me, she never took her eyes off Paige. As I stood I gave Paige a quick peck on the lips. "Be back soon".

As I went to join the men, I smiled as I heard Aria press Paige for a confession. "Girl . . . I want details."

I ENJOYED A GOOD CIGAR, as did the other men. It was just the three of us—me, Declan, and Carter. I took a seat beside Carter. The topic of conversation was fatherhood, and how becoming one had changed Declan's world.

"I'm telling you, *everything* I do has a different meaning since the baby was born. Even my business is more focused. I don't ever want that little girl to go without. It's crazy how much I love her. She's the most precious thing in the world to us."

Declan took a long drag off the cigar. As he exhaled he stared out at the sun hanging high above the horizon. He was deep in thought for a few moments. His legs were crossed at the ankles as his feet rested on the railing. His back slumped against the weatherworn Adirondack chair. This was the most relaxed I'd ever seen him.

Once again, he puffed on the cigar until the head of it glowed. For a few quiet moments, the three of us enjoyed the aromatic smokescreen.

"We watch her when she's sleeping, you know? It's difficult to explain. I look at her and can't believe I had anything to do with creating something so perfect. Aria says the same thing. Sometimes, it's hard to look at her and believe she's ours."

"I'll say," Carter chimed in. "I never expected you'd get married, much less have a kid. A lot has changed"

Declan looked at his brother. "What about you? When are you and Aimee going to make it official?"

"I'm not the one who's stalling. She's got my ring on her finger, but I can't get her to pick a date." Carter tilted his head toward me and changed the subject. "Seems Grey over there is with Paige."

Declan sat straight up. "Really. You're dating Paige?"

An unexpected grin curved my lips, but it wasn't because of Carter's revelation. I smiled because I wondered how they would react when they discovered Paige and I were married.

Declan took my smile as confirmation and fell back into the chair. "Well, I'll be damned." The corner of his mouth curled up. "Blake will be sorry to hear she's off the market."

"He already knows." My words were clipped, and the atmosphere chilled under the icy tone. Declan and Carter both noticed the change and waited for me to elaborate. I leaned forward, dangling the cigar from my fingers. "How well do you know Blake? Either of you?"

"I guess as well as most of our group except Declan. Blake was Declan's agent, so they had a friendship before the rest of us met him." Carter shrugged. "When Declan had the accident, Blake called all the time to see how he was doing. He was with us in Hawaii when Declan and Aria got back together."

Declan's expression sobered. "Why are you asking?"

I needed some answers because things with Blake didn't seem to add up. "Have you guys noticed anything odd about him?"

"You mean as far as Paige is concerned?" Declan asked. "Nothing big. Aria told me he was pushing her to go out with him. I told him to back off."

My spine stiffened having Paige referred to in the same sentence as Blake. Declan noticed.

"Why? What happened that you're not telling us?"

My jaw tightened. "When I was in Vegas, Paige and I ran into each other. I'd noticed her at Carter and Aimee's party, and everytime that I approached her Blake gave me dirty looks. I backed off because I didn't know the dynamics of your group. You know, who was with whom. Then Carter told me that nothing was going on between them. I found that odd, because he sure as hell acted possessive whenever I came around her. Territorial. In Vegas, Paige assured me there was nothing between them. We went out for dinner, and one thing led to another. We were together almost every day—sometimes twice a day." I gave Declan a grave look. "You say he was pressuring her to go out and you had to step in. He obviously didn't get the message."

Declan's expression grew puzzled. "I'll talk to him again. We've been friends for years."

"That's not saying much for your taste in friends,

Sinclair." My tone was accusing, causing Declan to react.

"If you've got something to say, Grey, spit it out!"

"I'm saying he didn't get the message!" Anger and a sense of protectiveness for Paige brewed a toxic mix in my gut, and my tone reflected it as I went on the defense. "He wasn't taking no for an answer. Not from her, and not from you. He was in Vegas the same time she was—stalking her, I would say. After one of our dates he beat her and tried to rape her! If I hadn't come back, he probably would have."

I'd blurted out what wasn't my story to tell, even though Paige and I had discussed it. I should have felt remorse, but I didn't. All I felt was rage. I didn't give a shit about friendships or business relationships. All I cared about was Paige, and though I knew that she would be pissed at me, I hoped that any threads of Carter and Declan's relationship with Blake would be completely severed.

Shock registered on the faces of both men, Declan more so than Carter. He was the first one to speak. "You're shittin' me, right?"

"No." My expression hardened as an image from that night revisited me. "I threw the son of a bitch onto the elevator and marched his ass down to hotel secu- rity. I told them to call the police and told him that if he ever came near Paige again I'd would break his fuckin' neck. The reason he spent only one night in jail was because Paige wouldn't press charges. I understand it, but I'll never accept it. The bastard needed to pay for his actions, but she's much more forgiving than I would ever be." I looked at Carter. "And he was on some-thing, I'm sure of it. Glassy eyes, pupils dilated—the works—but still, she wouldn't press charges. I wanted the bastard to pay for what he did, but she wasn't having it. That was why I was so pissed off when I got back from the trip."

"So that was the reason you were such a prick to me?" Carter asked.

"Yes. I was angry. Misdirected, I'll give you that, but I was pissed at the situation and pissed at her. Believe me, I wanted the bastard to rot in jail for a while, but Paige acted like it was all a big, fucking misunderstanding. It took me awhile to figure out what was really going on, but she didn't want to make waves. It damn near broke us, and it sure as hell took us a while to get past it, but we did. I thought he'd be smart enough to stay away from her after that, but then I found him here yesterday. While he thought no one was looking, he grabbed her. He's lucky I didn't snap his damn wrist. I dragged his ass out of here."

Burning anger had me hot around the collar. "Yesterday was his last warning. I told him to keep his hands off her or the next time I was going to kill him." I wiped my hands over my face while I tried to clear my head, then looked at Declan. "I know he's your friend, and now that you know this I hope you see him for the creep he is, but, regardless, I'm not letting him get near Paige again."

Declan's mouth tightened into a thin line. Carter's expression mirrored that of his brother's, except he looked like he wanted to punch something.

"Look," I said, addressing them both. "If after knowing this you, like Paige, still want to give this guy the benefit of the doubt, then at least consider the information I'm giving you. Something's going on with him. I don't know if it's drugs, alcohol, or something else, and I don't give a shit. What I do care about is Paige, and if I catch him near her again . . ."

A thick, sobering pause fell over our conversation. I knew they were mulling over the information I'd just relayed. Declan, looking pissed off, relit his cigar and took a few puffs. As he exhaled he stared at the thick ash on the glowing end and then redirected his gaze to me. He wore a troubled look.

"You're right. Blake and I have been friends for years. He was my agent and my friend. That being said, I haven't seen him on a regular basis since I've been married. I have no reason to believe you would lie about this—and if he was pulling some shit in my house while we celebrated my daughter, then I'm glad you dragged his ass out. I don't want that around my family."

"I believe you Fal," Carter said, his countenance and tone reflecting that of his brother. "You're one of the few people in this world that I really do trust. You're also pretty good at finding out somebody's end game. Any idea what his is?"

I shook my head. "No. Paige and I have gone over this. She says he wasn't always like this. I asked her what his association was with Manny Vallega and his wife." Shock registered on the faces of both men. "Well, she looked as surprised as you do now."

"What the fuck do Manny and Marisol have to do with Blake? Or Paige?"

Carter's outburst wasn't unexpected, but it confirmed to me he didn't know anything about their connection. "I don't know. In Vegas he was hanging out with Manny Vallega and his wife. I know the history you guys have with Marisol, and Paige filled me in with even more details." I looked at Declan. "I know about her obsession with you. I also know that Blake was Marisol's agent. He could explain away why he was with her, because that's a plausible excuse, but that doesn't explain Manny. He was rubbing shoulders with Vallega in Vegas—real buddy-buddy shit."

"Blake and Vallega?" Declan asked the question

then, confused, shook his head. "Yeah. Something's not adding up."

Carter nodded. "My thoughts exactly."

Declan paused a moment and then turned to his brother. "Can I hire you? I want you guys to check into Blake and Vallega."

Carter looked between me and his brother. "We're a security company, Dec, not investigators."

"I know that." Declan's tone was clipped and defensive. "I'm asking you if you'll bend your fucking rules and do this for me. If Blake's involved with something underhanded, I need to know. If so, I sure as hell don't want to do business with him—and I sure as shit don't want him around Arai or Karas."

Carter looked over at me. "You want to do this?"

I nodded, my behavior composed, but I was itching for a legitimate reason to make Blake accountable for his actions, and Declan had just given it to me. This was the part I loved. Hunting. Blake was an animal and all I had to do was scout him out, find his weakness, and tear the son of a bitch's life apart. I'd make that bastard sorry he ever fucked with my wife. By the time I was done with him, he'd be begging me to put him out of his misery.

Chapter 24

Paige

I'd lost track of time as I held Karas in my arms and walked through the house, going room to room, as I bounced her gently. Normally, I would have helped Aria and Aimee clean up, but Karas was a much more pleasant diversion.

"She's a beautiful baby." Falcon's deep voice raised goose bumps on my flesh. He came from behind me and looked at her. She was almost asleep.

"She really is, but then, look at her daddy and momma." I looked up at him. "Do you like kids?" He nodded.

"Always have. I'd like to have my own someday." He pushed the blanket down tenderly to better see her face. As he took her in, his expression softened.

"Me too. One day." He reached up and caressed my cheek and looked deeply into my eyes.

"One day," he agreed.

Falcon's green eyes were the color of moss and as bottomless as a deep pool of water. The love I saw there made me hope. I felt myself sinking into them. That one glance and I was drowning a peaceful death. Something happened to me when I was with him. I felt and thought things I'd never dared. I had hope my dreams would be answered.

I bundled up the baby and took her outside. Falcon held the chair while I eased into it so as not to wake her. He sat next to me and the two of us kept looking from the baby to each other. It was another peaceful day. Karas startled once, and we both froze. She was quickly soothed back to sleep by an ocean lullaby. He reached for my hand and held it firmly in his. We found tranquility in the company of each other. How we'd gotten from an undisturbed snow to the peacefulness of the ocean was surreal, but I couldn't imagine it happening any other way.

I was glad for these moments together. Soon the others would be joining us for what would be, at the very least, an interesting conversation. Although I hoped everyone would be happy for us, I was a little numb. My connection to Falcon filled a void in me that had become an almost incapacitating chasm. He was the balm for my battered spirit. I felt like I was learning a new means of communication because of him. Love had a language all its own. It was a discussion without words, a sentence of restoring apologies, a paragraph of healing hearts, and a composition of hope. It articulates when words aren't enough to become a novel written from emotions. It's a touch, a glance, and an understanding that, when treated with kindness, becomes a best-selling blockbuster in the universal library.

We enjoyed an uninterrupted moment in our own little world, but soon we had the company of Aimee and Carter. Declan and Aria followed, laughing. Something one of them said to the other that might have been an inside joke, I was sure. I loved that and secretly hoped for the time when Falcon and I would do the same. When Aria and Declan looked over at us and saw their sleeping daughter, they smiled at the two of us. Falcon never let go of my hand, and I enjoyed the way he declared our status as a couple to our closest friends.

"I'll take her." Declan reached over and lifted his baby girl from my arms. "This little one has had an exciting few days. She's not going to know what to do when it settles down to the three of us again."

He disappeared into the house to lay Karas down. The breeze was beginning to pick up, and Aria handed a light blanket both to Aimee and me, and we wrapped them around our shoulders.

"So you and Paige, huh?" Aria teased Falcon. "I can't say I'm surprised." She began to giggle. "I'm shocked, actually."

"What can I say? I'm irresistible to women." Falcon playfully grinned and waggled his eyebrows.

"Bullshit!" Carter choked on his beer, and Aimee and Aria burst into laughter. "You are one, ugly, son of a bitch! It's a wonder she didn't take off screaming!"

"Hey! You're no prize yourself, Sinclair!" Falcon returned his own rapid quip.

"Who's no prize?" Declan asked as he rejoined the group.

"I was just saying your brother's no prize. I think you got all the looks." Falcon shrugged his shoulders matter-of-factly while Declan's chest puffed out proudly.

"I knew you were a smart man, Grey. It's no wonder you landed Paige."

"So what's up with that?" Aria brought the conversation back around. "How did you convince her to go out with you? I've been trying to hook her up for years."

Falcon's eyes widened. "Well I sure as hell am glad you didn't have much luck!"

"Don't get me wrong." Aria waved her hands as if

erasing her former statement. "I didn't mean that in a bad way, it's just that she's really picky. You must be pretty special to have landed her."

"Or very drunk." I smiled at them.

"Drunk? You left out that little part of the story." Aria looked between Falcon and me.

"There may have been a little alcohol involved," he laughed.

I snorted.

"Did you just snort? Little Miss Perfect?" Aimee looked at me with eyes wide and mouth hanging open. "Oh my God." Her voice faded in the swell of everyone's laughter.

"Well, beautiful, that's something I didn't know about you. Snorting may be a deal breaker for me." Falcon made them laugh even more.

"Shut up!" I hit him on the arm.

"So there *was* alcohol involved." Aria confirmed her suspicions with a smug look on her face. "I knew she was coerced. She's always been so adamant about not wanting a relationship. Must have been *a lot* of alcohol." She winked at Falcon.

"Now, wait a minute!" Falcon put his hands up in a defensive stance. "*I* didn't have much alcohol." Everyone laughed again.

Aria turned to me. "And you? The prim and proper business woman?"

"Yes, Aria. I had alcohol. It was Vegas for God's sake!" I rolled my eyes, exasperated.

"You'd better watch it, Falcon. Our unattached friend might rethink having you as a boyfriend." Aria's warning made him chuckle.

"*If* she were unattached, and *if* I were her boyfriend, I might be worried." Falcon looked at me with mischief in his eyes.

"What do you mean 'if,' because *if I* know her, it's going to take a whole lotta convincing to tie Paige down."

"Guess I convinced her."

Everyone went silent while Falcon grinned.

"What?" Aria looked between us. Then, suddenly, understanding dawned in her eyes. "You're kidding, right?"

I shrugged.

"You've heard about those Vegas weddings. Well . . ."

"Holy shit!" Carter's outburst reflected what the others were thinking. They all stared in disbelief.

"Oh my God!" Aimee squealed. "Congratulations!" She jumped out of her chair and gave me a hug, then threw her arms around Falcon and gave him one as well. "I'm so happy for you!"

Declan and Carter followed suit, giving me kisses and slapping Falcon on the back. The only one who held back was Aria. While everyone else chattered, I sat next to her.

"Are you upset?" I asked in a low tone.

"You got married." She seemed sad.

"I know." I leaned forward in my chair because she seemed a little dumbstruck.

"You got married," she said again.

"I know. We've established that." I smiled at her. "Can't you be happy for me?"

"You got married, and I wasn't there." She pouted playfully.

"So, you'll be there for the babies."

"Babies? I can't believe you're married—I didn't think you trusted *anyone* that much."

"Ah . . . I'm working on the trust thing. It's a good thing I was drunk. It might not have happened otherwise." I looked over at Falcon, who was still being ribbed by the other men. "He's a good guy, Aria."

"He'd better be." She looked at him with determination. "Or I'll kick his ass!"

Chapter 25

Paige

It had been a week since Karas's christening. Falcon had convinced me to take off for a few days and he did the same. Although I'd already planned to take a day or two off to spend with Aria and the baby, he occupied most of my time. I apologized to her, but she understood completely, insisting that I spend the time with my husband.

Husband. Has a nice ring to it.

I half-heartedly rummaged through the closet as I prepared to go into the office. Mondays always seemed to come so fast. My fingers lingered on each hanger as I looked over my wardrobe possibilities and pushed them aside one by one until I found something to wear. Usually, whatever I wore reflected my disposition, but

I was more distracted than usual. Today my mood was light, though the events of the past few days had been taxing. My normal routine was about to change dramatically because of the over six-foot-tall, solid muscle, handsome man who was lying comfortably in my bed. I looked over my shoulder in the mirrored door and smiled.

Falcon was still here with me.

It felt like a dream.

This past week had been one I could get used to. Having some time off at home had been such a delicious change for me and not at all an inconvenience. I'd been accused of being a workaholic, rightfully so. The past few days I'd pushed off my responsibilities. Falcon and I'd had fun all week, and, for the first time, I didn't miss work at all. We got to know each other better in a more relaxed way, the way newly married couples do. We did our morning runs on the beach, after which I made breakfast. We showered, made love, ran errands, made love, worked out, made love . . . but he was leaving tomorrow. Business dictated he made another trip to Vegas and my schedule wouldn't permit me to go with him. As much as I hated to do it, I was leaving him on his own for a day. I had to attend to rescheduled appointments and the workload that had begun to pile up while I'd played the newlywed game with a man I both loved and respected.

We'd been together every day since the christening. Today he would be on his own. Of course, there was still a small, nagging voice that warned me that if I did so he might realize he'd made a mistake. That was just my insecurity talking, but the good news was I paid less and less attention to it. I'd even snuffed it out one night when Carter and Declan had insisted on giving Falcon a belated bachelor party. While the guys had gone out, I'd spent the evening at Aria's house with her and Aimee. We'd had such a good time just hanging out and catching up. Those two had grilled me for details while the baby had slept. Three women, three wine glasses, and three bottles of wine later, I'd told them most of what they'd wanted to know.

As I bent over to retrieve a pair of shoes, I bumped into a few purses and knocked them off a shelf. My attempt to catch them was unsuccessful and when I stood up I saw sleepy, green eyes watching me. It felt so natural. Falcon was the serenity I'd lacked in my life. I hadn't even known there'd been a void until he'd filled it. No matter what we were doing there was a peacefulness about it.

"Come back to bed. I'll warm you up." He patted the side where I slept.

"Tempting, but I have to go to work." I reached into the closet to put back the bags that had fallen on the floor. He leaned up on his elbow and the sheet fell down around his waist.

"Where are you going? To work?" His confused, smoky baritone made me want to abandon my plans and spend the day in bed with him.

"I'm going into the office today, remember? I won't be long. It'll do you good to have some time alone." His eyes grew dark.

"I don't need time alone. What I need is more time in bed—with you. Now get your ass over here." Something happened to me when he used that tone. It didn't feel threatening at all; it just made me feel wanted.

Abandoning my outfit, I laid it over the chair. All I'd worn to bed was an oversized T-shirt and panties. I laid down and turned over on my belly. Leaning up on my elbows, I gave him my full attention. I was admiring his sexy, morning look when he wrapped his arm around my waist and pulled me close. His eyes were awash with determination.

"You're staying here with me today." He growled playfully into my neck. I tried to wiggle away from his stubble-shadowed chin.

"Stop! That tickles!"

Obviously, that had been the wrong thing to say because he tightened his arms and attacked the same place on the other side. I tried to shove him off, but it was like pushing against a concrete wall.

"Stop! Fal! Knock it off!!" Laughter cascaded from me as my shrieks and giggles puddled on the floor. I tried to kick at him, but in one quick move he straddled me. He held my wrists above my head. With one hand he held my arms in place and with the other he pulled up my shirt. Using his stubble as a weapon, he motor-boated my breasts. I screamed mountains of laughter. He lifted his head and gave me a playful look.

"Still going into work?"

"I have to!" I shouted. "I haven't been there for a week! Now let me go!" I struggled, but he held me tightly.

"Wrong answer." He cupped one of my breasts with his free hand and stretched out on top of me. I was completely at his mercy. His rough cheeks and chin both tortured and excited me while I squealed with laughter. I bucked and contorted my body trying to throw him off. Unfortunately, it had the opposite effect, as evidenced by his growing hardness. His eyes locked with mine in a heated gaze. "Keep doing that, beautiful. It feels great."

"You're insatiable!" My hips rolled under him, but there was no chance of escape.

"And you're a tease." He used his prickly chin like a sex toy, waking my nerve endings with each brush of his jaw. He paid special attention to my breasts, the pleasurably painful abrasion mixing the signals in my brain. As his tongue flicked over my sensitive nipple, my back arched.

"Mmm. That's much better," he growled under his breath. He continued the sweet torture as he moved down over my hips and stomach only stopping long enough to torment me for his pleasure. He dragged my panties off as he lowered his chin. He gave me naughty looks when he peered up to gauge my reaction. Goose bumps rose where he licked, turning my skin pink as I chilled in the morning breeze. I shivered from the erotic combination of external chill and internal heat and gasped as my mind tried to grasp the extremes. He teased so effectively, I was unable to think of anything except the undercurrent of sensation that tightened my insides. I opened my eyes to see him on his knees between my legs, examining the result of his handiwork.

"Now, *this*, is a beautiful sight." The passion in his voice stroked my growing need. He came up on his knees, his hands coming to rest on each side of my shoulders. His face hovered above mine as he watched my reactions. His hardness pulsated against my entrance and he entered me slowly. Every inch he gave took me to a more pleasurable depth until I was drowning in ecstasy. His hands snaked beneath me, his fingers digging in as he eagerly gripped my curves. Relentlessly, he controlled every thrust for my pleasure as I sank deeper and deeper. The friction robbed my breath, and I gasped for air.

"Oh . . . Falcon."

"I love it when you say that."

I catapulted into a chasm of pleasure where sparkles of light splintered my vision. I moaned his name as wave after wave of pleasure pushed and pulled my body in a riptide of sweet death. Falcon rotated his hips to deepen his penetration as the pounding sensations bade my body to clench around him. He groaned as he released in an orgasmic tidal wave and he held me as we fell into the abyss of exhaustion together.

I LAY on my back listening to the sounds that soothed me, the screech of hungry seagulls searching for a meal, the distinct crash of liquid hitting the sand, and the roar of the ocean crushing the jetties. Falcon's arm crossed possessively over my midsection as his hand rested between my breasts. I didn't want to think about him leaving but asking him to stay would be selfish. He had his work and I had mine. He'd asked me how we should do this—two cities, two houses. I hadn't answered him because I'd had no clue. I'd always been such a loner, throwing myself into my work, but for the first time I wanted to breathe the air in someone else's life and not just live within the edges of my own.

"What's going on in that head of yours?" His hand slid around to massage the back of my neck, kneading the muscles. I smiled and brushed against his face with my fingertips.

"Nothing. Just thinking." He looked at me with interest.

"Now's not the time to start lying to me, sweetheart. Let's try that again."

I sighed and relaxed my shoulders, cupping his face in my hands. "I'm concerned about where we go from here."

"And you're worried?" I nodded and pulled me close. His embrace made me feel secure and comforted. "Where we go from here is anywhere we want, but no matter where that is, we're going together." He rested his forehead against mine. "We'll figure this out, Paige. I would never ask you to give up your life to come live in mine and I know you think the same."

"That's just it. I do feel the same." I nervously played with a loose thread on the edge of the sheet. "I want to be with you, but I don't want you to feel you have to give up what you've worked so hard for. I love you enough to give you space and I respect you too much to try to take it away. I wasn't being evasive when you asked me if I thought this could work. I honestly don't know the answer."

Winding his fingers through my hair, he tugged gently. My neck arched backward which forced us to look into each other's eyes. He wore a wide grin on his face.

"What's so funny?" I narrowed my eyes.

"You just said you loved me."

Shit!

"So I did." I needed a distraction. "What do you think about us living apart? Are you thinking long distance relationship? I'm not sure I like that."

"Paige, Paige, Paige." He humored me with a tsk, tsk, tsk sound as he brushed his thumb over my bottom lip. He was *still* grinning. "You're a smart woman, but you're not thinking. I'll blame that on the great sex."

A snort of laughter burst from my chest, and he smiled.

"Your business is set at the beach. That isn't the only real estate in the United States. Hasn't it occurred to you that since we're merging as a couple that we can combine assets?" He made a circling motion between us with his finger. "I have you and you have me. You have a business and I have a business. We can have a house in the mountains and a house at the beach. What's mine is yours, Paige."

The pace of my heartbeat increased as old insecurities jabbed my newly emerging confidence, but the tone of his voice and the look in his eyes quickly flat-lined my fears.

"Well?" His wicked grin teased me, but before I agreed I needed to have a question answered.

"Does this mean you have no regrets about our marriage, because I'd understand if you do?" I hated sounding needy, but I had to know.

He distanced himself far enough that I could see his scowl. "Do you?"

"No. I'd be lying if I said I did. When I came home I kept thinking of ways we could salvage what we'd started, but then I remembered you making the comment that you'd never been lucky in Vegas." His eyes softened.

"Beautiful, I didn't mean you. Finding *you* there was the best luck I could have hoped for."

He kissed me and took my mouth possessively. When he took my body he loved me so thoroughly I was assured our wedding at The Little White Wedding Chapel would make an interesting story to tell our grandkids.

Chapter 26

Paige

After a night spent in his arms, the morning mist was as salty as my tears. It wasn't like me to get emotional, but after a week spent secluded with my husband, the ache of having him leave stung my heart. The normalcy of real life had crashed our private little world.

Falcon had woken me early that morning. My wake-up call was a trail of kisses down the length of my body. Indulging in morning sex was delicious and decadent. His lovemaking was an intense, all consuming, sweet desperation. It eased the sting parting would cause. I enjoyed the way he wrote his every touch on the lines of my skin. He'd loved me so thoroughly, I'd walked into the shower on shaky legs. With strong hands he'd washed me tenderly, massaging my neck, back, and hips with sweet agony. His fingers kneaded and eased the battle scars of lovemaking. My body throbbed when he pinned me against the wall. We kissed like it was our last, as if we'd never love again. I hungered for the feel of his naked body against mine, so I could blanket myself in the memories. He never broke our kiss, lifting my legs and wrapping them around his waist. His muscles were tight with need and there was no mistaking what he wanted. Our love-making was explosive, leaving me shattered. When I didn't think I had an ounce of energy left he carried me to the counter, the marble chilling my skin, but his seduction scorched me with desire. I craved his touch because I knew our time was short, but his lovemaking was unhurried and intense and he, once again, drove us over the edge.

As we dressed in silence, he peered at me over his shoulder. He watched me as I slowly followed my normal routine, although nothing so far this morning had been ordinary. My life had been so customary and methodical until I'd met Falcon, and ever since it had been nothing but a wild ride.

When I was stressed, the repetition of certain tasks

quieted my nerves. I laid my makeup brushes out the way I always did, all in a row on the counter. Falcon came up behind me and lifted my hair away from my neck. When his lips touched my skin, I closed my eyes and savored the velvety feel.

"I'll make coffee."

His deep, whispered voice revealed a mutual misery. He gave me a few minutes to finish getting ready before he called my name, and when I walked into the kitchen he was waiting for me with a full cup.

"Thank you." I sounded detached, even to myself.

"You're welcome." His eyes were soft. "What's wrong, babe?"

I shrugged to conceal my gloom and hid my expression by dipping my face toward my cup. I couldn't help feeling the way I did, and I didn't like it. I had to put on a happy face despite the hollow feeling in the pit of my stomach. It was uncomfortable and made me feel needy, which was completely unacceptable.

We finished our coffee in silence. He rinsed out both his cup and mine and placed them in the dishwasher. As he walked by me he stopped, put his arm around my waist, and kissed me on the head. Such a simple gesture that brought me an inordinate amount of pleasure. The thing was, I didn't need to explain how I felt; he already knew.

My bruised heart and I followed him to the door.

He threaded his fingers through mine after he grabbed his duffle bag and jacket, and we walked outside together, hand and hand. I knew I was acting like a lovesick teenager and not the fearless woman I was, but I didn't care.

He opened the trunk and chucked the bag inside. I stood beside him, smiling as images of the past week replayed in my mind. He'd only brought enough clothes for a few days, but it never became an issue because he'd spent nearly the whole week out of them. That was a memory I'd rely on while he was gone.

I shivered. The fine spray that lingered in the air overpowered the skirt and sweater I'd chosen to wear. They weren't nearly enough to keep the chill away. Weather at the shore was erratic during a season change. Falcon noticed and pulled me close, running his hands up and down my arms and over my back to ward off the nippy air. His eyes were a storm of dark jade as he tried to hide the regret of leaving.

"I'm going to miss you." His voice was filled with comfort and tenderness. I wrapped my arms around his waist and gave him a weak smile.

"No more than I'm going to miss you."

"We'll be together in two weeks. I'll meet you at the airport. Remember. Two weeks." He gave me a sly grin. "I'll probably sext you. In fact, you can count on it." He cupped my butt cheeks with both hands and gave them a frisky squeeze. I returned the favor with a playful smack to his chest.

"You're incorrigible!" He pulled me closer, his voice low and sexy. "Hopelessly."

He kissed me one more time. If two weeks of affection could have been poured into a kiss, it was that long and deep. I bit the inside of my cheek to ward off tears. There was no point in postponing the inevitable. He closed the door and took my hand through the window. I leaned in.

"Be a good girl while I'm gone."

"Please be careful," I said seriously. "And please call me when you get to the hotel."

"I will," he promised.

I waved until he was out of sight then went back into the house. I wore the dull ache in my chest like a heavy overcoat. The further away he drove, the weightier it became. Being in love with him was so much easier than I'd expected and watching him leave was so much harder. He'd proven to me every day that one moment of real love erased a lifetime of hurts, and, for someone who valued her privacy, I couldn't wait for him to come home.

Chapter 27

Falcon

A year ago, I couldn't have predicted I'd be holding my wife's hand today. It had been a long two weeks. I was proud of the woman who sat beside me. Paige was a confident woman in every area of her life. Well, almost every area.

The truth was Paige was harder on herself than anyone else ever could be. All I knew was where she was weak, I wanted to be strong.

Her fingers curled around my hand. I ran my thumb in tender circles over her fingers. She alternated between looking at me and looking out the car window. There was no tightness around her eyes, no lines in her face. All I could see was a sweet air of contentment. A simple, relaxed happiness in the moment.

Our flight had been a good one. We'd met at the airport. Aria had driven Paige from the beach to Baltimore Washington International, and I'd driven down from the mountains to meet her. My home had seemed empty without her, even though she'd never lived there. We would soon rectify that. I didn't want to be apart and I knew she felt the same.

Once reunited at the airport, we'd gained an audience at the entrance. I'd pulled Paige into my arms and kissed her until we'd attracted the attention of the general public. Once we'd severed the connection, we'd checked our bags, gone through TSA, and had walked to our gate. Boarding the flight had been uneventful, but takeoff was another matter. Paige's fear of flying had evidenced itself in the fingernail marks on my hand. She'd gripped me to the point of pain. I'd been thankful all we'd had was a little turbulence, or I would have had puncture wounds to prove her anxiety.

Now that we'd had landed, we were on our way to the first of a few surprises I had planned for her. Our wedding had left little to be desired, but I hoped this time in Vegas would make up for it. As expected, Jorge had been waiting for us outside the Las Vegas airport.

"Mr. Grey. Mrs. Grey. It's good to see you both." Paige grinned at me as Jorge put our bags into the trunk of the car. I knew the origin of her beaming face, we hadn't yet been publicly addressed as husband and wife. Jorge then opened the car door for us and gave us a wide smile as we entered.

Now that we were headed to our destination, Paige wore a sweet expression.

"You're awfully happy, baby. What's going on?" I turned and stretched my legs out, resting my hand on her knee.

"Just Jorge. What he called me."

"What did he call you?" Arching an inquisitive brow, I played ignorant. I knew exactly what Jorge had said to cause her pleasure.

"He called me Mrs. Grey." Her eyes crinkled at the corners as playfulness tipped up and curved the corners of her lips. It pleased me, more than I would have thought, that she liked her new title. I played with her hair, my tone low and suggestive as my lips touched her ear.

"If it makes you this happy, I'll be sure to call you Mrs. Grey when I'm between your thighs."

The remainder of the drive was a study of self-control for me. I wanted Paige in my arms and in my bed, but I had surprises in store for her. Thankfully, I'd paid close attention to the things that brought her pleasure when last we were in Vegas.

Her eyes grew wide as Jorge pulled the car up in front of the Bellagio Hotel. Her response told me she was thrilled when she realized we were staying there.

The beautiful eyes I loved had more of a twinkle in them than they had a few moments before, and they continued to sparkle as we found our way to our room. The suite was more than I would have required, and less than she deserved. I wanted to give Paige the best of everything, and this trip was the first step in doing just that. It overlooked the Las Vegas Strip with a completely unobstructed view of the fountains. The décor defined the word luxury. My beautiful wife was speechless—and that made me very happy.

"Do you like it?" I closed my arms around her waist and pulled her to me. Her expression told me everything I needed to know.

"It's so beautiful."

Her voice was hushed and gentle. I placed a soft kiss against her temple. The sensation of my lips against her skin left me wanting more.

"I thought you might like it."

I watched her as she looked around the room, breathing in its luxurious air. A chilled bottle of champagne was on ice, accompanied by a large bouquet of her favorite flowers. I answered a knock at the door, and a gentleman introduced himself as our private butler. As I focused my attention on my wife, he opened the bottle and served us both. Paige's countenance was one of pleasure and appreciation, which in turn made me happy. With our glasses in hand, we stood face to face.

"To us, and the best life we can live." I clinked my glass to hers.

"To us," she countered, and we both took a sip. Her eyes moistened with unshed tears.

We dismissed the butler and unpacked our own clothes. An hour later he returned with our dinner. The dining area was set for an intimate meal. Candlelight flickered and danced in multicolored shadows as it caught the light in the gold veined marble. Paige went room to room, inspecting the suite, her bare feet padding softly on the cool stone until she took a seat with me on the sofa.

Our view was perfect. The desert sky was just beginning to darken in hues of cobalt, navy, and indigo. Though we could appreciate nature from this vantage point, I'd chosen this room for the view of the fountains. Paige had mentioned it in conversation on our first date. She'd said the carefully orchestrated water show was one of her favorite things about Vegas, though she'd only seen them from the street. I was glad that, tonight, she would have her own personal viewing. The first of many.

As we began to relax, the butler brought a scotch for me and a glass of wine for my bride. I put my feet up on an ottoman while she snuggled against my side.

There was a sweet bliss that had settled over both of us now that the unpacking was done. It was a depth of contentedness I hadn't experienced before. I was happy, plain and simple.

"Will there be anything else, sir?" The butler patiently waited while Falcon gave Paige a questioning glance. She shook her head no.

"Your name would be nice, but, other than that, we're good for the rest of the night," I answered.

"Oh, I'm sorry, sir! I thought you heard my introduction. My name is Luca. If you need anything else, please don't hesitate to ask for me." He tipped his head. "I'll leave you to enjoy your evening and will see you in the morning."

As I heard the private elevator close, I turned to Paige. "The fountain show plays every hour. Do you like your view?"

"Mm-hmm." She rested her head against my shoulder and drew lazy patterns on my thigh with her index finger. I put my arm around her shoulder and responded in kind, stroking her neck and throat with my hand.

"You've been very quiet since we arrived."

"I'm enjoying myself." She tilted her head to look up at me. "I feel like I'm on sensory overload, but in a good way. I'm not sure I can find the right words to describe why, all I know is that I love it. Thank you—for all of this."

As she turned her focus back to the window, I rested my chin atop her head. The silky feel of her hair combined with the sweet fragrance of her perfume played with my senses. I loved touching Paige, and it wasn't long before my hand strayed from her shoulder to the buttons on her blouse. I'd been away from her for two weeks and craved the feel of her skin.

One by one I unfastened them, taking plenty of time to enjoy and savor touching her. My fingers drifted, and she leaned back, allowing me better access. I toyed with her bra, running my fingertips under the lacy edges. I hooked my thumb in the top and stroked the nipple, teasing it until it pebbled. Paige's response sent blood rushing to my cock. Her eagerness matched my own and, as her desire mounted, I enjoyed the sound of her quickening breaths.

As I continued my exploration, a flush spread across her pale skin, giving her a rosy, pink glow. I took my time seducing her, playing with her beneath her clothes. She shimmied out of her blouse and bra, releasing her breasts. I cupped the full globes and strummed her nipples with my thumbs. The sensitive tips hardened, excited from my touch.

I played with her for a while. As I enjoyed her reactions to the brush of my hand, I equally enjoyed how she wasn't reacting to the soft light. I'd thought that she'd insist on turning off the lamp, but she hadn't. Her self-consciousness had relaxed, and that made me feel damn proud. I wanted her to see herself the way I did—beautiful, sensual, and feminine. Eventually, she would.

Paige turned her body into mine, and my heart clenched in my chest. Her full lips begged to be taken, and I complied. I stole them, crashing against her mouth like some carnal bandit.

A wave of lust crashed over me as she so willingly gave herself. I couldn't control my desire as she surrendered herself. This was more than a woman having sex. Paige was, physically and emotionally, giving herself to me.

The passion in our kiss demanded more of us both, and my cock turned hard as stone when she whimpered. Release would come in due time. I wanted to linger and enjoy the taste of my wife's submission. I made quick work of helping her out of the remainder of her clothes

Her eyes locked with mine, and our eyes never broke their connection, even when she bit her bottom lip, revealing a moment of insecurity. But my gaze commanded her body to relieve itself of fear. My erection was evident, the bulge painfully restrained by my zipper. When Paige's hand reached my crotch, a spark lit up her eyes.

Whether unconsciously or not, she grew wanton. The tip of her tongue licked at her lips as she savored the effect she had on me. I let her hands wander on their erotic quest, they roamed all over me, then she boldly stood naked before me, running her fingertips over her hips and ass. I followed the direction of her hands over her beautiful, lush curves. A smile played at her lips as I took a long sip of my scotch, the burn warming my throat and feeding the fire of desire that blazed deep in my core.

Paige kicked her clothes to the side and came toward me. Placing one knee on each side of my hips, she straddled me. I couldn't tear myself away from her beautiful eyes. The pupils pulsed and dilated as she rocked her sex against me. This sexual creature wanted to quench my thirsty libido, and she was all mine.

I cupped her ass cheeks, lifting her as my fingers dug into the luscious curves, and then dropping her on my dick. The only thing separating us was the fabric of my pants, but the hardness hidden inside them was unmistakable. She gasped. I kept my hands locked on her hips. Every little move she made pressed both of us against our most sensitive spots. Her soft mews were answered by my groans. She kissed me, and I sucked her bottom lip. When she went to pull away, I closed my teeth against the sensitive flesh, prohibiting her from moving. This little vixen was awakening a beast within me, and I planned to make love to her until it was satisfied.

In one quick move I wrapped her legs so tightly around me her cheeks were spread to their limit. Paige was as petite as I was broad, and I loved holding her in my arms and loved her legs around my hips even more. I kissed her neck, burying my face in the dip under her jaw. Her hair brushed against my arms as she lifted her chin to permit me better access. I craved her and loved the taste of her skin, I alternated nips and kisses as I carried her into the bedroom.

I sat her on the edge of the bed, committed to worshipping the body of the woman that had given herself to me. The moment I released her I shed my own clothing. There would be no barriers between us. Neither Paige's body image nor insecurities were a match for the love we had. I would crush anything that tried to harm her, but tonight all I could think of was being inside of her.

I sank between her thighs and sheathed myself in her heat with one thrust. A delicious moan escaped her lips, and I stilled to allow her to adjust to my size. Her head fell back, and I enjoyed the view of my woman. She was a warrior and had the battle scars to prove just how strong she was. She was braver than me, and I admired her for that fact alone. Her enemy came from within and tried to make her think less of herself. To others she may have appeared too tiny to be much of a fighter, but I knew better. She woke up every morning with the monster of insecurity, and at the mirror she looked that bastard dead in the eye. The outcome was always unpredictable. Some days Paige won the battle, hands down, and some days the monster wounded her—but my brave girl never stopped fighting. And now she had me to help her. I wouldn't just fight, I would slay the demons with words of love and affirmation, by reminding Paige of exactly how magnificent she was and how much she was adored.

I couldn't take my eyes off the sight of her. Moving tortuously slow, I dragged myself out of her with a long, hot pull. Once, sure that I'd pressed against every nerve, I again plunged deep and hard. Her body spoke a language of its own as she clenched tightly around me, closing her eyes to sink into the pleasure

"Eyes on me, baby."

She opened them and looked at me, her gaze reflecting how lust drugged her. She clenched around me again, and I began a synchronized rhythm with her. Goose bumps rose on her skin, which was now pink with desire. I drove hard into her sweetness and took away what was left of her control. She gasped, the mounting sensations causing her lips to part as she uttered a moan. She tightened her legs around me. With a fervor that equaled my own, she dug her heels into my ass. Her immodesty as she surrendered to me was an addiction. The more I pumped into her, the more I craved her. As the first waves of her orgasm approached, the spasming became unbearable as her insides made a tight fist and milked me. The viselike grip flipped the switch of primitive madness inside my brain. Lost in the sensations, I plunged harder and harder and surrendered to my release as she shattered, screaming my name.

BEAUTIFUL EYES, the color of rich, warm wood, were gazing into mine as I awoke. *My woman. My wife.* With one arm under her pillow, she draped the other casually across my waist. It felt so right. It felt like it had always been meant to be.

I brushed the hair away from her eyes. Neither of us said a word. The moment was consumed by touch as we enjoyed the simple intimacy of lying skin to skin, stroking and holding each other.

"I think we need food." Paige broke the silence. Her smile of contentment filled my heart. I kissed her forehead.

"Good thinking. I'll be right back."

I felt her eyes on me as I exited the bedroom. She was still looking toward the door as I came back with a tray filled with cheeses, bread, and fruit.

"How did you do that so fast?" She sat up, cross-legged, and pulled her hair back into a messy ponytail. No makeup, disheveled hair, and still I thought she was the most beautiful woman in the world.

"I had Luca make it before he left. It was in the fridge."

As she pushed the sheet away with her feet, I sat the tray between us on the bed, and when I leaned in towards her, she grabbed my chin and gave me a light kiss. I could get used to that.

"I love a man who plans," she said as she shimmied against the pillows at her back.

"Lucky for you I always have one."

I placed a small piece of cheese in her mouth. It only took me a moment to notice that Paige was slowly —without thinking—pulling the bedding back up to hide her scars. I gave her a stern look.

"I've seen every inch of you. Why are you trying to hide yourself?"

"I don't know." She cast her gaze down toward the tray and shrugged her shoulders. "Habit, I guess."

"Uh-huh." I tilted her chin up, forcing her to look into my eyes. "I want you to understand something: those marks mean nothing to me, but I know they mean something to you." I ran my thumb along her jawline. In turn, she pressed her cheek into my palm and closed her eyes. "I have another gift for you, baby. It's one that may make you feel less self-conscious about the scars. But you'll have to keep an open mind."

"What is it? Tell me." Her puzzled expression accompanied a cute smirk.

"No." I held a piece of cheese for her to bite into. "I'll show you instead. Tomorrow. Then you can decide if you like it. Pulling her onto my lap, I curled my fingers around her nape. I looked deeply into her eyes, our lips only a whisper apart.

"I love you, Paige. You are everything I want, everything I could want, and so much more than I deserve."

As if on cue, the moment I kissed her, the fountains came to life.

Chapter 28

Paige

As I walked down the Strip to meet Liz, I realized that for the first time in my life I was truly happy. Last night had been magical. I was so glad Falcon had a meeting this morning because I needed the walk. It gave me some time to reflect.

For someone like me, who was so methodical about everything, being spontaneous was uncharted territory. If I were to be truthful with myself, I hadn't known what I was missing. I'd always adopted the "it is what it is" attitude. That mindset had kept me going for years. Although I would never say my happiness depended on Falcon, I'd been much, much happier since I'd met him. From that first walk in the woods, he'd changed my perspective. He was also changing my view of my childhood accident. I wasn't a religious person. For as much as I believed in a god, I didn't believe he cared for me. I'd humored my parents' faith, and never disrespected it. My mother used to tell me there was a reason for everything. That God's timing was perfect, never early, never late. I'd listened but I hadn't really heard. When I'd become an adult, I'd remembered her words but never understood the meaning. Even though I'd been too young to understand faith, the accident had compromised my future beliefs. My mom had told me God was always with me, but then I'd wondered where He'd been when I was burned. It was so much easier to believe I was a peon in his kingdom of souls and had escaped his notice because he hadn't loved me. When I'd had this discussion with Falcon, he'd asked me to consider that I might be wrong.

I would never have considered my husband to be a man of faith. To look at him, he didn't look like a Christian, he was rough talking and tough looking and he was covered with tattoos. Falcon's body was a virtual feast for my underdeveloped sexuality. When I first saw him without his clothes, the tattoos had captured my attention. A thick tribal band circled his bicep while a sunburst with an Asian flair exploded over the right side of his chest and continued over his shoulder to his back.

I'd always believed that Christians didn't get

tattoos, so I'd thought that, when Falcon had told me he was a believer he was simply paying lip service to a denomination. But his faith was much deeper than I'd known. He'd given a good argument. He'd talked about his deployment to Afghanistan and he'd told me how much he'd had to rely on his faith. He'd said that when you were on the front lines you had no choice but to rely on God and your fellow soldiers. On the battlefield, that statement was to be taken literally, but in life your front line could be any situation that tested your faith because that was when it either grew the strongest or failed you. You made the choice. It sounded good, and I was happy he'd found something he could rely on, but I still couldn't relate to his conviction. He'd asked me to consider the accident might have made me who I was. I'd said it defined me just as much as being bullied had refined my personality. So then he'd asked me to, just once, look at everything I'd gone through from a different perspective. What if God hadn't done it to me, but had carried me through it? The concept was speculative at best but certainly worth exploring.

Interesting conversation was just one thing about him I loved, and I was thankful my friends back home cared for him too. Elizabeth really liked him. She'd asked us to go to lunch. I was meeting her now, and Falcon would be joining us when he was finished. Now that our secret was out, she was anxious to see us both. I'd caught her up on the details of everything by telephone, but this was the first time I'd seen her since my life had unraveled and then was mended. Now that my marriage wasn't considered a Vegas mistake, Falcon was certainly helping me to stitch it back together with colorful thread.

It was gorgeous Las Vegas morning, as sunny as my new outlook and as warm as my introspection. After lunch, Liz had gone back to work, and Falcon, not wanting to miss a business opportunity for MarSin Falcon, had added another appointment to his itinerary for the day. I was on my own for a while. Although Jorge had been more than willing to drive me wherever I'd wanted to go, I'd chosen to walk instead. It was too lovely to do otherwise. The streets were a little less crowded in the hottest part of the day, but certainly no less interesting. Most people were so focused on getting to their destination they never paid attention to anything but themselves, but I wasn't one of them.

I was enjoying my walk down the Strip when a commotion from the side street diverted my attention. I wasn't too far away to see what it was but was shocked at what I saw. Blake was leaning against the corner of a building and it looked like he'd kicked a trashcan over, most likely the source of the noise. He was as relaxed as I'd ever seen him. His head was tilted back while he blew smoke rings, his cigarette dangling from his fingertips. Anger quickly sparked within me. Why was he here, now? Was he following me? It felt like more than a coincidence, and it was the last thing I'd expected.

I silently fumed and my temper was quickly escalating from irritated to irate. Suddenly, everything came back to me in a blinding double punch—the attack in Vegas *and* his presumptive attitude. Rational thinking was something I had in short supply as I started toward him. He was so into himself he didn't even notice I was coming. I was running a race with sanity, I was much too close to back down and not far enough away to use common sense. He was an unpredictable douchebag, and I was alone—and I didn't care.

"Blake!" My hands curled into fists as I shouted at him. He jumped to an upright position and jolted out of his stupor. It was obvious from the look on his face he was shocked to see me, so I dismissed the thought he was following me. Still, I wanted to set him straight once and for all, and when I was done with him he'd never want to come near me again.

He looked to the left and right before he noticed me. I was waiting for his cocky attitude to surface, but instead he looked agitated.

"Get out of here, Paige." He wore a scowl. I presumed it was because Falcon had nearly kicked his ass.

"No! I'm not leaving until we get a few things straight."

I was foolish.

This was ridiculous.

He was crazy.

I stopped right in front of him, my hands on my hips. "Why are you in Vegas? Are you following me? Because if you are, you're going to stop!"

"What?" He looked at his watch, and to the left and right again. Then he focused on me and became incensed. "No! I'm not following you. Now, get the hell out of here!"

He started to walk away from me, but he wasn't getting away that easy. I grabbed his arm, and he spun around, giving me a deadly look. As I looked into eyes that were empty, black, and cold, an unwelcome shiver went down my spine, threatening my vigilante frame of mind. He looked down at my fingers as if he couldn't believe I'd touched him. Without missing a beat, he wrenched his arm free and pushed me. I stumbled.

"I said get the hell out of here! I'm not telling you again!" His chest heaved furiously as he took breaths filled with anger and indignation. I concentrated on regaining my balance.

"Who the fuck is this, Matthews? I told you to come alone."

My head spun in the direction of the harsh voice. I could barely see the shadow of the man who'd jumped back into the building's shade. By the look on Blake's face I could tell he recognized the man, and the two were supposed to meet.

"I did come alone. She's leaving." He spat the words to the hidden man, and the air grew thick with tension. I couldn't see the man's face, but I saw his gun. As my eyes fixed on the metal in the man's hand, Blake's head flipped back-and-forth between us.

"She just showed up!" He shrieked his explanation, and I knew something devastating was about to happen. The man turned in my direction, but all I saw was his hand.

"That's too bad for her."

His voice was an eruption of evil. In the span of a breath I was looking down at the barrel, the click of the trigger detonating in my ears.

His unforgiving bullet annihilated my happiness and massacred the bliss I'd just begun living. I jumped, but something hit my face, and my mind exploded into jagged grains of pain as the cement walkway cradled my fall.

"Oh my God!" Blake screamed. "Why did you do that?"

His voice came with the sound of another discharging bullet, and I felt something fall at my feet. I remembered the breathing that had calmed my panic attacks and I slowly inhaled and closed my eyes. Someone came near me and kicked my foot, and, for the first time in my life, I was thankful to the girls who'd tormented me. I'd learned to lay limp as they kicked and hit me because I'd known if I didn't move, they'd lose interest. I prayed the same would happen with the assassin.

"Paige!"

I heard an angel yelling through Falcon's voice, but I didn't dare move. Adrenaline fueled my terror-filled thoughts, and every one of them was about him. If I was dying, I prayed God would take me quickly, so I could plead with Him for my husband's life. The last thing I heard was my soon-to-be-widowed husband calling my name as I spiraled into blackness.

Chapter 29

Falcon

The gray concrete turned crimson as I approached the devastation. Though I moved quickly, I felt like everything moved in slow motion. Whoever had pulled the trigger was now running away. I would have gone after him, but my only thought was reaching the woman who held my heart. All systems were on overload as I struggled to get to Paige in record speed. My eyes burned, my jaw was clenched, and my heart thundered so violently I thought it might beat its way through my ribcage and out of my chest. One mantra looped over and over in my head.

· · ·

Don't die.

Don't die.

Don't die.

"Paige!"

I yelled her name as if it were the last thing I would utter on this earth. The sound of my voice made her assailant run faster. *I'll kill him!*

I couldn't remember when I'd pulled out my gun. My thoughts were a jumbled mess between getting to Paige and wondering how this had happened. There were too many questions and no answers. *Why would someone want to hurt her?* I tried to sort through them as I closed the distance between my wife and me. I was confident of one thing, I would find the son of a bitch who'd dared hurt what was mine, and I wouldn't have far to look. It was Las Vegas. The best surveillance on the market was on every building, street corner, and traffic light. I'd dissect every frame I could get my hands on to find out who'd hurt Paige.

Shaking off all thoughts that weren't of imme-diate importance, I found myself close enough to her that I could see the rise and fall of her chest. *Thank God!*

"*Paige . . .*"

My voice was a pained whisper as I dropped to my knees beside her. The blood was coming from the side of her face. It pooled beneath her head, soaking her hair in a gothic shade of garnet. As I turned to check over the rest of her body I recognized the person beside her. Blake.

Blood poured from the bullet wound in his chest. It was obvious he'd been shot after Paige was injured because he'd fallen across her feet. His wound looked to be to the heart. The amount of blood was far greater than hers. I shouldn't have cared at all, but my military training took over once I determined that Paige was still breathing, and I automatically checked for casualties. I placed my fingers on the area of his neck where a pulse should have been. I quickly determined he was dead. Selfish bastard that I was, I didn't care.

I quickly turned back to Paige. I removed my jacket and lifted her head. As gently as I could, I placed it beneath her. I'd expected the worst but saw that the bullet had ripped away the flesh from her cheekbone. It burned through the indent below her earlobe but hadn't gone through her skull. *It hadn't gone through!* I tried to talk to her.

"Paige . . . baby, can you hear me?" I turned her

face. She was pale. I reached in my pocket for my cell phone and dialed 911. Giving them a clipped order to get to this location, I never took my eyes off her.

"Fal?" Her eyelids barely fluttered, and I could sense her confusion.

"Stay still, baby. Help's on the way."

I didn't want to move her but cradled her in my arms as best I could. I spoke out loud about anything and everything that would cause her to focus, but visually I assessed and processed the scene. I was already coming to conclusions. What I couldn't figure out was why Paige was with Blake. She hated him. *Had he forced her into coming here? Did someone other than me have it in for him? Did he draw her into the line of fire?*

It was a good thing Blake was dead because I could think of fifty ways I wanted to kill him. I would have congratulated the shooter for taking the piece of shit out of existence except he—whoever he was—had hurt Paige in the process. And who the fuck was he? Was he supposed to have shot them both, or was Paige just collateral damage? And would he come back to finish the job once he discovered she wasn't dead? *No fucking way that's going to happen!*

I needed answers, and Paige was the quickest way to get them. Once I found out who he was, I'd hunt the bastard down. For now I had to minimize any report of her survival, and I had to keep my hands clean—but I had contacts. *And some of those motherfuckers were far deadlier than me!*

THE HOSPITAL ROOM that Paige occupied was isolated, far away from the Emergency Room. I had insisted on it as a precautionary measure. It was imperative that I keep her out of harm's way. The beeping sound of the monitors attached to her formed a sick tune that played in sync with her heart. She'd been sleeping for over an hour, but that hadn't been the case when we'd arrived. An adrenaline rush had roused her and thrown her into a severe panic attack. I'd rung for the nurse, and she was quickly administered something to calm her down.

While she'd slept the nurses had cleaned the blood and dirt from her face. I peeled the tape away from her skin and lifted the gauze dressing. The breath I was holding rushed out as I finished looking and gently pushed the covering back into place. Satisfied the wound looked better than I'd expected, I determined that it was deep but short—miraculous, really. Just a few stitches. I could barely believe it when the doctor said that antibiotics, salve, and rest would have her good as new. *But would it?*

Feeling doubleminded, I ran two trains of thought.

First, would the incident send her into a tailspin and cause her hair pulling, and second, how quickly could I find the person who did this to her? Now, while she was sleeping, I concentrated my efforts on the latter. I was with the doctor when he spoke to the Las Vegas police and insisted on having their spokesman run the press release by me. Between me, the doc, and the County Sherriff, we came up with a plausible story that reported severe head trauma. With any luck, curiosity would flush out those involved. Hopefully, when all of this was over, she would seriously consider the proposal I'd made to her.

"Hey, babe."

"Hey, yourself."

"What are you up to?" I listened to the sound of paper being rifled in the background.

"Just looking through some contracts. You?"

"I was doing the same thing a little while ago. Just got back from dropping them off at Carter's." I put the call on speaker as I walked to the kitchen. "Did you eat today?"

"Yeeesss . . ."

"Good." I smiled at the annoyed tone in her voice. Paige worked all day without eating and then got too overtired to eat at all. I'd come to learn it was a trigger

for overthinking, which led to anxiety, which led to hair pulling. Knowing I was a pain in her ass, I changed the subject. "Can I run something by you?"

"Sure. What's up?"

"I know we said we'd work out the distance thing, but I have an idea that could make this work for us. What states are you licensed in?"

"Maryland and Delaware."

"Good. So you could set up shop here, if you wanted to."

"Yes, I could."

I could tell her interest was piqued. "What do you think of this? If I get you familiar with all the areas in and around Deep Creek, you could do business here as well as the beach. It's something to think about anyway."

"I'm never opposed to any business proposal, Fal, but what's in it for you?"

"You." Silence hung in the air. "Hello?"

"I'm here."

"You know we already handle some things for Declan down on the Eastern Shore. I'm sure I can pick up a few more accounts. The whole fucking area is nothing but small businesses. You and I can go between the two cities."

"So, if we travel between the two, we can spend more time together? Is that what you're proposing?"

"That's about it."

"I love you. You know that?"

"And I love you. I think it could work. It's always good to diversify and Deep Creek is as good a vacation spot as Ocean City and Rehoboth."

"The idea certainly has merit. I'll think about it."

Again, there was a lull in the conversation. I lowered my voice. "So tell me, what are you wearing?"

"You're crazy!" She laughed. "But I miss you too."

PAIGE'S LAUGH was a sound I'd grown to love. As I looked down at her I saw that she was awake and watching me. I took her hand in mine. "How are you feeling?"

"I'm fine." Her voice was weak and strained.

"So you said." She rolled her eyes at me. "I know you should rest, but I need to know what you remember."

"I said I'm fine. All I have is a banging headache. But, to answer your question, I decided to take a walk after our lunch with Elizabeth. That's when I ran into Blake." She looked from side to side, taking mental inventory of the beeping and buzzing equipment of the intravenous pump and heart monitor. "I'll tell you more when you get me out of here."

"We're not going anywhere until the doctor says

so." Once again, she rolled her eyes. "You know, you're going to make yourself dizzy."

"I am not. When are they going to get all this stuff off me?" She held her arms up in the air as she sneered at the IV and monitors Apparently, now that the fog had cleared from her head, she was back to her old self.

"As soon as all the tests come back from the lab."

"You know I don't like hospitals," she huffed.

"I can see that." I leaned down and kissed her on the head. "Humor me, will you? I want to make sure you're okay."

Her expression softened as she relaxed back against the pillows. "What's next? I know you won't rest until you know what happened to me."

"You're right about that." I smiled and squeezed her hand. "I'm not sure, baby. I concocted a story. The press release states you've suffered head trauma. I'm hoping that will put the shooter off your trail for a while, but knowing perps like I do, they'll want to see for themselves. My gut's telling me you weren't supposed to be part of what went down. I think Blake was the target."

"Was?" Concern shadowed her face.

"Yeah. Was." I watched as a shroud of sadness fell over her. "Paige . . ."

"I know what you're going to say. I didn't like him, but I didn't want him dead."

She looked off into empty space. I had no words of consolation. I was glad Blake was no longer a threat to the woman I loved.

"When you get out of here, we can get back to our plans. Specifically, our living arrangements."

She looked up at me. "And if I say no?"

"Not that simple, sweetheart. You're not leaving my sight."

"The way you say it sounds like a threat, not a promise."

"However you want to take it is fine with me." I leaned over the bed and pinned her down with a kiss. She'd have to do whatever I say. No way in hell was I going to let anything happen to her again.

Chapter 30

Paige

I was fine. I was up and moving around—and going stir crazy. Falcon had made me rest in the suite for over a week, and now I had no idea where he was taking me. Once I'd convinced him nothing was wrong with me, he agreed to my relentless hounding about getting me out of the hotel room. I thought we'd be flying back to Maryland. Instead, he'd asked me to wear something loose-fitting because we were going out. Who knew what fake names we'd be using, but no matter what the surprise was, I couldn't help but be happy to see something other than those same walls. Although he'd warned me I might not like whatever it was, and that I shouldn't get my hopes up too high, I couldn't imagine him planning something for me I'd hate. For a tough guy, he had a very tender heart. Especially when it came to me.

A smile filled my lips. You'd think that being shot and knowing a killer might be after me, would make me want to cower and hide, but it didn't. Each new day proved to me I was overcoming my personal demons. I didn't want to be that person anymore.

I had trouble recognizing the tortured woman I'd been just months before. Whether brave or crazy, I was tired of running away. Instead of internalizing my emotional monsters I tried to think up new coping mechanisms to face things head on. Falcon didn't have a problem with that but wanted me to do it his way. Too bad.

I loved that he wanted to protect me, but I wanted to live life out loud, not hide away in the dark corners of my mind. While he respected my choice, he didn't like it. His attitude was that we'll agree to disagree. It was the only source of contention between us. *At least we're putting aside our differences to have a nice day.*

I'd been puttering around in the suite for most of the morning, or at least I had been until Falcon snuck up behind me and swatted my butt.

"You have an hour to get ready."

"Give me fifty-five minutes."

He laughed. It was a sound I was growing to love more and more. It lightened my heart.

We walked out of the hotel hand in hand. The sun was shining, but instead of the oppressive desert heat a breeze cooled the temperature. I wasn't a fan of the cold winters near the Atlantic Ocean and felt fortunate to be able to escape to the warmer climate a few times a year.

Falcon tugged my hand. Looking into his eyes I saw a future filled with love. It was the greatest feeling and added something wonderful to my outlook. Even Vegas looked different to me. Everything was so colorful and crisp and, though I knew this was the most beautiful, pigmented, man-made city, I couldn't help but think that a brush with a bullet had colored my opinion of the world, in a positive way. It was the little things that gave me pleasure. *Like now.*

I loved how small my hand felt in his. I moved my fingers around his palm and committed the feel to memory. He opened it and interlocked our fingers. I didn't care about the dangers that could be lurking for me around any corner. I was confident Falcon wouldn't let anything happen to me.

Though it was early you wouldn't know that by the sound of traffic, horns blared, and motors revved. Though he wouldn't tell me where we were going or what we were doing, he led me to Planet Hollywood. I was silent as we walked through the lobby and meandered through the hotel. After pausing in front of a few stores to throw me off the scent, he stopped in front of a tattoo shop.

"What's this?" I grinned, my expression one of bewilderment.

"All I ask is that you keep an open mind and listen to what the man has to say."

Falcon's plea piqued my curiosity. I'd never been inside a tattoo parlor, but when we walked through the doors any preconceived notions I might have had disappeared. The inside of the shop was pristine. What looked like massage tables were sparkling clean, as were the stools and chairs. A very handsome Latino approached us.

"Paige, meet a friend of mine. Dee Sanchez."

The man extended his hand to me. "Nice to meet you."

"Dee, this is my wife, Paige."

The man's head jerked up. "Hey! You didn't tell me she was your wife, man. Congratulations!" I watched the exchange with a smile. Wife. It was the first time someone had addressed me as such. I liked how warm it made me feel inside. Dee slapped Falcon on the arm and then motioned for us to sit. "Let's sit down, and I'll show you what I've got." We followed him to a small consultation area, and Dee pulled out a sketchbook. He turned the book around and placed it in front of me.

"Falcon said you have some scarred skin that you might want to have covered up."

I gave my husband a challenging look. "He did, huh?" Falcon smiled and shrugged his shoulders. I gave him a smirk and then turned back to Dee. "He's right; I do have some scars."

"We can do something about that, if you're game."

Confusion crept into my thoughts. "I've had plastic surgery, so they're the best they can be—or at least I thought so. To tell you the truth, I've never thought about tattoos. You can tattoo scarred skin?"

"Sometimes you can, sometimes you can't; it all depends on the skin. I've done tattoos that covered some pretty nasty scars, and my clients haven't had any problems with it. I've seen women who have their entire chest and back tattooed after mastectomies. If the skin is willing to take ink, anything can be done." It was obvious from his tone he was confident in exactly what he could or couldn't do. I looked over at my husband, who was unusually quiet.

"I don't know how much Falcon's told you about me but I'm also a business woman. As much as I can appreciate the art form, there's still a certain stigma attached to tattoos." I didn't want to offend the man, but I thought voicing my reservations up front would be the best approach, so we wouldn't be wasting each other's time.

"That's true," Dee confirmed, "but he also told me that you're very good at covering them up by the way you dress. If that's true, then you shouldn't have any trouble covering up the artwork."

I shrugged. I had nothing to lose by keeping an open mind. "Okay. Let's see what you've got." I leaned forward. Falcon placed a reassuring hand on my knee as we both looked at Dee's portfolio. As he turned several pages, I sucked in a breath.

Sketch after beautiful sketch, expanded my understanding of what body art was. Each piece of paper held a drawing of a woman's body—different page, different angle. Though the body lines were loosely drawn, the designs were exact. The first was a view of the back. A floral design trailed over shoulder blades, mid-back, and down into the curve of her backside. It was almost exactly in concert with the places where my scars resided. With a graceful flow, the branches of a tree held delicate flowers. Some were full, some closed, and some in mid-bloom, but all were shades and hews of pink. The detail was amazing, so much so that the bark looked almost three dimensional.

"This is unbelievable." I was so moved that my voice was a whisper. Dee smiled.

"I'm glad you like them." He looked over at Falcon. "He said that cherry blossoms were your favorite."

Misty-eyed, I inhaled the loveliness that could

replace the violence in my life. I didn't have any idea when Falcon had met with him, but he must have described to Dee the location of each of my scars. Looking closely, I saw the side and neck area all held different twists and turns of nature's beauty. It was beyond my comprehension how designs so intricate could be transferred to skin because I was completely ignorant of the field of ink to flesh. When I got to the last design tears stung the back of my eyes. Butterflies!

Drawn with wings fully expanded, as well as some side view images, they were positioned on the blossoms of varying flora. Some looked as if they were drinking nectar, some were in mid-flight. They were stunning in blues, whites, yellows, oranges, and black. One even had a small tear in the wing. Damaged. *Just like me.*

I examined the drawings, noting that what attracted me and made them so beautiful was that the shading underneath them made them appear three-dimensional. I was speechless.

"I don't want to get up in your business," he said matter-of-factly, "but Fal said butterflies remind him of you."

The stinging in my eyes graduated to pools, and my throat tightened with emotion. I looked up into my husband's eyes. "They do?"

He nodded. "They do. They start out as one thing and become something else. When they've matured, their heart is the same, but they've transformed. There is beauty in the struggle, but eventually they become what they were destined to be—exquisite.

I felt the tears trickle as they spilled down my face, and Falcon brushed them away with his thumb.

"What do you think, babe? Want to go for it?"

Daring to hope, I gave Dee a questioning look. "I don't know if it would work on my skin."

"C'mon in the back, and I'll take a look." He winked at me and cocked his head toward a private room.

I followed him. After exposing myself for his examination, he decided within a few minutes a tattoo was possible. We went back to the front of the shop where Falcon was waiting. I looked into his eyes.

"I'm going to do it." My voice was a convoluted mix of both positive and negative thoughts. It sounded a bit hesitant. Falcon came over to me and warmed my upper arms with strokes of his hands.

"Don't overthink it, but if you have reservations, don't do it. I arranged this merely as a suggestion." There was such tenderness in his voice that my heart clenched.

"I want to. I really do." I paused to take a deep breath. "Dee said he would resize the designs to fit my skin. If he can make something better out of what I see in the mirror, I want to do it. I don't think anything could make it look worse." From the corner of my eye, I saw Dee prepping his table. I turned back to Falcon.

"He said this could take a while. You go, and I'll call you when he's finished." He was concerned. His eyes became a rich emerald and, right now, that depth came from his concern for me.

"Not gettin' rid of me that easily, sweetheart. I'm staying with you."

I stood on tiptoe, my lips brushing against his. "I'm fine. I'm not a little girl anymore and, unless he has hot oil in that thing, it's nothing I can't handle."

"Yeah. Not buying it. Besides, I almost lost you a little over a week ago. But if it makes you feel better, I won't watch." He dragged a chair over to Dee's private area and turned it around, sitting in it like a sentry to guard the opening. "I'll be right here."

Chapter 31

Falcon

I waited inside the tattoo studio while Dee worked on my wife. It had been over a week and no leads on who'd killed Blake and injured Paige. Nothing more had been reported in the news about the incident. Law enforcement officials who I'd had been working with were hopeful that curiosity would flush out the perpetrator. That didn't happen. The person was still out there.

Though I'd collaborated with Dee, I'd decided not to take him up on his offer to come to Paige and me at the hotel and take her to him instead. If there was someone out there watching her, I'd catch the bastard. I couldn't help but think Blake had been the intended target and Paige had simply been a victim of circumstance. She didn't know it, but I had eyes on us everywhere.

I hadn't anticipated the intricacies of the design Paige was getting in her tattoo. Dee had been working on her for a few hours. The sketches were more detailed than I could have seen in a quickly read email. Having sat for hours to get my own tattoos, I was a little concerned. There was no denying the pain Paige must have gone through with the initial injury and then the recovery from plastic surgery, but this was her first ink. When I checked in to see if she was okay, she said she was going to get the entire design in one session. *Strong girl!* She was going to be sore. I'd have to keep my hands off her until she gave me the all clear. I consoled myself with the knowledge that Dee's work was flawless and, as long as she was happy with the final product, I could be patient while she healed. No matter what. We had a lifetime to make up for a short period of inconvenience.

"Hey, boss. What's up?"

I'd seen him coming. He was big and mean—the perfect man to watch over my wife in my absence. At about six foot six inches, Herbert "Tank" Sherman was about as bad a motherfucker as they came. Ex-Army Ranger, Tank had seen his share of combat and had led his team through some sticky situations.

"Hey, Tank." I stood and clapped him on the shoulder. "Thanks for coming here on such short notice."

"No problem." He tipped his head toward Dee's private area. "She in there?"

"Yeah. She'll be in with him for a while."

"She know I'm here?"

"I poked my head in and told her that I had to run out and that one of my colleagues was her bodyguard until I got back."

Tank laughed. "Bet she loved that." Tank's eyes scoured the perimeter of the tattoo shop, noting entrances and exits before turning his attention back to me. "Go do whatcha gotta do. I got this."

I nodded, completely confidant in his ability to protect that which was most precious to me.

As Tank took the seat I'd vacated, I stuck my cell in my pocket.

"I won't be long."

Although I was hesitant, I left knowing full well Tank wouldn't let anyone near Paige.

As I made my way back to the hotel I couldn't help but speculate how events had worked out to my advantage. I'd spoken with the police chief about the shooting. With no credible leads, there were things I needed to follow up on. Paige was a bit desensitized when it came to attacks, and, although I understood it, her cavalier attitude about her own safety bothered me. The flip side of that would have been for her to be so afraid it hindered her everyday living. I wasn't sure which one I'd have preferred, but it didn't matter what I wanted. All that mattered was her safety. Her history with bullies may have put her under the illusion that if she acted tough, she was tough. *But tough doesn't stop bullets.*

Her altercation with Marisol was the most recent in a long line of unfortunate events. It unnerved me that she wasn't the least bit apprehensive when recounting what she did remember to the police. With each new day she remembered more of the details, yet she said she'd never seen the shooter. I guess she figured that since she hadn't seen him no one would come after her. Sadly, shooters didn't follow Paige's rule book. Little did she know, other than Tank, there were two other undercover bodyguards watching her.

After the doctors had released her from the hospital, we'd gone back to the hotel. She'd insisted on showering, directing me to order food. I'd smiled at her tenacity and did as she'd asked while also putting in a few calls to trusted people. I'd informed my partners what had transpired. Though Marcus and Carter had been shocked at the news of Blake's death, neither of them had seemed too sad about it. A few days later I'd read the autopsy report. Blake had had cocaine in his system at the time of his death. I'd put in another call to Carter and Marcus, and they were following up behind the scenes. The conclusion we'd all come to was the connection between Blake Matthews and Manny Vallega had more to do with dealing drugs than with Blake's representation of Marisol. The problem with that was we were the ones with the questions and, even if we could get Manny to talk to us, we were sure he wouldn't be offering up any answers.

Jorge had picked us up from the hospital. That was when Paige had begun to confide the truth of what she'd remembered. It was more than she'd disclosed to the police. She was jaded when it came to law enforcement, and she had good reason to be so. After Paige and Aria had been violently attacked by Marisol, the courts took over. It was believed that Marisol would spend years in jail—but that didn't happen. Paige's faith in the judicial system had been rocked. She'd told me in the car that she was only talking to me. I was the one she trusted. As her mind cleared so did her memory, and she recounted the details to me. The details had become clues, what the shooter had said to

Blake, how tall he'd been, the sound of his voice, and the sound the gun had made when it went off. It had been only a matter of time before all the pieces had fit together to give me a clear picture. I'd used Declan as a means to find out if Blake had been dealing drugs. Because I didn't want to alarm Paige, most of our communication had been via text messages. I'd used Carter as a liaison between Declan and me. As soon as I got back to the hotel, I called him.

"Carter?"

"Yeah. How's Paige?"

"Better. What did you find out?" I reached into the drawer of the hotel desk for paper and a pen.

"Something you're not going to be happy about." His serious tone made the situation even more sober. "Your suspicions were on point. One of the models was hysterical about Blake's death. She confided in Declan that he was her cocaine connection. She said Marisol was her initial contact, but since Marisol spent most of her time in Columbia, Blake distributed. That's just hearsay. No doubt that Marisol was his connection, but there's no proof."

"Shit!" The pen flew from my hand, sailing across the room.

"Yeah. My feelings exactly." Disgust dusted Carter's words. "I checked the hotel records. Blake was registered in a room right next to Manny and Marisol. For all appearances it looks innocent enough—like they were on vacation—but I did some inquiries. Seems the DEA was watching as well. They suspected the cocaine connection. They've been following the trail longer than we have. Like a few thousand kilos longer."

"I knew it. Fuck!"

"I don't think Paige knew anything. At least not anything other than that Blake was an asshole."

I closed my eyes and ran my hand over my face. "I don't think so either, but the drugs in his system would explain the aggression."

"And his erratic behavior," Carter added. "You didn't know Blake until my party, but he used to be a pretty likeable guy. A little egotistical, but that's normal in his line of work. Declan told me the girl that exposed the drug connection told him there were other people involved as well. You know models and being thin. Apparently, Blake was supplying the drugs."

"He may have been their connection, but he was a gopher, I'm sure of it. And the DEA is tailing Manny?"

"Yeah. They have been for a while. I'm not sure how far they're gonna let us go with this."

"Damn it!" Frustration heated my blood. "Manny has got to have some loose end that we can trail. Maybe if we bait him . . ."

"Don't do something stupid, Fal," Carter interrupted. His tone issued a warning. "Leave it be. I'll talk to the Feds and see if we can offer any assistance. Other than that, we have to back off."

It took me awhile after the phone call to compose myself. Something about the whole thing wasn't sitting well with me. Paige was pretty intuitive, and I couldn't give her a reason to suspect anything was wrong—I had to come up with a plan.

Tank had been giving me updates from the tattoo shop. True to form, Paige was weathering the session well and hadn't asked to take a break. He'd overheard her say she couldn't wait to show her friend Elizabeth the final product. I went one step further and as I headed out of the suite I called Liz, asking her to meet me so we could see it together. While Paige showed Liz the ink, Tank and the other guys could give me an update. I only wished I didn't have to be so secretive about the steps I was taking to protect her, but it was for her own good.

Frustration over my conversation with Carter was still biting me when the elevator doors opened.

"Well, well, well."

I looked up, and into the face of Marisol. With the

new revelations, it took everything I had not to haul her ass back to my room and interrogate her. Instead, I expended all my energy in being civil. I walked past her, but she couldn't let it be.

"Does it come naturally for you to be this rude, or is it just your reaction to me?"

As I kept on walking she shouted down the hallway, drawing attention to us both.

"I hear you have a new pet bitch, and that she has some interesting markings."

Son of a bitch! I spun around and glared at her. She wore an evil grin.

"You can thank me later."

Marisol spoke in riddles, never directly admitting guilt for anything. I closed the distance between us. "You're nothing but a shrew. Somebody should put you out of your fuckin' misery." I spat the words through gritted teeth, my jaw clenched so tightly I thought the bones might shatter.

"Aw . . . now, now, Falcon. That's no way to behave. Of course, I wasn't really responsible. I wasn't myself when she went flying through the window, though the recollection I have of seeing Paige sail through glass is rather amusing. I was just happy to give her something to remember me by."

"You're pure evil. Why don't you go crawl back up Manny's ass, Marisol? You reek of him."

"Oh, there's no need to be hostile. I didn't even know about Paige's scars—although I'm happy to take credit for putting them there. Blake told me all about them. Seems he saw them when he was riding your whore."

My hands balled into tight fists. All I could think of was wrapping them around her skinny neck.

"You mean when he tried to rape her. Good thing he's not alive to tell the story to anyone else. If I were you, I'd shut my mouth. I don't take kindly to people talking about my wife."

She ignored my comments, not even flinching when I mentioned Blake's death or my marriage. Instead she remained cool and continued to bait me.

"I hear the scars have given her a very distinct look," she said, her narrowed eyes adding to her sly expression. "Don't worry, Falcon. I understand some men are attracted to freaks."

"Fuck you!"

I wanted to wipe off her smile with my fist in her face but turned my back on her instead. As I continued down the hall I ignored the small crowd that had witnessed our exchange. I hated recalling Carter's words, that there was nothing we could do. My gut told me Marisol had something to do with Paige getting shot. The shitty thing was there was nothing I could do about it. Until we could make a case I had to stand down and let Marisol and Manny run amuck with whatever it was they were doing and let the Feds handle it. That would take time. In the meantime I could collect intel. Maybe, one day, I'd be able to help them connect all the dots and, hopefully, both of their sinister asses would rot in jail.

Chapter 32

Paige

Freedom.

Though he didn't yet realized the impact, my tattoo was the best gift Falcon could ever had given to me. As I watched my skin heal I couldn't help but feel that my battered soul had joined in the process. With each passing day the area had grown less sore. Falcon had inspected it each day, the smile on his face revealing his thoughts.

We'd sacrificed the remainder of our honeymoon to my healing. There would be more days ahead to live, love, and be happy. For now I was content to share coffee and conversation, to get to know my husband. Having someone to love and to be loved by, was more than I could ever have dreamed, and it was a dream I hadn't dared to hope for. I reveled in the discovery of newfound feelings of happiness and contentment.

It was almost three weeks to the day since I'd gotten the first of my "ink," and I was certain I would follow suit with most of the other scars. Not everyone was as lucky as me. I'd learned that not all damaged skin is eligible for the process. Falcon admired them as much as I did. As I looked into the mirror, gone was the dread that had accompanied my reflection for as long as I could remember. In its place was a sweet kind of conceit. The artist's needle had injected not only pigment but the gift of grace and elegance into my skin, beauty from pain. After years of loathing my reflection, I found myself staring in the mirror with an appreciative fascination.

Falcon was uneasy that Blake's murderer had not yet been found. One night after dinner in our suite he revealed the measures he was taking to ensure my safety. I listened with intent as he listed the names of three men who'd been watching me around the clock. During another time in my life I might have been frightened, but, strangely, I had no fear. At my request, he'd agreed to arrange a time in the near future when I could meet these protectors. I didn't quite understand the change. For too many years I lived in shadows, most of it of my own making. A newfound confidence had made me bold, and I was growing more so every day. A crazed shooter hadn't done any worse to me than I'd done to myself. I refused to live that way anymore.

When we'd returned home from Vegas, Falcon had told me he wanted to do something special to mark our wedding. Nothing big, simply a small celebration. After kicking ideas back and forth, we decided to have a dinner for our friends and family at one of my favorite restaurants.

The name threw him off—The Hobbit—but then it did the same for most people. All Falcon could picture was a quirky place with gnome-infested décor. He was pleasantly surprised to find an elegant venue with a lovely view of the Bay. By the time we'd finalized the plans, he'd acted as if the location had been his idea. All of this had occurred one week ago. Luckily, all our circle of friends and loved ones were able to attend, and we'd be seeing them very soon.

I smacked my lips after applying my lipstick. A little touch of eye shadow, a spritz of hairspray, and I was ready to slip into my outfit. At first, I was a little nervous about my choice of "wedding dress" but there was no way I was backing out now. I liked what I saw when I looked in the mirror. Instead of victim, I saw a victor. As my newly discovered boldness settled in my bones, I grew impatient to show Falcon my dress. He was waiting for me downstairs in the living room.

"Are you ready?" As I called out to him I heard the deep rumble of his laughter.

"Yes. Are you going to make us late?"

Closing my eyes, I sucked in a deep breath. Funny how I wasn't at all nervous about a shooter yet was apprehensive about what Falcon would think of my appearance. Never in my life had I exposed this much of me in public, but I reminded myself I was no longer a broken sculpture, but a work of art. I descended the steps and stopped on the last one. The distance nearly equaled our height.

"Holy shit!" Falcon's eyes widened. I was pleased by the stunned reaction. I looked down, my hand gliding smoothly over the satin fabric covering my belly.

"Really? You like it?"

He held out his hand, and I took a step down. He slowly twirled me so that he could see the dress from all angles. When we were face-to-face he closed the distance between us. I shivered when his fingers trailed down my spine. He gave me a chaste kiss.

"You look stunning."

I bathed in the appreciation of his words. The satin material was an ivory color. Modest in the front, it draped in a deep cowl dip in the back, revealing my skin until it nearly reached the tip of my spine. The butterflies and blossoms of my tattoo peeked with my every move. I looked into my husband's eyes and saw myself exactly as he did. Blinking back a tear, I swallowed the lump in my throat as he pressed his lips to mine with another tender kiss.

"Don't cry. You'll ruin your makeup."

"I won't." I smiled at him. "Do you really like it?"

"If we don't leave here soon . . ."

I laughed as he teased. Moving past him, I picked up a small, beaded bag and looked over my shoulder to see a smoldering look in his eyes.

I WAS COMPLETELY COVERED. A jacket matching my dress fell tastefully over my frame and hid the revealing dress underneath. The material was designed so that it looked like a dress all by itself. I wore it throughout out the meal.

"I'm so happy for you." My mother hugged me in a sweet embrace.

"I told you about the tattoos so you wouldn't be shocked." She then put an arm's length between us, her hands resting on my waist.

"I can't see anything, Paige. I honestly didn't know

what to expect when you told me, but you look nothing but demure."

I tapped the small clasp at my neck. "Once I unfasten this, you'll be able to see most of it."

"I'm sure it's beautiful." She gave me a peck on the cheek. As I looked into my mother's eyes, I could see the delight dancing there. "But, then, to me you've always been beautiful."

My mother, as always, calmed my fears. No one else suspected. My outfit covered everything.

Excitement coursed through my veins. I felt like a kid on Christmas morning who couldn't wait to show off her presents. As soft music played in the background, Falcon took my hand and led me to our wedding cake. The seven tiered Smith Island confection was topped with a miniature "Welcome to Fabulous Las Vegas" sign. Obviously, my husband's idea of adding a lighthearted reminder of the best mistake we'd ever made.

Falcon handed me a glass of champagne while the restaurant staff filled those of our guests. He clinked it with a fork until he had everyone's attention. I looped my arm through his. As the time approached for me to reveal myself, my body hummed with a heady mix of excitement and happiness.

"Thank you all for celebrating with us today." He took my hand and looked deep into my eyes.

"Paige, before I met you, I lived a very plain life. Everything to me was black and white. But somehow, on a snowy walk, you did something I never expected—you filled my life with color. Marrying you in Vegas was the best jackpot I ever won."

He kissed me and turned to our guests. I winked at him as he placed his fingers on the clasp at my neck. As the satin fell off my shoulders, he tossed it over his arm. I heard a few gasps, but I only saw his handsome face. His eyes glistened, reflecting love and pride.

As I looked over the room, I smiled at my parents, my brother, Aria, and the remainder of our friends. There were tears—happy ones. Some knew what I'd just done. Others had no clue. Though I wanted to add to his toast, emotion choked me with unshed tears of joy. It was impossible to articulate how this man had changed my life. He placed his lips to my ear.

"You're such a show off."

Only I heard the playfulness in his whisper. He brushed my hair aside and planted a kiss just below my ear where the scar from the bullet was healing. Wrapping his arm around my waist we looked to our guests. His voice was loud and full of pride as he held his glass up for a toast.

"I'm one lucky son of a bitch," he bellowed. As he turned to me I saw eyes full of love and a smile that made my heart soar.

"Here's to my wife. The most beautiful woman in the world."

Keep reading for a preview of the next title in the
Imperfection Series

No Perfect Bitch

Preview

No Perfect Woman

An Imperfection Series Novel

Book 5

DD Lorenzo

Prologue

Marisol

On nights like this, I wondered if anything I would have done differently would have changed the outcome of this circumstance. Nights when the black of a midnight sky stole my sleep and flooded my veins with the thick tar of speculation. My thoughts tortured me giving me no rest from my endless speculation of what could have been. What should have been. What I did know for sure was that loving her had energized me, fueling me to be the best version of myself.

I'd failed her miserably.

I didn't deserve her.

She was, and would always be, the part of me that desired to be the best. For her.

Love had made me a better person, and loving her allowed me to live happily with myself in blissful ignorance. Erasing any sins from my past. Even though her sweetness blessed me with an inner light I'd never experienced, no matter how I tried I couldn't wash the condemnation from my soul. I would have spent every day for the remainder of my life paying and seeking absolution if it would have meant I could have kept her forever. Since that would never happen, I would have to be satisfied with holding her in my heart.

It was either a travesty or fitting justice that I might never be healed by the sweetness of her forgiveness.

Chapter 1

Perfect!

There was something decadent about perfection, and I was looking at it. A nursery that was fit for a princess. *Our princess.* All my plans had turned out just as I had pictured them in my mind. The room was full of color. Unimaginable hues of pink mixed with smatterings of coral, yellow, and white. The walls were painted in such a way that the colors graduated seamlessly and beautifully one into the other. The illusion it created was of the morning sunrise in my home country, Colombia.

The smile on my face was genuine. As my gaze traveled from one pretty thing to another, I imagined that some would argue that the space was excessive. I wouldn't agree, nor did I care. This was our baby. I intended to lavish this child with the best of everything.

A wash of exhaustion lingered over me. Manny and I had been traveling extensively. He had his sights set on the presidency of Colombia, and our social activities were planned with that goal in mind. Just the night before we had hosted a dinner party for fifty guests. Hobnobbing with the elite of society. Most were affluent in large social circles both in Columbia and abroad. We spared no expense in taking the necessary steps to assure Manny's victory. Knowing that presenting ourselves as a stable family would further our ambition, we decided it would be best to add a little one to our family.

Accepting that I would be filling the role of a mother took some time. I didn't think that I had a maternal instinct in my entire body, but a person's outlook can be changed when they are given the right incentive. Once I accepted that having a child would be in our best interest, I warmed to the idea.

It was decided that last night's event would be my last until after our child arrived. Manny would carry on without me as he fulfilled our social obligations. Strangely, that pleased me. I had been in the spotlight for far too long and, though I thrived on the attention that the media gave to me, the idea of sequestering myself had appeal. In time, Manny and I would reemerge with our little one, and I looked forward to the frenzy.

Today was the first that I was able to sit back and enjoy the fruit of my efforts. Nothing was too good for this baby, and I was looking at the best that money could buy. One of the walls was painted a soft cream, with built-in bookshelves filled with children's stories. A tiny dressing room, mimicking my own, was off to the right of the crib. I took the few steps necessary to travel within and sat down in the overstuffed rocking chair. It was powder blue and hugged me as I leaned back into it. A miniature crystal chandelier hung in the center, just over a dressing table. It was an island made specifically for dressing a baby and to accommodate the design of it I had filled it with diapers, powder, and lotions. One wall was littered with built-in shelves stacked with tiny shoes, and the hanging bars were filled with outfits from the world's best designers. The child of Manny and Marisol Vallega deserved no less.

Joy was an emotion that I had just recently added to my repertoire. The feeling was foreign. Nonetheless, I could only deduce that what I was feeling was happiness. I couldn't help but be. My husband indulged my every whim. An addition to our family was his suggestion. The idea held little appeal at first, but becoming a mother was a small price to pay. I relished the security and protection that being Manny's wife afforded me.

The media painted a picture of our lives with a broad brush. Because of my bipolar diagnosis, I became the face for Manny's philanthropic efforts in educating the public of mental health diseases and disorders. Within a short period of time his efforts paid off and he shed the shadow of his association with my father. His drive and ambition were respectable and h announced that he was setting his sights on the presidency of Colombia. The harsh spotlight on us had softened as the focus became more positive than negative. No longer were we seen as two isolated people driven by selfish desires. Now, accordingly to the public, we were delighted, expectant parents. The power of media was once again at work. We were embraced by our country.

Strange how the mention of a child could sway the public.

To keep reading, purchase a copy from your favorite online retailer today!
No Perfect Secret (Book Four)

DD Lorenzo is an award-winning author of Women's Fiction and Romantic Suspense novels. She loves coffee, long lunches with good friends, and fresh flowers to balance her obsession with anti-heroes. You can find her most days plotting and planning her character's lives from her beach house on the Delaware shore.

To stay updated with DD's books, please visit her website at www.ddlorenzo.com and sign up for her newsletter. Want the inside scoop? Join DD's reader group, DDs Diamonds, at www.facebook.com/groups/ddsdiamonds

Stay connected with DD

Website:
www.ddlorenzo.net

facebook.com/ddlorenzo.author

x.com/ddlorenzobooks

instagram.com/ddlorenzobooks

pinterest.com/ddlorenzo

bookbub.com/authors/d-d-lorenzo

amazon.com/DD-Lorenzo/e/B00GA5ARJ8

goodreads.com/D_D_Lorenzo

Other Titles by DD Lorenzo

The IMPERFECTION Series

No Perfect Man

No Perfect Time

No Perfect Couple

No Perfect Secret

No Perfect Woman

No Perfect Beginning: An IMPERFECTION Series Prequel

The ROCK HILLS Series

Boundless Hearts: A ROCK HILLS Origin Story

Bone Dust: Rock Hills Book 1

Standalones

Indiscretion

(An Aleatha Romig's Infidelity World Novella)

Heels, Rhymes, & Nursery Crimes

(A multi-author series)

Twinkle, Twinkle Little Star: Fragile Flower to Femme
Fatale

www.ingramcontent.com/pod-product-compliance
Lightning Source LLC
Chambersburg PA
CBHW031742180726
48283CB00005B/1626